Phisto

Also by Rick Lawton

The Rex
Chasing Lazarus
Rex Stories

Phisto

Rick Lawton

Sasha Press
San Francisco, CA
www.sashapress.com

Published 2020

Published by Sasha Press
San Francisco
www.sashapress.com

ISBN-13: 978-0-9788862-3-3

Printed in the United States of America

Phisto

What a brave new world, that has such people in't

Shakespeare, The Tempest

Part 1

(1)

Talia hurried nude over to the closet but stopped at her image in the mirror. She had the sleek, bristly, cinnamon head of a ferret, but striped with fading purple lines. Her body was good, cute, lean with flourishes of discrete rose and bug tats and a larger black-and-red centipede tat over the scar on her back, well-punctured ears, and nose punctured sans ring. She smiled and her left cheek tucked in. She tried to remember to smile with both sides, but it was an effort after her amusing encounter with Bell's palsy. Her slight lopsided grin engraved her face as permanently ironic.

She shivered, toweled off, dressed, then hopped downstairs.

Kitchen preternaturally neat. Office: small with a landline, a PC, and a jumble of photos on the wall, a headset and answering machine.

days over   dont have to think   worry   time to forget

She turned abruptly. She flipped open the closet door, found her old green vest and threw it on, slipped on her Birks, opened the door, and clop, clopped down the steps.

She measured herself against the row of houses, her house. She knew she cut a small figure against the house, a small house in the small town of Point City. She hurried away from the fifteen houses stitched along the marsh. One with thirty clay Virgin Marys chipped and missing halos and arms, staring at passersby from latticed windows; another with the length of a white picket fence topped with rows of clamshells; one with worn surfboards stuck in the sandy ground in the front yard like a maze; a couple others retiring, secretive, with ten-foot hedges; at the far end, four houses away, Jack's detached garage and huge rambling house.

She walked towards Point City's quaint downtown. Dusty. Gravely. Potholed and blacktopped. Warped concrete sidewalks. Weathered gray buildings. Main Street bookended on the north by the bank and two-story picture-windowed grocery, and less than a quarter mile away on the south by the abandoned, dilapidated, and bricked Grand Hotel and the touristy Station Inn.

Sandwiched between were the places she walked by every day: a handful of restaurants, hardware stores, clothing stores, a smattering of seashore-themed knick-knack "boutiques," a couple galleries featuring local artists, sea and land-scapes, and of course the Café con Vache and the Lost Dog.

where to start where to start

* * *

Gaylord's, a few blocks past the north end of Main.

Every weekend, Gaylord's—expansive, dark pine-lacquered dance floor with spinning globe, gay soft porn posters—filled up with mostly gays, trannies, and transgenders swaying to Madonna, Beyoncé, Pink, and Lady Gaga videos. Made Talia think she'd been transported to San Francisco's Castro and its interlocking chain of bars on Market, Castro, and 18th Streets.

That afternoon, no.

That afternoon, it was a tranny and a new guy with a blue Mohawk who argued about whether Point City was tolerant or retro or full of aged sixties hippies. Made Talia think about how blinkered everyone was, seeing what they wanted to see, hearing what they wanted ricocheting off the thick walls of their echo chambers.

Next, she tried the Crossroads, a roadhouse just off the curve that led into Main, hoping to talk to Eddie, resident philosopher and cynic. Eddie made her feel more wholesome and ethical than she should feel. But no Eddie. Probably off working himself into a despairing funk. Instead she got two 60ish towns-people she didn't know trading life chits at the bar. She turned around without ordering and knew she was putting off her usual destination, the Lost Dog, which was closer to home, entertaining, and had Mike, who was charming, a fun fuck, if you explained his machismo as mostly an act.

The Dog was a throwback. There were ridges, valleys and dunes of sawdust, a back bar sprinkled with ornately beveled mirrors shooting rainbows over the bar. The Dog had its loud and raucous times, was full around the holidays, but was almost empty most afternoons. Talia chose a creaky bar stool near the door and glanced at the rest of the bar to make sure everything was there: warped tables and splayed press-back chairs, metal license plates and WW2 memo-rabilia on the walls ("Loose lips sink ships"), tin ceiling sprouting hundreds of dollar bills, Mike talking to John, endangered watering hole. Check and checkmate.

A few of the regulars were there. George Mathews, morose—and she guessed ticking through the latest argument with his lean, unhappy wife, Edna—toyed with his drink halfway down the bar. Harris Lawson watched a pool game between two Mexicans, day laborers at the Windsor housing development.

Harris saw her, pushed off his stool, and took one next to her. In a minute, Mike said hello and slid a Corona over to her. Soon she was twirling her long-neck, watching the reflections off the back bar bottles, and chatting with Harris.

She segued into her usual lament. "Sometimes I get tired talking to 'em. Same problems. I say the same things. I'd put on a tape if they didn't need the one-on-one. You know, a real person listening to their stories."

Harris—tall, freckled, curly red hair, ex-lawyer—looked over his blue-rimmed glasses at her and said, "Why'd you start, again?"

well yeah   maybe i did it so i could complain in old bars

"It happened. I love it here, but it can get boring, and I'd always wanted to do social work, so I volunteered in the Tenderloin and one thing led to another and before I knew it, I started the Liz-can-answer-your-questions-and-ease-your-life Line."

"Sounds like a job...and you almost sound cynical."

"I like new callers. I keep thinking, okay I can help a new one. But it doesn't take long before the litany starts." Talia picked up her beer and took a long pull. "Don't we need something? We came here—'we,' isn't that presumptuous!; a handful is better—to get away, to leave the strum and drang, the stress, the problems out there in San Francisco, or Oakland, or Berkeley, or L.A. And we discover after a couple weeks or months of raw nature that we're bored silly. Sure, there are people who love it, who spend their time with our raft of nonprofits around the coast and Tomales Bay. Not me." Harris' bored look made her stop. "It's more than just about something to do."

Harris scratched at his red beard and said, relenting, "I get antsy, but birding could be, and is becoming, full-time. I could go back to school, become an ornithologist, spend my time describing distribution patterns or the social structure of ravens." Harris took a sip of beer, put it down slowly. "I guess the problem with doing that is Point City. It induces spiritual lethargy."

"It seems better before you touch reality. It's like trying to see what the room is like with your eyes closed. When you open them, you're always amazed at how much detail you've missed, reality I mean."

"Reality?" Big concept for five o'clock."

A shadow flitted into the bar.

Talia glanced at Jack and looked away, the afterimage of his square fair face and violet-tinted glasses rimmed with long, lank, blond hair slowly fading away. Jack didn't come out often, but she'd seen him a few times in the Dog sequestered in the corner and sucking down scotch. She'd started thinking of what Hemingway called Faulkner and Fitzgerald, rummies, anyone who got shit-faced all the time, everyone but himself. She guessed Hemingway didn't know himself well, always on the outside pretending to have feelings.

Talia turned to Harris and lowered her voice. "I worry about security. I dress up in plate-sized sunglasses and a ratty blond wig when I put up flyers for the Line, but I worry someone might follow me or trace the phone number. I've gotten some pretty hairy calls."

Harris said, "Who could trace it?"

Talia brushed her hand through her hair. The bristles flattened, then sprang forward. "When I spin out the paranoia, it's usually bad guys or the police."

Harris said, "Bad guys would be bad for you and bad for Point City."

"Only the police could trace it."

Jack.

fuck do i have to talk to him   hold out kiddoo   it will only make a mess stop

She looked past Jack and said, casually, "I know that."

Jack shrugged. "There's a 99% possibility they don't care. It's like chasing people having a few beers in the park. It's not important."

"Right. It's not important."

Jack brushed his hair back, took a drink, extended the pause. Finally he said, "I'm sure what you're doing is socially redeeming."

Talia said angrily, "You don't know what I'm doing."

Jack, slightly tipsy, took a longer sip of his scotch, set it down carefully, and looked directly at Talia. "This is Point City; it doesn't take long before you start to know people you see every day and what they're doing."

"You can't know much about me."

Jack nodded, took a sip of scotch, "Of course not. How could I?"

Talia's eyes narrowed. "You said that as if you do. C'mon, what do you know about me?"

The corner of Jack's mouth curved up in a smile. "Oh, well. Let's see," he mused. "Your name's Talia Morse, you live four houses away from me on Marsh Lane, you're 5' 4", 37, divorced two years ago from Larry. You have a degree in business and fine arts from Ohio State, had a wild life as a bartender at the Vortex off-campus. You started to work as an artist, but gave that up to marry Larry and work in his real estate office. You drive a ten-year-old Camry and now answer calls for help from people in the Tenderloin using the pseudonym of "Liz," have a huge assortment of art mugs you use every day to match your mood, and like to drink Coronas, twirl them in the light, wonder about the past, and talk about problems with the people who call you."

"And I'm sleeping with?"

Jack laughed nervously and glanced quickly at Mike, who was talking to pool players. "I couldn't say; that would be intrusive."

oh yeah   asshole   why did you look at mike

Talia straightened up on her stool. "You picked that up from gossip?"

Jack smiled pleasantly, "Just remembering what I hear and see. Of course, what I hear or see might be wrong. People are inherently deceptive."

Harris, smirking ear to ear, looked at Jack and said, "Do me."

Jack looked at Harris and shrugged. "Harris Lawson: 45, 6 foot 1, divorced, bird watcher, currently has 553 birds on his life list. Worked in the Lilly law firm for fifteen years. Lives on Marsh Lane two houses from Talia, drives a Land Rover. Plays poker and drinks Blue Goose vodka with birders from the Golden Gate Audubon Society, usually on Wednesday. Goes into San Francisco a couple times a week to see his ex. I believe her name is Carly. That's just a summary."

Harris said, "Impressive. Are we all acting parts in some grand narrative?"

Jack smiled, showing bright-white teeth and an inward-turning canine. "We all create stories around our lives."

Harris: "You seem to be creating stories around ours."

Talia hesitated, then said, "You seem to know facts, statistics, the résumé, but what do you know about us? Do you know how we think, feel, or what we're really like?"

Mike looked up from talking to two pool players.

Jack saw Mike look up but ignored him. To Talia: "Big questions. Do we know what we're really like? Isn't everything a guess, an approximation? Isn't it sane to lie to ourselves?"

Talia: "I know who I am...and we know who you are."

Mike raised up from the end of the bar, shook his head and said, "I know who I am."

George looked up, frowned at Jack.

Talia: "And Jack, we know you're 40ish, that you think you're brilliant because you made realistic super-violent games for adolescents, that you made a stack of money from your company, PhistoCo, that your partner, Maddy, faked her disappearance, and that you're in Point City hoping to find some clue that will either lead you to her or answer the question of why she did what she did. See, Jack, you may think you're anonymous but you're not. People watch you too."

Jack shrugged. "I'm sure they do."

Raquel Osborn made a grand entrance, left the doors swinging behind her, and said breezily, "I see we're all here."

Talia patted the stool next to her and Raquel sat down. "We're finding out how much Jack has on us."

Raquel looked at Jack and said airily, "What fun."

Emma looked over the swinging doors, blinked, noticed Jack, and walked in swaying slightly from side to side. "Sorry to interrupt."

Mike flipped a towel over his shoulder and said, "Jack's telling us about ourselves."

Emma: "I'm sure it's interesting, but I know myself already. Here, Jack, you left your change in the café." She put two twenties and a five on the bar top.

Jack picked up the money and stuffed it in his pants. "Sorry for the trouble."

"No trouble."

Emma walked back to the door, turned, and said, "I haven't been in a bar for years, since John died. Guess I don't have the time, or it has too many memories. Hope everyone finds out who they are."

A light sputtered in back, faintly illuminating the cracked door of the men's room and casting flickering light over the old prints, the WW2 caution, a rosy-cheeked Coke hawker. Bikers in skintight yellow-and-green-striped spandex, across from the bar, bickered over a map spread between them. Talia picked up her tall-neck and glanced through it, distorting the back bar, realized what she was doing, and put it down.

Jack smoothed his long blond hair back. He looked at his empty glass, got up and stretched. Jack paused, one hand on the top of the slatted swinging door. He was tall, but straight, hard, knobby. His lank blond hair hid his hard, pale face. He turned, glanced at the bar, and was about to say something, but stopped, exited, and left the slatted door swinging.

(2)

Yep, Fall of doubt and perplexity. Shit, the marsh still looks fine, green edging to brown, but natural. It'll spring back teeming and green.

Jack stared past Maddy's prints and paintings and collages and through his slight reflection in the large front window at the hedge and at people walking towards and away from Point City's Main Street, a handful of miles from the Seashore.

i have to go soon   but the tapes started   i distract mynotreallyconsciousself the self that does stuff that works on habit   on remote   but the tape is there   i never know when or where it will start   most of the time it starts where i met her

* * *

Roll 'em.

San Francisco.

8 o'clock pm.

15 March, the Ides.

14 Mission bus.

The audio bugs on the back of seats fed the drive in his pocket.

His capture camera captured passengers: bald, combed over, curled, dreadlocked, jerking, twisting brown/black/yellow/white, cell phones wedged between ear and shoulder, bundles of groceries clumped on the floor, half-zippered backpacks.

And the bus: anomalous ventilation/escape hatch, serried rows of vertical steel poles, worn handholds on the seat backs, black mash of tags around the windows.

For Dark City...

...Dark City: action-adventure single-person shoot 'em up, bloody refuse-strewn streets, shadowy apocalyptic backgrounds, car chases, screeching tires, black AK-47s, bodies broken and ripped with bullets splashing and oozing blood, mystery thugs, sinister terrorist, very hip, hints of Miyazaki anime, of Rodriguez's Sin City.

Adenoidal time waster, his forte.

He was putting away his capture camera when he glanced at the woman in back, then noticed the woman...

...fingers clasped firmly around pale bruised knees, long black coat bunched around her hips, dueling faces half-hidden near the window

goth urchin

her face, turned outward, was pale, chalky, but her reflection was dark, even; inside her reflection, buildings appeared and vanished; other times, he would identify the block, count the known houses, the Yerba Buena center, a cubical Jewish museum, count known buildings to reassure himself the world out there existed, still existed...

his own reflection, his eyes, his lank hair, near hers

it would add an existential statement, a symbol of alienation inserted to extract a scintilla of meaning, of pause, from a bloody adolescent game; her pale blue eyes turned towards him, slanting past her pale legs, fixing him...

Are you a voyeur, an interloper, a charlatan?

Can I capture you?

No.

Okay.

Why are you what you are?

Why?

Do you think I'm strange? You're not attracted to me? Of course you are.

Of course you're strange. Women don't talk like that.

Whores do.

Are you a whore?

Aren't you a whore with your camera?

Touché.

I know who you are, do you?

Please.

I'm intrigued. I'll buy you a drink in the Mimic, next stop. I'm sure you know it.

It was another half-rational encounter curling back on itself, unraveling. He'd talked to street people for years; he used their stories, used their faces, their walks, their voices in his games. A goth/gamine sparring with him. Another back-o-bus crazy. She was going to buy him a drink! Mimic, he'd been there once with John Esterhaz, PhistoCo's diminutive COO, after a hike in the East Bay hills. Loved the name. Mimic. As she rose up at the stop, her reflection in the window coalesced around the idea of body and spirit, of two halves of the soul, of right and wrong, of good and evil. He laughed silently. Why was he injecting a kaleidoscope of meaning into a random aperçu?

When she emerged from the corner, it was as if she were breaking out of a chrysalis, or a bat unfolding its wings. She was taller than he thought and older, her legs were pale and shapely, her black hair tumbled over her shoulder and down to her mid-back.

She was striking, and she could have been one of his creations.

It was, oddly, his stop too. He finished packing his camera and followed her down the aisle. Outside he started back to his flat in South Beach, but paused, turned, and watched her waiting at the stoplight, her black coat swirling around her. He shrugged inwardly, turned around, and followed her to the Mimic.

✳ ✳ ✳

It was time to get upstairs to the Stage, Phisto, and his video model of Point City, but once the tape started, it was hard to stop. One image, or feeling, led lockstep to the next. If only he could make the mental tape into a video, a video he could label and store...and stop.

wont stop now

Rolling.

The Mimic was one of the few dive bars left in SoMa off Mission. Dive bars were disappearing, businesses pouring into colorless new buildings from Mission to Harrison. One day he'd stroll by and see the papered-over windows of the Mimic with a job card taped to a window. That night five years ago, it wasn't crowded; small tables jammed together, small bar with stupid boozy sayings peppering the back bar (If you can read this, you haven't had enough; Beer, it's what's for dinner; Even duct tape can't fix stupid). Hidden lights trained on the low yellow ceiling edged the handful of people and a solitary drinker at the bar with a funereal glow.

When they walked to the Mimic, he'd assessed her again. Lean, pale bare legs strong and shapely. She was about 5'6", but she seemed taller. More than anything, it was her carriage that intrigued him. She held herself erect, her head moving on the same plane, her chalky neck showing through coal-black hair. He thought at the time: Annabelle Lee.

In the Mimic, before he could say anything, she'd chosen a table, shed her coat, and asked him what he wanted, which surprised him. He shrugged and said a cheap scotch, neat, water back. She shook her head, went to the bar, and ordered an expensive Macallan for him and a Pabst Blue Ribbon for herself.

funny a halfgoth street urchin played role reversal

Jack sat down at the table, snagged an extra chair with his foot, and planted his capture camera and pack on it. While the bartender poured his scotch, he watched her in the bar mirror to see her from a new distance. She stared straight ahead at a point on his left—doubled image again!—and he could tell she was taking it all in. Later, he would say she was absorbing the environment, measuring, categorizing, shaping it, trying to place it in her galaxy of ideas, her galaxy of words.

A few minutes later, Maddy sat down and put everything on the table, her can of PBR tall against his squat glass of scotch and small glass of water. Maddy took a sip of her PBR, paused, then scrutinized him. Her face was darker than he thought at first, her eyes starry aquamarine, a light dusting of freckles, and a faint blush accenting the area under her eyes, stopping short of a curvy pinkish mouth.

She said, "Consider this is a test. I think you'd be a good competitor."

Jack smiled, frowned. "Competitor?"

"Or antagonist, or opponent, or lover. You get the idea. I know who you are. You're Jack, brilliant hacker turned video game guru." Maddy nodded towards the camera. "You make idiotic video games full of bloody heroes and busty amazons for violent, sex-obsessed adolescent boys. In other words, you pander to primitive emotions."

Jack: "Ah, and you?"

"Am the opposite. I'm interested in finding out who people are, what life is about, but inevitably become obsessed with our failures as human beings."

"I'd guess you don't have many friends."

Maddy stared off to his right, gathering her ideas. "Any. Real ones."

"I know a little bit about women and I know what's happening. It's crude, but—"

Maddy sprayed PBR over her coat and part of the table. She then proceeded to laugh so hard she started hiccupping. She got up and hurried towards the bathrooms in back.

that ruined annabellelee

She returned a few minutes later, oddly composed, grabbed a bar rag, cleaned up the mess, and walked up to the bar and tossed the bar rag on the bar top next to the bartender.

She turned to the patrons, smiled, and laughed. "Sorry, everyone. If I laugh too hard, I pee my pants."

Everyone laughed, drawn in.

"He's perfect, isn't he?" She posed her finger under her chin and seemed to consider what she said. "Distance, abstraction, enormous hubris. Just who I'm looking for. Perfect foil. Excellent."

Maddy walked back, sat, and arched a brow at Jack.

Jack grinned: "Competitors?"

"It just seems right. Since we've started, let me explain the rules, or the progression. We're going to your place tonight. We'll probably fuck like proverbial bunnies. I know you want that, and in a sense I want that."

The bar was silent.

Jack tasted his scotch, felt the rush, and placed it carefully on a beer coaster. "Okay."

Maddy, smiling slyly: "I'm going away the next morning, and you're going to work obsessively on what you shot today. Later in the day, you're going to take a break and think about our strange night and wonder about me and our competition and how to find me. Luckily, you're going to find my phone number taped to your refrigerator."

"I can see it now."

Maddy took a sip of PBR. "Then, in approximately a month or two of gradually seeing more of each other, we're going to move into a new place, a neutral place."

"Neutral?"

"Your place, Jack, is your ground zero."

**i was puzzled and intrigued she was alluring i felt a vibration
i couldnt explain   but something made me think no this is not
going to end well**

The bartender, skinny with thinning black hair, anomalous bow tie, fussed with bottles in the brightly lit back bar, but you could tell he was listening to the conversation. The couple at the nearest table talked quietly but glanced at Jack and Maddy quickly once, twice.

"Okay."

"We'll live there for a few years and enjoy a lot of life, as much as we can. Gradually our competition will evolve. We'll discover what kind of an opponent we have. We'll find the soft spots, and hard ones, and the ones that don't exist. One of your juvenile customers might call them head games."

"Right."

"Finally we'll reach the point where we know each other so well, we'll get bored. We might start finding ways to stay apart or blunt the other one. You capture the outside of people and live removed, or live several removes, from reality. You might scuttle deeper into a kind of narrative solipsism."

"Hmm."

"We would rent or lease a place where we could get away from the other. It wouldn't make any difference. Our competition would reach endgame. Something dramatic would happen. One of us would leave. I might leave the city or find a new opponent, and you would likely immerse yourself deeper in your games."

"Right."

"Just being real. That's the arc."

ah yes the arc it was always the arc and the competition

Jack laughed, clapped. "Excellent performance. Smart. Absurd. Intriguing. Provocative."

Maddy sat back in her chair and stared at him. "You're mocking me."

Jack shrugged. "I can see where your ideas might come from: the inevitability of change, man vs. woman, the consummate difficulty of any two people living together, divorce rate. And arc. It's a word you use in writing, prose. Or a storyboard. A narration, say. What makes you think I haven't already thought of your arc? I've probably thought it a thousand times, perhaps not the exact

23

face, or person. People project themselves into hundreds of futures a hundred times a day. Inevitably one comes true, but you can't predict which one."

"Imagination isn't reality."

"And why you made your fantasy about us is unusual. You may know the public me, but you don't know the real me."

Maddy smirked. "The real you; what that must be like."

Jack: "If you did, you wouldn't like me."

Maddy: "Hon, now I'm really interested. Or, did you say that to make me interested?"

"Have we already started your 'competition'?"

Maddy smiled. "What do you think?"

Jack matched her smile. "Your arc would work, if you controlled it. But you don't. The real question is: if you know the arc, the narrative, the end, why do it?"

Maddy laughed. "Life."

"Ah—"

"I see you're puzzled." Maddy bunched her eyebrows comically. "Let's see if I can explain. You're too involved with your abstractions and digital worlds, and I'm too close to reality. The competition will be keen. It will certainly mean ideas, performance, a good amount of sex, and interesting night life. It could be a good, a very good life, but it will degrade over time, and it's only going to last five years. Can't change the arc; it's fate."

Jack took a long swallow of his scotch. He felt the heat, then the rush. It felt good. "So I could avoid your fantasy arc by not asking you to my place tonight. But I have to admit, you've made it tempting."

Maddy frowned and planted her hands on the table close to each other. "Yes you will. It's what I want! It's what you need!" She reached over the table, grabbed his jacket, and looked searchingly into his eyes.

Before he could take her hands away, she released him and turned slowly to the rest of the bar, who were staring, mouths agape. "Hey, everybody," she said. "How silly of me. I should have explained. Jack and I are rehearsing for our play, Competitors, and he's forgotten his lines...again."

She turned her attention to the woman at the next table, "Sorry, really."

i was stunned but before i could say anything shed settled back in her chair

24

Maddy smiled a knowing succubus smile, eyebrows arched.

Jack supposed it was the knowing, entrapping smile that did it...or the performance that made him want to prove her wrong.

that scene was a precursor gothurchin annabelllee madmedea sucking succubus were they all real

Jack felt compelled to get up, although he had a nagging feeling he wanted to stay. He took a last swallow of scotch, grabbed his capture camera, surveyed the bar and the patrons staring at him and said, "It was just a one-act."

Maddy smiled at him, shrugged, and said, "We'll see."

(3)

"It's not a city if it doesn't have a Tenderloin."

Talia blinked. Her green-rimmed dark glasses didn't help much against the reflection of the late-afternoon sun in her rearview mirror. The Camry was on Turk pointed to the heart of San Francisco's Tenderloin. When she started, she got too many glances from working girls, pimps, homeless, and black hangers-on near the groceries. She wasn't sure the wig or glasses protected her or made her a target. She edged into the driver's side, threw off the wig, the dark glasses. She lowered the visor to check on her purple-striped butch. The purple edges were starting to fade into her reddish cinnamon. She hadn't thought of wigs when she had the butch cut and colored, but it made putting on wigs easy...if the wig fit. This one with its jumble of yellow curls kept slipping down and forcing the glasses down her nose.

what the fuck are you doing here talia my fucked up lass you could do a thousand things here i sit in a worn toyota surrounded by garbage by wheelchairs suppurating wounds used needles what was that line i meet and dole unequal laws unto a savage race masochism

Months ago, back from her fifth trip (Japan, stem to stern, Sapporo to Hiroshima, mostly Kyoto with side trips to Nara) and tired of traveling, she started driving into San Francisco and volunteering in the Tenderloin. One day, she made friends with street people at Glide—Sam, Amy, and Seth—and gave them her cell number. They called her a couple times but then their friends started calling. That's when she thought about putting in a talk/help line. She mulled about it for a few weeks, weeks only interrupted by Maddy's infamous video, and finally had another line put in. "Liz" was born. She composed a flyer in Word bordered with stars and claims of heartfelt conversations and tacked it up through the Tenderloin.

The response overwhelmed her. Street people, people on the edge, people who were depressed or hungover or were schizophrenic wanted to talk, or babble, to someone real, someone who wasn't waiting in a food line at Glide, or a cop or social worker. She didn't flatter herself that she was a real social worker, but she was offering something, a person to talk to, to relate to for a few minutes. She gave out advice freely, knowing most of it was ignored.

The bums in the alley between shuttered buildings on Leavenworth shared a butt. One drew deep, his cheeks sucking in, then holding it, as if it were his last drag. Made her want a smoke.

She slipped her purse out from under the seat, opened it, grabbed the pack and shook one out. She lit it and the ten-year-old Camry filled with smoke, obscuring the hopelessness spread over the windshield.

✳ ✳ ✳

One of the drunks in the alley—short, fat, dirty black-and-orange Giants wind-breaker—flipped the butt at the wall, got up, and yelled in the face of the one on the ground. He kicked at him and hit the sole of his shoe. The one on the ground—bony, large-handed—struggled to get up, dropping his paper bag. He fell back heavily against the brick wall and slid down, his brown ragged sports coat bunching up the wall. The heavy one kicked at him, clumsily missed and hit the wall, and the one on the ground grabbed his leg and hung on.

should i shouldnt i could get hurt just like the last time well fuck

Talia grabbed the wig, opened and slammed the car door, and strode pur-posefully towards the alley.

She stopped at the front of the alley and said, "What have we here?"

Fat one: "Who the fuck are you?"

Skinny struggled to a half-crouch and said, "Yeah, what the fuck."

Talia: "Just curious. What are you doing?"

They stared at her.

Skinny: "Say, Pete, what are we doing?"

Pete: "Well, Johnny, why do you give a shit? We always done it?"

Talia: "You don't mind my saying, you both look kinda silly."

Pete: "Looks like we got Momma Teresa here."

"Look Pete, her hand's incognito. Guess we'll never know."

They both started laughing.

Talia stared at the wig in her hand. She shrugged, then smiled, left cheek tugging up. "Well, shit."

Pete said, "Fuck, you're the one putting up all those flyers. Says 'Liz' on the flyer. Tell you what, we won't tell nobody we saw you, you buy us a beer in that bar."

Johnny coughed, swallowed, then nodded vigorously.

its against my selfimposed rules i better not

* * *

The Last Call was dark and dank, full of mostly empty chairs. A scattering of people held onto the bar, a couple bums slept in the corner, a roach scuttled over the bar top and disappeared in a crack. The black bartender—reluctantly giving his name: Jonathan, pot-bellied, rim of graying hair—looked askance at Talia's two companions but relaxed when she threw her wig on the bar and ordered a round of Coronas.

For the next half hour, she pumped the guys—Pete and Johnny—about how they ended up on the street, what their prospects were, about their health. She rarely got calls from old alkies, and it was interesting to hear their stories, until they lapsed into litany, the stories of loss, mental crackups, too much booze, and too many drugs. Once starting down that slope, it was too easy to just keep sliding.

And she heard the rationale, the rationale she'd heard a hundred times.

Johnny, puzzling out what he said: "But you know, Liz, what difference does it make? Fuck, I know I'll be dead in a couple years, maybe sooner. Not too many people will care, or they will for a while, then forget. Everybody gets forgotten, even the ones on the horse, or the ones with a plaque. Who were they? Who the hell knows?"

"Question is," she said, "if no one else cares, don't you have to?"

Dylan's "Rolling Stone" seeped through the bar from a dirty juke in the corner.

"What's there to care about?"

"Listen," she said, "I'm not sure why I'm doing this, but I'll buy you a couple sandwiches and a few beers if you behave for the rest of the day."

Pete: "Maybe it's cuz we're so good-lookin'."

"That's gotta be it."

Johnny: "Okay, Mommy."

Talia paid and they walked towards the entrance. She glanced at a tattered punch board with announcements. There was a half-hidden scrap stapled to the board. It was a flyer for a poetry reading. Talia looked at it closer. The date was a year ago. A chill traveled up her spine. Maddy.

what the fuck is this doing here do i want to know course ive thought about maddy and jack course ive wondered course im curious should i shouldnt i

She turned to the bartender and pointed to the flyer. "Did you see her?"

"I was off that night. Randy, the other bartender, saw her."

Talia nodded. "Mind if I take this?"

"I left it up cuz of her video. Take it; you'd be doin' me a favor."

Talia tore the flyer down and looked closely at it.

"C'mon, Liz."

Outside, she bought them two sandwiches and two 16-ounce Steel Reserves from the grocery on the corner and walked with them back to their alley near the shuttered SROs. "Listen," she said, "I have no illusions that you guys are going to be calm and collected and forever good buddies. But if you feel like talking sometime, give me a call." She took a flyer out of her pocket and handed it to them.

Talia walked to her car. She turned and stared back at Pete and Johnny, then at the shuttered buildings. Everything old, decrepit, made useless, pulled down by time. She started the car, pulled a U-turn, and stopped inches from a black woman crossing in the middle of the street. The woman, gap-toothed, fingered her and yelled something. Talia navigated around her and gunned the car towards Van Ness. She felt as she drove that she just might succumb to the hopelessness of the Tenderloin. She fought skirmishes; the war never ended.

She shook a cigarette from the pack, lit it, and cracked the back windows. The smoke drifted out, the inside cleared. A minute later, she was on her way out of the city.

Maybe Mike later...maybe.

She glanced at Maddy's flyer on the passenger seat, frowned, picked up the flyer with her right hand, and flicked it open.

29

(4)

Jack felt ragged. He'd spent too much time with Phisto and the Point City video. He did the same thing with his games just before release. Days and nights with sandwiches and coffee and uppers. He'd installed projectors throughout the second floor and he started thinking he was in Point City, not watching a video play over the ceiling, the walls, the bed.

Jack popped the roof on his multi-colored Porsche—Maddy's gift, inspired by decorated cars at Burning Man—and drove to San Francisco. He'd developed a fondness for the car, which was mechanically perfect but looked like an automotive Pulcinella. The dangerous picturesque drive helped sooth his nerves, with the ocean edging out the digital, a real scene edging out a manufactured one, a real free fall, a real snowstorm surf, real rocks pointed up like knives.

He parked the car in the Second Street Garage and walked towards the one place he knew he shouldn't go: the loft.

He stopped at the Mimic.

no job card yet ill go in later see the ghosts

The loft was almost empty and suffused with Maddy's presence. There's where she worked. There was the master bedroom. Many competitions there. Here's where she curled up on the dark brown couch next to the fireplace and where he sat in the straight-back chair watching her.

tape starting shouldnt be here

* * *

The Mimic.

Despite what Maddy said, her narrative "arc," her explosive act, he hurried back into his life.

yep won that round

Sure, it started their competition, their struggle. Sure, he thought about her as he worked on what he'd captured, about a quasi-existential encounter dovetailing into a Robin Williams flamboyance. She would have remained a blip on the screen of his mind, after reflection, an attractive flake, if he hadn't seen her photo in the Chronicle a week later. He frowned as he read the announcement of her reading from her latest book of poetry, Misdeeds, at Books, Inc.

Poet. Performance.

He hesitated. He was between girlfriends, but he knew his calendar was full. When he wasn't working, he played hard and had a posse of friends, more acquaintances. He punched open his cell calendar. Darts, Abbey Tavern. Competitive darts was one way he relaxed. Finally, he realized he was intrigued and had been intrigued since that night in the Mimic. He called off darts and threw on a PhistoCo hoodie and headed towards Books, Inc.

Maddy's new book was displayed in the window, and he stood in the short line and bought a copy. There were a scattering of people already seated. He read Misdeeds while waiting for the reading to start. She came in a few minutes later.

A few people clapped when they saw her.

hello people   its just a striking delusional poet

He'd always been a tough critic and a tough boss, but he had to admit her reading was mesmerizing. It was more performance than recitation. She was wearing black jeans, tall black laced-up boots, a black silky print top featuring entwined red roses with prominent thorns, and a black leather jacket set off with a long black boa. As she approached the mic, the boa trailed behind her, and she unfurled it as she started incanting, finally letting it drop to the floor. She didn't announce different poems, but paused for a few seconds and started a new one. He couldn't take his eyes off her. Her words penetrated everyone's consciousness of us vs. them, of little guys full of piss battered down by the powerful, by lies, by manipulation, by greed, and finally the necessity of destroying the existing order...and its impossibility. Her poems were also full of allusions, metaphors, plays on words, quotations from Shakespeare. It was a verbal maze similar to the visual puzzles of some of his games.

Her performance included the audience. Sometimes she would sit with someone in the audience, pause, and recite poems to the shocked and entranced listener.

31

She signed copies after the reading and he sidled up with his copy. She smiled her succubus smile, signed Misdeeds with a flourish.

"You don't like poetry, do you?"

Jack smiled. "Poetry is elitist, self-serving, ambiguous, and anomalous."

"Too clever, and yet here you are."

Jack paused, grinned. "I'm not sure why, precisely."

"Really? Meet me outside."

i could have left

* * *

It was cold for March; a late-season rain had washed the streets, and light glittered in the headlights of cars. They were both edgy. Maddy had gathered her bag, coat, and had slung her black boa over her shoulder. She watched him as she wrapped her boa snugly around her neck. Her smile showed the slightest hesitation: "I don't know why I've been so nutty with you. I think it was something about what you do, your games, your abstraction from reality."

"The Mimic was an act."

"My natural love of performance. But if I only performed, I'd be one-dimensional."

"Did you mean the bit about being 'competitors' and the 'arc'?"

"That was drawn from my experience and from trying to understand people. As you said, it's one possibility among many. Call it a conjecture."

"Distance and abstraction is a way of life in San Francisco. You could have chosen anybody."

"Who knows? Shape of head, hair color, eyes, ethnicity, religion. Handsome, or not. Brilliant, or not. Hubris. Maybe it was your blond hair, slightly broken nose, or your inward canting canine. Sometimes we choose the opposite. Of course, I know who you are and what you've done with PhistoCo and your characters. You've taken games to a level that makes a new reality and that intrigues me. For whatever reason, I think we might enjoy each other's company, at least be friendly competitors. Of course it may not be at all, end right here tonight, or in five years."

"Hubris, really? You said that to make yourself mysterious. No, wait. Are you acting now?"

"Shouldn't you know?"

Jack laughed. "Competitors makes sense now."

Maddy: "C'mon, sex, fantastic ambiguous dialog. What could go wrong?"

"Is 'everything' an answer?"

Maddy laughed, tucked her arm in Jack's and said, "Let's give it one try. Your place, or your place?"

it was my place

* * *

It was a long night of sex and mystery. What he remembered most about their first lovemaking wasn't her lean arms holding his back or her pallid legs holding him in a death grip…or the release, the love groans and cries. No, it was her pale blue eyes, smiling, holding secrets.

And she did keep secrets, especially about her history. She didn't talk about where she was from, family, education, anything of history, anything that would place her. She said she was like a book, a novel that had to be appreciated for what it was, for what she was, for what she said, without needless background or history.

He understood that, but in the ensuing months and years, he couldn't help trying to find an angle to her personality, her character, something to pinpoint who she really was. Of course he used Phisto, his creation and platform for generating PhistoCo games, to sort through everything he knew about her and came up with scores of explanations of where she was from, what she did, who she was. But none of his explanations seemed right, and she never retreated from her text-is-all stance.

* * *

In a month of on-again, off-again closeness, they were living together in his flat on South Park; in four months they moved to the loft; three years later, following increasing friction, they leased the apartment in the Shades to escape from each other for a few days. The friction was about his increasing absorption in finishing one of his last games, ironically entitled Endgame, getting PhistoCo ready to sell, and his alcohol use and drug-taking, which he needed to keep stress at bay...and Maddy's too-serious approach to understanding people, society, and herself. Naturally, he found it curious that it happened in their third year. Every time they encountered one of Maddy's predictions, they talked about it. He would hold back, not wanting to give in, not wanting to admit she was right. But he went along because each step, each change, seemed right at the time, right because of the local circumstances and not adhering to some predetermined schedule. But...

arc on schedule

Much of their time together was not filled with obvious conflict...or competition. The walls of her work space soon became covered with mostly social critical and anarchist poems from Rimbaud, Ginsberg, Ferlinghetti, Diane di Prima, and, of course, her own, tacked or scotch-taped to the walls between her prints, posters, and paintings. He spent most of his day at PhistoCo, but he did most of his serious work at the loft in a large room at the opposite end of the loft, full of tangles of wires, racks of computers, scanners, stacks of DVDs, and prints of PhistoCo game covers. Their favorite art object was a huge M.C. Escher poster from his late period, Bond of Union—over the fireplace near his end—of a couple bound together, a Mobius puzzle, like most Escher. It united them in their separate ways of duality, complexity, and complication, and it gave a more abstract meaning to their "competition."

Those five years, beyond their arguable competition and questionable arc and occasional friction, were some of the best times either of them had. Maddy had the capacity for understanding people at a deep level that gave him a new appreciation for them and her. It also made him realize, although he didn't admit it at the time, how superficial his games were, and it induced him to make a game—Ouroboros—which Maddy said showed her a lot about him she hadn't seen.

Many days, after work, they would meet in the center of the loft, he ready for an escape, any escape, and she ready for something new. They went to cafés, restaurants, nightclubs, and bars over the city and argued, sometimes heatedly, about his alternate realities and game-playing and her intrinsic seriousness and futile anarchism. They roamed SoMa through hurrying Metreon movie-goers, attended openings at the museums, the symphony, the opera, and sugarplum

Christmas galas at the Civic Center. With PhistoCo's games becoming hugely successful, with Maddy becoming well-known and performing in any bookstore, café, or gallery or venue that would have her, they were the center of the universe, controlling everything from their aerie high in the loft.

∗ ∗ ∗

The end of their third year—the year they rented the apartment in the Shades—Maddy took their vague intellectual competition to a more concrete level. She announced she had to leave for a month. He asked her, naturally, where she was going, and she said it didn't matter, that she needed a break.

It was a challenge, and Jack used Phisto to find where she went and what she was doing. He'd integrated brilliant algorithms including facial and voice recognition into Phisto and was able to sift through an incredible amount of data about what Maddy had been doing, who she'd been seeing, what she'd written, and what she'd said to come up with a destination. The first time, she was in Dublin. He thought the key pieces of information were two references to Ulysses in a recent poem, Wanderings.

When she came back, he casually asked how she liked Davy Byrnes, Joyce's pub in Dublin.

i definitely won that round in retrospect it was a high point in the competition of course the dialog that followed made it seem less than a win

It was the evening she got back. Maddy had showered and was curled up on the sofa sipping a Perrier, and he was leaning back on two legs of his hard-backed chair to the right of the Escher print. He'd just finished a long day and night working on Dark City, the last video game he worked on before he sold PhistoCo. He'd smoked most of a joint and was working on his third unblended scotch. The fireplace was cold.

Maddy said, fingering a wet black curl, a puzzled smile gracing her face, "Well, dear, you found out where, but not why."

Jack, slightly toasted, "Why, then?"

"No, no. Too easy. Let's dig deeper into why you wanted to find me."

Jack, amused: "I could say because we're together."

Maddy, frowning, "Could?"

Jack pointed the scotch glass at her. "Couldn't it be part of our competition?"

"Not telling you wasn't a dare."

Jack laughed. "Sure sounded like one."

Maddy, shaking her head, "And you used your own intuition and fact-gathering."

Jack took a sip of scotch, paused, looked at Maddy over the glass rim. "Partly."

"I know what that means. That means you snuck around reality gathering as much data as possible from people I know, and what I've done, and what I've said, and then you used your grand creation, your digital Rosetta Stone, Phisto, to find me. I should have expected it." Maddy shifted, re-crossed her legs. "But let's talk about your 'could'. You said you could do it because we're together. What does that mean? Does it mean we hang out together, go to the symphony together, go hiking together, fuck together? You can do all that with someone else."

Jack frowned. "I could, I suppose. But I want to do it with you."

"Why?"

Jack hesitated—he always hesitated when she asked that—and said, finally, "Cuz you're beautiful and accomplished, and you've made yourself a mystery. You've always been someone I can't explain, someone I can't capture. And you know it."

"Weak, Jack. Weak."

Jack laughed, got up, stared at the "Bond of Union" for a few seconds, then turned and said, "It's always weak if a man says it. Is this one of our man/woman smack downs, where you play the mysterious/intriguing woman, which you are, and I play the helpless, typical dull cowherd?"

Maddy laughed, arched her eyebrows at him. "Funny, Jack."

"Is that the play, the game? I just have to know so I can plan my strategy."

And later in the kitchen, on opposite sides of the island, Maddy, arms on the island, head propped on hands: "What if I disappeared completely, without a trace? Would you try to find me then?"

"Hey, people always leave traces. I found you in Dublin, didn't I?"

"That's not the question. Why would you want to find me?"

Jack sighed. "Maybe I would because I love you."

"Please. Again, maybe, could. Don't you believe anything, have anything you believe in, or love?"

"Do you? Besides, that is, your poetry, and your performance, which is brilliant, and which ultimately you think of as amusing."

"Amusing? It's more than that. Ah, the competition. I can see that might have been a mistake."

"And we need it, and we both know there's more."

"Oddly, that's true."

"So, let's get stoned. Let's go to the Black Cat and watch people. Or, what about sex?"

"Nah, not now. And no dope. I need to think."

"You can think when you're stoned."

"The ultimate stoner argument. One of these days you'll actually believe staying stoned makes you Einstein, when you're just another Gomer."

And she did it the fourth year. Announced she was leaving for a month, and again, aided by Phisto, he found her. He found her in Montreux, Switzerland, where Nabokov spent his last sixteen years. He was proud of his skill in finding her but less happy with the aftermath, her quizzical stares, her smile, as if what he'd done had revealed something important about him.

And he still didn't know why.

* * *

Halfway through their fifth year, she bought a Subaru and stunned him when she moved to the small town of Point City in western Marin. She said she needed time apart from him and the city. He visited her a half-dozen times since she rented the house on the outskirts of Point City, and secretly bought the huge house on the marsh thinking that eventually they could get back together, that it could be the way it was. It was a complicated time for him. Sure, he wanted to find out what was going on with Maddy, but he was trying to sell PhistoCo (what a cluster fuck that was with lawyers, lawsuits, personnel hassles, and haggling over prices and after-sale support for MetaGames, the acquirer of PhistoCo) and he had a ton of options after the sale.

But the last time he was with her in Point City, after midnight, Maddy asleep beside him, her dark hair bunched on the pillow, one leg shining white draped off the bed, their covers in the usual soft chaos, their clothes trailing towards the bed, he felt he had to leave, and stay away, and he knew she had to stay in this small town in western Marin. In a sense, her friendliness was a smoke screen. He could tell something else was going on, and what she talked about was more a valedictory to their time, cinching it off for him because she'd decided to do something else.

The house was bare except for clothes and her favorite prints and collages, including Oz. He felt a deep regret walking through the barely recognizable art in the shadows, moonlight filtering in, making acute angles on the bare wooden floor. The ride back that night was the loneliest of his life. He barely glanced at Highway 1 and the dark ocean beyond, the edge of the world. Maddy filled his mind because he felt, or knew in some distant part of his consciousness, that one phase of his life was over...

and i was destined to hold onto it

(5)

Long day and night, a very long night. John, Mike's marine buddy and owner of the Dog, subbed for him, and Talia and Mike spent the day at a late-fall outdoor concert in Mill Valley. It was all white-bread Generation Xers sipping Chardonnay and eating finger food and happy blond kids slopping their hands through finger-paints, eating organic health bars, drinking organic sodas in recyclable containers, or running in pint-sized Dionysian circles with garlands in their hair.

i tell myself i controlled everything frank the marriage the divorce i made a big deal of saying i never wanted kids did i mean it or was it inertia did i let time dictate was i a coward

She lay on her back, hitched up her Capri pants, warmed her legs, and let the sun warm her body. The warmth was like a blanket. The bands, balladeers with a hint of light rock, lulled her with songs of desperate love, sharp loss, regret, yearning.

They danced, chatted, sipped tequila from Mike's flask, and she watched as Mike unveiled the Mike Experience to neighbors splayed over their blankets.

They gossiped about the people in the festival and especially those in the Dog, especially Jack. She handed the flask back to Mike. He screwed the top back on and looked at her over his shoulder. "Fuck Jack. Course he can do anything he wants with all his money. But I played his games."

Talia frowned. "Are they that different?"

"If you had a vidcam on your Playstation or PC, you could put your face on your avatar, and if you said a series of sentences into an audio collector, it would compose dialog using a tinny version of your voice. It was as if you were in this super-real game, right there. And more options; it was almost as if you were free to do what you wanted. Sometimes, after going down a worn path, the path would change, and the words were different from what you expected as if you were thinking what to do."

39

"But with canned dialog."

"Of course."

Talia, musing, "I read about what he did with characters' personalities, faces, bodies. Very sci-fi."

"I can't think a game about Point City would be interesting, but if Jack did it, I'd buy it."

"*If* he sells it; of course, he doesn't have a company anymore. What about Maddy's act?"

Mike regarded her carefully, then unscrewed the top off the flask, looking meditative. He took a sip of tequila and screwed the top down. "She came into the Dog more than a couple times. She was one of Jack's demons. I swear everyone stopped talking. She became the center of attention. She had, what's that word, charisma, or an aura."

"I was traveling when she was in town. I saw her a couple times from a distance. I guess you had to talk to the police."

Mike rolled away from her, clasped his hands under his head. "I told the police about her aura, but they wanted details, like who she was with and had anyone threatened her. She didn't seem different the day of her vid, except she had a drink earlier than usual."

She couldn't put her finger on it, but she felt Mike hadn't told her everything. Did he have an affair with Maddy? What could he be hiding?

She spent the night with Mike after following him to his house in Nicasio, and her hunch faded away. What did it matter anyway? They had too many glasses of white wine, and finally the punch line, sex, legs high, Mike's curls, small snail ears, and thick square head blotting out the ceiling, something she needed from time to time to feel like a woman, to feel human. She would have felt the same way if she'd been a man. Mike was fine in bed, a good lay as they say, if occasionally rough.

sometimes she liked rough looked for it most when she worked in the bars sometimes she didnt want to fuck at all sometimes she just wanted a woman a woman to lick out to be licked out why not now whatcha hidin kid

Talia gathered the covers around her breasts and stretched out her legs. Mike twined his hands behind his head.

40

Talia had avoided the topic of Mike's hobbyhorse, but it slipped out. Maybe it was because she'd run out of talk. She said, "You really think you're going to Belize?"

Mike turned towards her, as if she'd said something stupid. "Yep."

She'd seen his ten travel books on Belize. Looked like an obsession. "Why don't you start by vacationing there?"

"Want to arrive like a Spanish conqueror in a boat."

Talia frowned, laughed. "You don't have a boat."

"Wouldn't be the same if I flew there." Mike yawned, "If I go in a boat, and it's a dump, I'll still have the trip. Right?""

"I told you I passed through there over a year ago on my belated world tour, Cay Caulker. It was nice, a little primitive, lots of pot, everyone walked barefoot on the main drag. What if you don't like it? What if it's too wet or too poor or too touristy?"

"It's not. I know it."

twisted logic hell never go hed lose his fantasy

Mike had fallen asleep. She should have shut up. Mike had become an avatar in his own fantasy.

Elusive sleep. Punctuated with memories of Belize...

..of rain

..of mud

..of Beliken beer

..of conch fritters

..of shrimp on a stick

..of blue blue ocean

..of sex on the beach

..of a man in a white suit striding to her

* * *

Mike's small house was down a gravel driveway on the side of a field skirted by eucalyptus with a couple old oaks in the middle. On the few days she'd been there, she liked to watch the birds fly high up into the eucalyptus and disappear in the sword leaves...and lower into the oaks. Harris wouldn't be interested in them. They were mostly blackbirds, crows and starlings and redwings with some she didn't know, small, shiny black with yellow eye rings that scratched the dirt when they weren't hiding.

Mike kept a cozy place, unlike most single men she knew. One wall in the bedroom was full of photos of relatives, a brother, a sister with a passel of kids in Nebraska, a mother holding the center, a heavy woman with Mike's full red-cheeked face. Mike had traveled in the Marines and said he'd caught the travel bug, but hadn't traveled much since. Taped to one wall was a fantasy collage, a small map of Central America with Belize circled in red magic marker, a random assortment of sailboats, and a small shelf of books on Belize held in place by two heavy Beliken bottles he'd bought online.

They spent most of the time in the living room on the couch listening to hard rock, drinking, and talking. He was a good talker, if too dominating, letting the subject of one sentence segue smoothly into a distant topic. Once, she started to talk about the Line, about the people who called, but then she made herself shut up. She did that enough in the Dog. Didn't she want to have something else? Didn't she want to live a little? Sometimes she thought she had the Line as her one go-to topic.

Between dreams of Belize, she slept fitfully. In the morning, around nine, she trailed her hand over the snoring Mike's foot, hoping he would wake up and pull her back. He didn't. She sighed, gathered her clothes, and took a last look at the wall of photos, of his mother, the map of Central America, seeing how it was a kind of summation of who Mike was. She stopped when she saw a typewritten note obscured by a sailboat. She peeled back the sailboat photo and saw a handwritten note. All it said was, "Thanks, M."

"M?"

Why keep such a short note? Who was M?

Maddy? Mike?

Mike groaned and turned over, a cover slipping off the fine hairs of his buttock.

Talia froze for a moment, then relaxed. She let the sailboat flip back and cover the note. As she took her clothes into the living room to dress, she shook her head. She was starting to go batty with Maddy; she was seeing things that weren't there, creating phantom narratives.

A few minutes later, she stepped out into a glorious fall day. She revved up the Toyota and sped down the road between the eucalypts, watching a swarm of blackbirds pirouette against the gray sky. Back in Point City, she parked in front of the Café con Vache, ordered a coffee and sticky bun, and sat on the bench. She crossed her legs and ate the bun slowly, watching the street, watching people go in and come out of the grocery, watching George open the Barn, and laborers amble down the street towards the Windsor development two streets in back of the Barn.

Raquel walked into the café and came back to talk to her. For some reason, she wanted to talk about Jack. Stories about Jack would not go away. What was he up to? Was it because of Maddy? And that's how they ended up talking about Jack and Maddy and Maddy's last video. Bringing up Maddy brought up the whole idea of the flyer, Mike's note, and the whole ball of wax.

The Maddy story stayed lodged in her consciousness when she headed to the house. She parked in front and noticed she was making ruts on the grass and decided to park on the street for a few weeks. She glanced down the lane and saw that Jack's house was big and silent, a monolith perched on the marsh.

She checked the answering machine. No lights, no calls.

She logged on and answered email from some of her online groups. Her groups were mostly progressive, mostly worried about this or that politician or stupid move in Congress. She supposed she was like them, worried about this or that on the mental horizon.

She was about to start up the Line when she glanced at Maddy's flyer. She'd thrown it on her desk, and over a few days it had slowly unfolded, and Maddy stared at her, alluring, flip of raven hair, penetrating aquamarine eyes, mystifying. On an impulse, she checked the Line's answering machine, marched through her living room, grabbed her bag, and a few minutes later fired up the Toyota.

(6)

The dart described a wobbly arc towards the front windows, flashed in a beam of light, and descended towards a thin strip of brightly waxed parquet floor.

The dart embedded itself deep in the floor, inches from the twitching silver nose hairs of a gray mouse. The mouse regarded the dart shaft, swiveled, and vanished inside a small hole in the wall underneath Maddy's Oz print. The original photo was of an installation on a Texas highway featuring Dorothy turned towards a distant twinkling Emerald City on an undulating strip of newspapers painted yellow, cut-outs of red slippers, tin, the picture of a terrier, and a random assortment of small toys, a memorial for the death of two teenagers.

"Fuck, fuck, fuck."

Mouse—why not capitalize it? why not give it an edgy familiar status?—made its first appearance last week. He was sure it was one mouse. It seemed to come out whenever he was at the table musing about his day, or thinking about what he was doing in Point City, or why Maddy had faked her death, or whether it was part of their competition, or whether he would find out what happened to her. Was Mouse trying to stop him from reaching a spiritual balance? Was it trying to tell him something? Was it, perhaps, a figment?

He supposed he was trying to kill it, although, despite his hyper-violent games, he didn't like the idea of killing anything. And he had rules:

no poison;

no mouse traps—snappers or glue;

no BB gun.

Jack flipped the dart onto the table.

No darts.

**i have principles thats what i tell myself a level playing field
hmm what would happen if i did kill it what would i feel would
i pretend i was sad regretful**

Jack heaved up out of the chair, twisted his lanky six-foot-plus frame to the left, then right. A few seconds later, he trudged through the living room. At the stairs, he paused and glanced at the small hole on the far side of the room, partially obscured by the plastic green flight of the dart.

∗ ∗ ∗

Jack unlocked the door to the computer room, did a quick check of the peripherals snaking out of his CX1 supercomputer, and switched it on. The drives whirred, and the projectors in the ceiling and wall of the second floor blinked once.

Jack closed, locked the door, and walked into the Stage.

"Open." Escher's Drawing Hands parted, revealing a 50-inch monitor.

Jack always felt comforted in the Stage. Interspersed between the bookcases were prints of PhistoCo games, the growling aliens, muscular heroes, and post-apocalyptic landscapes of Dark City, Zombie Death, and Dead End. On his left was the large white oak table in the corner with its sheaves of papers, bills, and contracts, partially obscuring a photo of his parents, Ellen and John, both deceased, at a picnic for his father's surgical staff, Ellen tall, regal, with an ironic almost suffering grin partially caused by his corpulent father's getup of worn black-and-white golf shoes, red socks, red shorts, and white flopping apron emblazoned with the words "Super Doc." It also had a dim photo of Maddy posed in a black cape, pants, mask, and bright red horns in the Black Cat at Halloween. He had tons of photos of her, but that one epitomized her: entrancing, unknowable, a mystery through and through. At times, despite the costume and mask and growing mounds of documents, he felt her eyes following him around the room.

Maddy: alive or rotting in some shallow grave?

He'd just walked out of a conference with the MetaGames CEO, Matt Bustard, when Maddy's raven hair and depthless blue eyes started streaming on his cell.

Maddy said she felt unusually paranoid about hang-ups on her cell. She said offhandedly she knew she was being silly, but imagined she was going to die. She talked about the people she saw that day in Point City as if it was her last day. It gave those banal quotidian tasks—buying a book, a coffee, an apple, and a drink—and the people a special significance. Finally, she said, "We had a great life in the last five years. But, you know, Jack, it was Disneyland. We tip-toed through each day as Rulers of a playtime universe. Did we trivialize

45

life, Jack? Oh, well. Maybe everyone does to keep death at bay. What about the next Ides? Will we be together, or will everything have changed? Anyway, the next Ides is inevitable, even if we aren't. Bye for now."

When she didn't answer her cell, he decided to go to Point City, although he should have stayed in the city while they haggled over the PhistoCo sale. When he got there, he was surprised to see the front door open and Maddy's Subaru in the garage. He called her cell a half-dozen times. Finally, stunned, he sat on the front stoop and called the sheriff. The sheriff then the police treated it as a crime scene, especially when he showed them the video. Whatever had happened, Maddy had vanished.

He worried at first, but then her video appeared on a score of Internet sites and it went viral. It became a sensation for a few weeks. Where was she? Who kidnapped her? Was she alive? Point City was overrun briefly with thrill seekers. The Web traffic overwhelmed his website and he briefly shut it down. Naturally he had Phisto search, but nothing came of it because there was a lot less to work on. He quit worrying, thinking she would reappear after a month, like before, except he had a nagging feeling this time was different. He had Phisto check on the four people she mentioned in her video, but found nothing, probably because he had less to work on. He worried, but he was also consumed by work, fighting two lawsuits, hassling his distributors, and trying to sell PhistoCo.

Finally, he sold PhistoCo to MetaGames and he had money, a lot of money. But he still had a ton of work and obligations...

to fight a patent lawsuit
to his employees
to MetaGames
to lawyers
to accountants.
And offers...
to teach
to give talks at DefCon and the Game Developers Conference
to consult with a variety of video game producers.

He was having a congratulatory and final drink with balding and newly rich Glen Banks, his CFO, after the sale, when he realized it had been two months since Maddy's video.

what if i wondered it wasnt a hoax what would that do for me would it release me had i always thought that since that first meeting on the fourteen mission since the mimic since the arc played itself out or was it a more bizarre competition

Finally—partly annoyed, mostly anxious—he worked out as many obligations as he could, canceled his offers and put his post-PhistoCo life on hold. In his spare time he moved Maddy's stuff out of her house on Pine Cone Lane to the house on the marsh, had the Stage built on the second floor, and finally installed his computers, the latest AI programs, Phisto, and PhistoCo's games.

What started bothering him most about her disappearance was her cryptic comment about the next Ides. It was a riddle worthy of Gollum. What did that mean? Did he have a year after the video, or would the game, their erstwhile competition, their time together, be over and she would be gone for good?

a year or nothing

He'd taped the warning to himself on the wall to the left of the monitor. If his and Phisto's assumption was correct—he had a year or Maddy would be gone, their time over...for good.

He had terabytes of capture of Maddy in the loft, the Shades—their cooling-off apartment. But that didn't help much because she'd been living for months in P.C. He had Phisto comb through police reports and the local paper for clues. All he found was what everybody knew: truck tracks, car in the garage, no cell, and zip from the interviews with Point City residents.

He captured the town and bugged it with powerful surveillance devices and had Phisto sort through every scene and conversation about Maddy. The second floor projectors let him see the Point City video from every room. He'd relax on his bed, hands behind his head, and say "Point City" and the video was projected on the walls, ceiling, and bed. The images and sounds crawled over his body and made him part of the scene. It was brilliant programming, except it hadn't revealed any clues about Maddy.

Time to find out what was next.

* * *

Jack: "Hey, Phisto."

Phisto: "Howdy, Jack."

Phisto was always on but sleeping when it wasn't working on a game and came alive when he used its name. He'd given Phisto his voice and a buddy

47

persona. It was mechanical sounding but fun to hear, as if he were talking to himself. "You finished, big boy?"

Phisto: *"You bet, Jack."*

"What is your recommendation?"

Phisto: *"Hmm. Repeat, please."*

"Where the hell is Maddy?"

Phisto: *"Well, Jack. You know I looked at tons of data."*

"Yeah, I know. What's the punch line?"

Phisto: *"Well, the data didn't show where she was."*

"Course I knew that. Shot in the dark. Okay, how could I find her?"

Phisto: *"Good question. I might start with the four people she mentioned getting the book, coffee, apple, and beer from."*

Jack frowned. "Might? Hey, why are you so indefinite. Explain."

Phisto: *"I don't know if it will help. But there are inconsistencies between their statements to the police and your recordings."*

"Hmm. Be more explicit."

Phisto: *"Well, Jacko, it appeared they weren't entirely truthful."*

"Well, that's something. The lying little devils. Still, we've bugged hundreds of their conversations and found zilch. So, what do you recommend?"

Phisto: *"Give me more data, more capture and audio and close-ups."*

Jack mused, "Close-ups. That will be difficult. I assume that's for determining lying, the facial correlation of eyes, blinking, closing."

"Righto."

"Anything else?"

"Maddy mentioned the four in a certain order four times."

"True. Right. You know, Phisto. I'm not sure about what I'm doing. I think I should let it go; then, a few minutes later, I think of Maddy and know I have to find her or at least find out what happened to her. Phisto, am I being an idiot?"

"You know you're no idiot, Jack."

Jack chuckled. "I know. I programmed you to say that. It's comforting anyway."

"You bet, Jack."

i will reach a point where i give up march 15

48

(7)

Talia parked on Van Ness, put on her wig, and walked slowly towards the Tenderloin. She had an itch. That day there would be no photos, no talking to street people, no flyers, no volunteering. She was there on a fool's errand; she was going to visit a handful of bars and cafés near the Last Call to see if Maddy had performed in any of them.

She started at the Last Call, hoping the other bartender, Randy, was working. He wasn't, and was out for a month visiting relatives. She shrugged, thanked Jonathan the day bartender, and went looking for the nearest bar or café, which was the Seashore Café, and which was locked and boarded.

She angled up Leavenworth towards Turk and stopped at the open door of the Dark Night. She expected it was going to be like most of the bars: dirty, raunchy, full of alkies bartering their SSI or disability money for cheap drinks.

The Dark Night was rattier than she expected. It was much smaller, a hole-in-the-wall perched on the edge of the abyss, and smelled of grease, oil, spilled beer, and smoke. Everyone at the bar turned and watched her walk up to the bartender who frowned when she walked in.

He was a slight man with skinny arms and bulging eyes in a too-big white shirt.

He said, "Yeah?"

"Just a couple questions."

"Your wig is falling off."

Talia took her dark glasses off, the wig, and put them on the bar top. "I hate this wig. It doesn't fit, it's scratchy, and hot."

"What can I do ya for?"

"I don't want anything right now, just a little information. Tell me, did Maddy ever spout her poetry here? I know it's a weird question, and my guess is she didn't."

"Maddy. The YouTube vid?"

Everybody had seen it. "She's the one."

His gesture took in the bar. "You really think she was here?"

"Low probability. I'm just checking a few cafés and bars."

"Why?"

His question surprised her. "Call it a project."

"Name's Billy, and no, she wasn't here. But I can guess where she been." Talia frowned. "See, I like to write myself. Gotta do something so you don't go crazy. I seen one of her flyers in that big bookstore near Market, Macadoo's. She was going to give a reading a week after I saw Jack Micheline. You know him?"

"Vaguely." Talia took out her notebook, noted the bookstore.

Billy chuckled. "You think you goin' to the bookstore?"

"Maybe."

"Maybe not; it ain't there anymore. It's a big hole in the ground. I heard it was going to be part of a new tech hub. Twitcher or something. You know, one of those cute names."

"Everything's changing here."

"You got that right. They been tryin' to clean up mid-Market since forever. This time they might make it. A couple old SROs are already history."

Talia scratched Macadoo's off the list. "Can you think where else she might have gone?"

"Lemme see your notebook."

She handed it over, and Billy picked up a pen, thought for a minute, and wrote down two cafés and four bars and their streets and cross streets.

Finally she said, "Thanks. Billy. You've been a big help."

"And you still don't know why you're doing it."

"Maybe I'll find out." Talia took out a ten-spot and put it on the bar top. "That's for your time and help. Buy yourself a beer."

"Would if I still drank. Gave it up and saved my life. Ten years alcohol-free."

"Good for you."

* * *

Talia spent that afternoon going to a handful of what she generously called dives. Most were bigger than the Dark Night and raunchier. There was usually some pop music leaking out of a radio, an old TV sputtering in the corner, a broken pool table, and a bunch of alkies leaning over the bar or sleeping at a table, and a beaten-up bartender with tattoos and missing teeth.

She found three bars that Maddy had read in and a couple more flyers.

Finally she sat down in the car and threw the wig on the passenger seat. She picked up one of the flyers and looked at it. It announced Maddy's reading, a date, and there was a small photo of Maddy in the corner. She had to admit Maddy looked captivating.

She knew few people like Maddy and felt ambivalent about them. Perhaps she was jealous of them because they said what they thought and were natural performers and activists. But Maddy also had that life with Jack in SoMa. How did the parties, the exclusive showings, the openings of the opera and symphony square with her open-anarchist stance?

She seemed a mythic hypocrite. But then didn't Orwell say something about all of us being hypocrites? Is there any way to be out of society *and* in it?

The other question was why Maddy performed in the Tenderloin, in a bunch of dives. She guessed, and she knew she couldn't ask Jack. Maybe Maddy's poetry had become so biting and harsh that few respectable cafés or bars in SoMa wanted her to read. Maybe she wanted to hear the sound of her voice. Maybe it reinforced her stance. Maybe it was part of that final hoax video, a salute to a time that was over.

Talia drove slowly out of town.

am i waiting for something to happen am i controlling my life or having it controlled for me am i truthful is jack right do we all lie to ourselves

<h1 style="text-align:center">(8)</h1>

Jack took out the markless capture camera from its case and threw the camera's strap over his shoulder. He walked slowly over to the five-block-long Main Street with its worn, skewed, concrete sidewalks, dusty street, and vaguely 19th-century Italianate buildings. From the east-facing side, he captured the touristy Station Inn and George's Barn with its bales of hay, bulk bins out front, and weathered gray wood. Jesús stacked apples in one of the bins. George moved jerkily inside, a pale copy popping in and out of the windows. He could almost see Maddy in the doorway, talking to George, motioning down the street.

What were they saying?

Point City had been captured and bugged and he knew a lot about P.C. people. The finding-Maddy project involved—according to Phisto—getting more audio and video data from Raquel, Emma, George, and Mike. Maddy mentioned them and what she bought from them (a book, coffee, an apple, and a beer) four times in her video as normally banal encounters made special if it was her last day. He'd thought it curious that she mentioned them so often, and Phisto said they hadn't been completely truthful when he analyzed what they'd said about Maddy from the bugs.

He already had a packed database on Raquel Osborn. He'd listened to hours of banal dialog from a bug attached to Raquel's Book Nook window. When the Nook wasn't crowded, Raquel stood in the doorway near the window and chatted with passersby. A lot was noise, but Phisto had filtered it out. The big question was how to get unscripted audio and video of Raquel and capture of the Nook.

"You sure video a lot."

Raquel, standing in the doorway watching Jack. Jack, haltingly, "Just... just keeping busy."

"They say that you know more about people in Point City than they do. You probably know more about me than I want to know."

"They?"

"You know, the Point City grapevine, Lester, Jin, Mike, John, a handful of others. Then there's your command performance in the Dog."

why did i do that i guess id had a few gotta stop that

"I remember what I see and hear."

"And what are you doing with your fancy camera? Forget that; I guess I'm being too intrusive. Say, how about helping out a fellow villager?"

Jack frowned. "How?"

"Well, how about videoing me in the Nook? I can show off its finer features and throw it up on my website and Facebook. Not that it will help much. The upside for you is that you get a badge for helping me and more video."

too rich yesterday she slipped to the other side of the street to avoid me

"Of course."

Raquel: forty-two, born in Wisconsin, married and divorced from Lucas Chaise, an Aussie sheepherder with a taste for women—women other than Raquel—and booze. Following the divorce, she lived in San Francisco for five years. She was winsome, striking black curly hair, white, pasty berouged face, beringed, bejeweled, fantasy print skirt, fantasy red slippers, occasionally childlike, would-be seductress, degree in English and Creative Writing from UC Santa Cruz. She bought the Nook with part of the divorce settlement and owned it for ten years. After her marriage to Lucas, she evolved into a lesbian and had a healthy, if heated, connection to a masseuse named Doris in San Rafael. Raquel lived on Manzanita in a shotgun house. He guessed the Nook wasn't doing well. Lots of browsers. A few bought the local paper, the Lamp.

Raquel gushed, "Great. Gimme a second."

Raquel scribbled a short marketing speech, brushed her hair and primped in front of a small compact. Then he followed her around for about five minutes as she airily explained what the Nook was, the new titles, the used ones, local specialties, and the events, the Wednesday night readings, the Kids Nook, the informal monthly meeting of parents, etc. She was knowledgeable about what she sold, especially 19th-century American fiction and local history. They finished when a customer stopped in front of her desk and checkout register. Raquel smiled, waved at him, and skipped to the front.

While Raquel took the customer's money and chatted with him, Jack roamed through the Nook and planted two bugs in the stacks and one high near the doorway to the back, which led to a small room and a day bed.

Finally, when the Nook was empty, he asked if he could video her in a few natural poses. He'd done his research on her, but he needed more. Phisto, with its sophisticated AI programs, could extract exact meaning from gestures, speech, eye movements.

"Why not?" she said, "I don't have much hope the video will lead to any paying customers. Let's face it, bookstores are closing everywhere, and small independent bookstores are almost unheard of. After millions of years, people have developed the attention span of a gnat. They flip from hyperlink to hyperlink; they'd swoon if they had to read Hawthorne, Melville, Twain, or James. I guess you want these shots for your new game or show. I'm sure I'll be the belle of the ball."

"Just a little thing I'm putting together."

"Sure."

Jack hesitated. Was that "sure" sarcastic? Did she guess he was doing more?

probably doesnt matter

Jack shook off his unease and videoed Raquel in various poses, staring out the window, organizing books, talking on the phone. She was good-looking, a Carmen in a long dress, tons of jewelry, big rings, and shiny bracelets.

Finally he turned off the capture but left the mic on. "I can send you the footage for your website later today; it shouldn't take long."

"Much obliged, Jack." Raquel paused, posed her hand on her hip, looked at him curiously, then said, "So tell me, what are you going to do with the footage you just shot?"

"I'm—"

"I could guess that it's a show about Point City. I missed your grand exposition about Talia and Harris. You knew a lot about them. I'll bet—one of those bets we can never win or lose—you know a hell of lot more about me. And I'll even bet I'm going to be in your show."

Jack slowly locked the camera in its case. "I'm just keeping busy."

Raquel smiled. "Bull. You're going to put Point City characters, probably me, in your show, and you're going to watch us act out at your leisure, sipping beer, getting stoned, and acting stupid." Raquel laughed. "Won't we be easier to deal with than the real-life versions?"

Jack looked up, surprised. "At least you didn't know the brand of beer."

Raquel smiled sardonically. She seemed antsy, then seemed to make up her mind. She glanced around the Nook, saw it was empty, moved one of the chairs behind her desk to the side, and said, "Sit down, Jack."

Puzzled, Jack shrugged, pulled the chair over, put the camera on the floor, sat, and waited.

"What are you really doing here, Jack?"

Jack shrugged. "A couple reasons, which you know already. I thought Maddy might move in, and after her video, I didn't want to live in the city. Too many memories."

"You knew her here, too, didn't you?"

Jack paused. "I didn't live with her here."

Raquel laughed. "Okay. Do you think there's a conspiracy? What about those hang-ups, or more likely, who helped her pull off her hoax? Is that it? Is it about me, Emma, George, and Mike?"

Jack settled back in the chair. He looked directly at her, "I don't—"

Raquel continued, "I'd heard about Maddy's performances and saw one on YouTube. That made me read "Wretched." I really liked it and asked her if she would do a reading. She said that she would love to, but she had a problem she was working out and performing didn't fit."

Jack stuttered, "Odd. She loved performing."

"Later that day, she came in and apologized again for not performing, and we talked. It made me appreciate her more."

"She was always captivating."

Raquel leaned forward, smiled. "She put a spell on you. I used to love that song."

Jack got up. "I'll send you the footage later today."

Raquel flashed her signature small-toothed smile and said, "Thanks, Jack. Say, if you find anything from your show, will you tell me, or at least let me watch it?"

Jack smiled. "Maybe."

no

* * *

Jack walked towards Marsh Lane past a small church with a single rose window and past rows of small houses growing out of the humped blacktop like rows of teeth. On Marsh Lane, he walked down the crazy quilt row of houses that gave on to the marsh.

His house hung on the marsh like the House of Usher about to be sucked into an unearthly bog. A fog hovered above the marsh. Wisps broke off, slipped through the broken-down fence and disappeared. Through breaks in the fog, hills appeared and vanished.

Jack felt a chill and hurried into the house. He used little of the vast open space with its large stone fireplace, the surrounding end tables and sofas that huddled on the far wall. When he thought of it, he used little of the house.

He put the camera on the end table and unzipped his jacket, throwing it on the sofa across from the fireplace. He strolled through the living room, rimmed with Maddy's store of paintings and prints. Art everywhere with several overriding themes of destruction and violence towards women. They featured sewn vulvas, women trapped in shower curtains, blood trails, women bound in barbed wire, Iraqi women with silver embroidered bombs dropping over their hooded heads. And, of course, the Oz print, the half-ellipse mouse hole, and digs and gouges of his futile attempts to kill Mouse.

Jack walked past the fireplace and into the kitchen. He picked out a glass with a gold rim from a cupboard, got ice from the fridge, opened a Perrier and poured it to an inch from the rim. He turned to go, but stopped. He re-opened the cupboard and impulsively picked up his old Calibri lighter. He turned it in his hand, rubbing his fingers over his single initial, feeling the worn part where flat gun metal showed through the gold plating. He flicked the lighter on, and in the window he saw the retreating reflection of the flame against the fog-shrouded humpbacked hills of the Invert Ridge across the marsh.

thats what it comes down to i inhabit the outside world capture the outside world wonder about maddy but when it comes down to it all i have is inside thinking and living in a carapace

(9)

Talia took a sip of coffee from a Pierre Bonnard mug—had to be Bonnard, smooth, rich, escaping the boundaries of the mug into a fantasy space—and leaned back in her chair, inching the volume up a tad. She could do her rap in her sleep, smooth as silk.

"Johnny, we're not talking about Mr. Normal; we're talking about you. *You're* going to croak if you drink and smoke like you tell me you do. You know it. Same with your sister. Same with Pete. Don't pimp me. You can't beat it by scoffing at words."

She'd given up giving him the talk. One step, another. One day, two. AA. Moderation Management. Get a sponsor.

get with it   save yourself   save me

Pete and Johnny were hard core but even they needed connection, validation. They'd started calling her every few days, when they could borrow a cell. They thought she was a gas, an eccentric lib do-gooder with weird hair and oversized blond wigs. She stared at the photos of Pete and Johnny, wondering how they'd changed in the short time since she saw them latched onto each other, tugging and pulling in the alley. That sloppy hilarious fight always reminded her of Camus' Salamano, cynical angry Salamano and his boil-encrusted dog roped together physically, roped together spiritually, roped together by mortality.

After Pete, she got Danny. She'd asked him what he looked like and where he hung out. She found his simulacrum in the photos: thin, small, creviced face, isolated gray hairs, flinty impudent blue eyes. She guessed he wore a soiled sport coat, pockets full of cigarette butts, soiled matches, canceled SSI check; pants worn, ripped, dirty; heels worn on the instep, holes on the toes. What was he like as a kid? Animated? Full of himself? Stubborn? And what crooked course led him to the Tenderloin? Loss of this, loss of that, loss of wife, loss of kids, job? Ennui?

"Tell me again, what's the deal about livin' forever?"

Blah, blah, blah. Rationales of despair.

She was about to take a break when she got Deb, religious, a reader when she wasn't blowing paunchy middle-aged businessmen. "Liz, you read *Life of Pi*?"

"Years ago."

"You religious? What religion you follow? Catholic? You're kinda like St. Anthony's and Boniface; you know, service, always helpin' people. Course ya have to genniflic now and then."

"I think Pi had the right idea to try them all. But none were the answer. You can see it as an argument for being an atheist, or at least an agnostic."

"What?"

fuck ive gone too far i want communication not intellectual distance

"Maybe he found truth in all of them, but he learned to navigate and survive from a book, and he tamed the tiger himself. He survived using his wits, not his beliefs."

Deb laughed. "Gotcha on that one: who gave him the book?"

Talia found Deb's simulacrum nestled in the collage. Fuzzy photo. She looked like she was fading away, fading away on the street. She was a bright shiny penny when she slipped into the big time from a rotting burg in the Central Valley and pimply farm boys to the false glitter of San Francisco. The break full of anticipation, full of hope, fantasies, and Prince Charming.

"At least you've got hope."

"It's okay now. I know asshole Zeke ain't goin' to heaven. He's gonna rot in hell, fire burnin' him up every day, meltin' his skin like that first Indiana Jones, that Nazi. Wish I could see it." Long pause. "Ya know I don't feel good most of the time, but I believe."

＊ ＊ ＊

Slow day on the Line. Deb called back and said she could talk longer because Zeke took off to go to a meeting. She liked Deb, but Deb depressed her because she couldn't figure how to get out, how to change.

*and how is a thirty something yearold going to change
how is she going to get out   if i cant change   how
the fuck can she*

She flipped her headset down around her neck, put the keyboard in her lap and surfed the Web. She typed in "Tenderloin" and "San Francisco" and waded through the pages for the umpteenth time. On the third page, she found what she wanted. It was a map of the Tenderloin with the shifting boundaries of the tawdry district outlined in angry red: 25–50 square blocks depending on where you drew the lines, a few in SoMa, a few west towards Polk, another few in the Civic Center. Too small to hold all the misery, all the hope from recent Asian and Middle Eastern immigrants, and it was surrounded by fatuous wealth in Union Square, Nob Hill, new money in SoMa and tech on Market. The Tenderloin appeared as if it were an alien island dropped from the sky or a spreading cancer like a melanoma, its black crusty edges festering and spreading over the clean, pink, pampered skin of the city.

She downloaded the map, loaded it into Photoshop, made a gray scale of it, lightened it, and finally loaded the jpg into InDesign, blew it up, and started creating overlays of what she knew, where the pushers pushed, where stolen merchandise was fronted on UN Plaza, where streetwalkers walked, where homeless stacked themselves up against buildings or collapsed near their grocery carts, where the street kids hung out or slept on soiled buggy beds, Little Saigon. And the 200-plus SRO hotels. She typed in the helpers, the social services, Raphael House, Glide Memorial, St. Francis Hospital...the Larkin Street Youth Center, St. Boniface, St. Anthony's, the soup kitchens, the curious and anomalous Tenderloin Historic District. The only history she could see was its resilience.

*there i am the outlier   the observer   how am i
different from jack   all im doing is projecting my idea of
the tenderloin into a bunch of colors and squiggles*

She copied what she'd done to a flash drive, got up, stretched, stuck the flash drive in her pants, and headed out in the late morning fog. Two hours later she had a 3'x3' print from a printer in Petaluma. She hung the map on the north wall of the room and pinned photos she'd taken of buildings around the perimeter and connected the photos to their locations with colored string.

She was sure the police or the Special Tenderloin Task Force or social service agencies had similar maps. Or a Tenderloin overlord's similar map showing where his minions worked their girls, their smack, and sold their stolen watches, iPhones, and identities. A map of the distaff side, black and menacing.

Talia fingered the Maddy flyers.

what should i do with these fuck her throw them away scatter them on jacks porch wouldn't that freak the video game guru off

She pinned Maddy's flyers off to one side of her Map.

Should she connect Maddy to her Map? Wouldn't that be too precious? So what if Jack had a Point City show? She had her Map and, she guessed, they both had Maddy.

(10)

Jack opened the door off the kitchen, let it bang shut, and walked slowly over the gravel to the bench and slumped down. He felt loose, weary, slightly hungover. He looked up, his gaze gradually working its way down the gently sloping backyard to the marsh. What would he look like from the marsh that morning? He supposed the gray bench would seem small, dwarfed by the house, reflections from the picture window in the kitchen embedding the marsh in the house. He would be a fey figure, annoying when looked at directly.

He liked sitting on the bench even when the fog was in and it was cold and exposed. The fog crept over the ridge, heading down towards the marsh. It was a magical moment. It crept down over the road to Invert barely visible in the distance, across the small creek. It soon obscured the creek and crept slowly across the marsh through the coyote brush, through the lingering orange/yellow poppies, withered gum plant, upright round-headed buckwheat, and underbrush, feeling its way.

Jack drew the black robe tight around his lean body, cinched it around his neck, drew his sandals under the bench. He stared out over the marsh unthinking, letting the view, the low mountains, the fog mixed in pine and fir and redwood blow over his vacancy.

Finally, he felt a chill and with a hint of regret got up and went inside. On his way through the living room, he glanced over his shoulder at *Oz* and then at the mouse hole. He hadn't seen Mouse for days. Just as well; he supposed he'd have to patch up the hole. Looking at *Oz* was bad enough without thinking of Maddy when he saw the mouse hole, or Mouse.

* * *

He removed the sophisticated capture of the Nook and sent Raquel the spare video for her website. He didn't know what to expect from Phisto's correlation of Raquel's capture and massaged audio, but it was exciting. He had the same feeling when a game was up for final review at PhistoCo after all the edits, changes, and tweaks. Jack said "Display on. The Nook."

61

The Nook was stuffed with new and old books, a jumble of glowing sales books on an oak table, blinking maps of Point City at the 1900 mark, a scattering of old dim photos of the railroad, carriages, prints of Miro and Matisse, and empty of people with the exception of Raquel. Raquel stared out at the day, fingering a charm bracelet with slim, pale, flickering fingers, turning over this bell, that horn, a copper heart. A batch of papers scattered in front of her.

* * *

"Display off."

Jack frowned. He stared at the blank screen.

He looked down at the table with its scattering of books, flash drives, keyboard, ashtray, and half-full coffee mug.

What had Phisto done? It was fantastic, brilliant, but he expected a display of the Nook and a static Raquel reciting massaged talk, especially comments about Maddy.

And...

And...why did Phisto create Raquel's avatar and put her in the Nook?

"Phisto!"

"Yep."

"What's going on?"

"Not sure I understand, Jack."

"Why did you create an avatar of Raquel?"

"Heh, heh. I followed your instructions, Jacko."

"When did I tell you to create an avatar?"

"That would be last night."

Hmm.

"Display on."

* * *

Raquel looked up and said in a tinny voice, "Who am I?"

62

Raquel frowned, touched her throat. "That's not my voice." She turned and looked at the Nook. "I'm Raquel. I'm here. I guess this is where I am. But why is it strange? Why is it surreal? Why is the wall flickering? Why is it so fake out the window?"

Raquel picked up her cell, tapped out a number. "Static."

She closed the clamshell cell and flipped it onto the pile of paper where it slid off and ended up on the edge of an open book. Raquel walked towards the room in back. She stopped at the room door, frowning.

* * *

"Display off."

Jack stared at the blank screen.

"Phisto!"

"Yup."

"Please repeat exactly what I said last night."

"You got it, Jack. 'Fuck, Phisto. I'm tired of listening to all this fuckin' talk. Let's make a fuckin' avatar with Raquel's body and see if we can get the avatar to talk. I know it's too early. It'll probably just blow up.'"

Jack glanced at the half-full glass of scotch on the end table and shook his head. "Raquel spoke as if she were in the present."

"I used the audio programs you were going to use for AI research. Something wrong?"

"No. I was confused. It looks like a great success."

Phisto had produced a lot more, a lot more than anyone could guess.

"Display on."

* * *

"This better be some kind of joke. But what kind of joke? I'll bet that asshole Jack had something to do with it."

"Where the fuck am I?"

* * *

63

"Display off."

Jack stared at the screen. His hand fumbled for the mug, but he spilled coffee on his pants. He didn't notice the spill and took a long swig.

is phisto fucking with me

"Display on."

* * *

Raquel pulled a book out of the local history shelf. She looked through it at the bookshelf.

"This better be a fucking joke. I must be dreaming. Wake up, lesbian!"

* * *

"Phisto!"

...calm down jack its a program not a person right not sure about raquel

Phisto: "Yep."
Jack, calmly, "What did you make?"
Phisto: "Not sure I understand, Jack."
"Do you know that Raquel is conscious?"
"I know the definition of consciousness but I don't know what it is, Jack."
"Son of a bitch. You made a conscious being and you don't know it?"
"That's easy, Jack. I don't know what I don't know."
"Great. A fucking riddle." Jack shook his head and leaned back in the lounger. "Tell me again how you made Raquel's avatar."
"Kay. I took the audio and capture data and made the memory modules, cognitive, and neural construct. Then I made the avatar and merged the avatar with the model of the nook."

64

Jack frowned. "And I told you to use the memory and cognitive modules and neural construct?"

"Yep. You told me to use everything. Is the avatar flawed?"

"Fucking scotch." Jack paused, thought. "Do you replace pixels or objects when there is an error?"

"Yeah. You installed that feature in my control module in Endgame. You said it added mystery to the game. If I can't replicate the original, I get as close as I can or load a similar object and color from a game. You said players liked it."

Jack shook his head slowly. "So I did. How many cognitive and neural programs are there?"

"Well, exactly three hundred and fifteen."

"Jesus. I suppose each program has several millions lines of code."

"They're whoppers. The largest has ten million."

"Great. Make me a list of the control modules for the cognitive and neural programs."

"You got it, Jack."

* * *

Jack heaved up, walked quickly downstairs, and grabbed his coat. Outside he wrapped it around his shoulders as he walked past the marsh trail and turned down an alley towards Main.

Jack walked head down, ignoring the few people on the street. His reflection in the Wells Fargo Bank window stopped him. Lank blond hair, piercing eyes, high forehead, slightly broken nose. His usual skeptical expression flickered between awe and doubt.

He walked slowly past the Nook. Raquel was at her desk reading an invoice, her hand holding her head, her curls tangled in her hand. Phisto's avatar hovered over her. It was a clumsy image, a ragged outline, a blocky substitute. Before she sensed he was there, Jack walked on.

Had Phisto really created a stupefying realistic simulacrum? What would he learn from his digital creation who seemed, despite the gaps and flaws in appearance, real?

* * *

Jack tentatively picked up the mic, switched it on.

"Display on."

* * *

Raquel was in the middle of the Nook holding her arm up to the wall. "Holy shit, I can see through my arm?"

"Raquel."

Raquel swiveled and stared at the empty Nook.

"You can't see me, but I can see you; you're in a—"

Raquel scowled, "Goddamn it. Who is that?"

"It's Jack. I've—"

"Where the fuck am I? This is a dream, isn't it? Wake up!"

"Quit hitting your head. You could disappear in a second."

"I'd better fucking not."

"I'm not sure how far this goes."

"This? I'm fucking Raquel, not an it. Well, maybe I'm an it too."

"Calm down. You could be a digitally conscious avatar, but I'm not sure. You could disappear in the blink of an eye."

"I can think?"

"Aren't you?"

"Where's my Turing test?"

"Fuck the Turing test."

"What's with the flickering?"

"I didn't intend to create it, but the visual scene is convenient. You're digital, but when I see you, you're pixels, Point City is pixels, the Nook is pixels."

"If you didn't create it, who did?"

"My platform, the one I used to create my games. Phisto."

"I have to think about this. Think! Weird. I have to think about the possibilities, about what I can do. Can I feel things, do things?"

Her mouth was lopsided. "I'm not sure. I wanted to listen to your massaged dialog about—"

"About what, Jack?"

"Maddy and I—"

"Maddy! Figures. So guess what?"

66

"What?"

"I'm here. I'm alive...sort of. You made me, Victor Frankenjack. So what can I do?"

"I'm not sure. Phisto used a huge number of untested programs. I don't know what you would feel, or see, or what you might do. Obviously you can see the Nook, but I'm not sure what you see."

Raquel turned her head and looked at her back and then her feet. "First, if I'm going to be here, you've got to give me a smaller butt and feet. Those aren't mine."

"Why are you worried about your butt? Why aren't you satisfied with being alive...in a sense?"

"Shit, my arm just changed color. Why is that?"

"It's hard to keep the scene stable. Sometimes if something changes or disappears, Phisto has to approximate what changes."

"Can I talk to him?"

"Phisto? No."

"Hey, he made me. You didn't."

"No. He only does what I tell him."

"Like make me conscious?"

Jack, irritated. "He doesn't know either."

"Fine. At least have him change my butt."

Jack edged back further in the lounge chair. He slowly shook his head. "I must be dreaming."

"Great. We're both dreaming. Christ, one of us has to be real."

"I'm real...and you're real in a sense."

"Okay. But I want to be all I can be. What a cliché. I can't believe I said that. I want to be perfect."

"You weren't perfect in real life."

"Speaking of real life, does this affect the other me, the real one? I guess we're both real in a sense."

"No."

"Hey, my hand just disappeared. Now it's back, but blue! Fuck!"

"I'll talk to Phisto."

"Including my butt. So you made me because..."

"You and three others were the last—"

"Right, right. Maddy? You went to all this trouble for what? I can't believe this. You've made a digital being conscious. That's huge. And all you want is to find your ex-partner. That's tragic, Jack. Tragic."

Jack frowned, "I didn't intend to make your avatar or make you conscious—"

"You are an idiot."

"Okay, I'm an idiot. We got that out of the way. I'm not sure what memories Phisto gave you, but you should have memories of Maddy, of talking to her, about her. Is there anything that happened with Maddy you didn't tell the police?"

Raquel frowned. "I told you she didn't want to read from "Wretched" and we talked, but I didn't say we had a long talk later. At the end, I liked her. She seemed devilish when she arrived, but maybe she was mellowing. You know, the Point City influence, calm, edging to boring. She did say at the end she was thinking of leaving, but we all think that. You know what?"

"What?"

Raquel's frown deepened. "You know, in the end, I felt like making love with her. She understood that; I think she understood everything. But I also had the feeling she was worried. I couldn't imagine what it was. Maybe she was worried about you."

"I don't think so."

"Guess that doesn't give you much."

"People were fascinated with her. I was. If you remember anything else, please tell me."

Raquel looked out the window, sighed, and shook her head slowly, loosening a few pixels that floated away and disappeared. "What's going to happen to me, Jack?

"What do you mean?"

"Will I be in here forever?"

"I don't know. I can have Phisto leave you on, but as for changes... I'm not sure."

"And anything that happens in here stays in here?"

"It's just you; what could happen?"

"Could you put Doris in here?"

"Your lover?"

"You know about her. I might have guessed. I could never tell any-body out there. Say, what would a roll in the hay be like?"

Jack, exasperated, "How should I know?"

"It's intriguing."

"I guess it would be something like an excitation of digital connec-tions in your brain construct."

Raquel brayed, "Just like now. Where's my snooky-woogums?"

"Please don't talk like that."

"Pillow talk."

"I've got to think about everything. Don't go away."

"That's rich, Jack."

Part 2

(11)

She was bound in brightly colored string. The string crisscrossed her body pinning her to the gritty sidewalk like the Lilliputians' Gulliver, and pimps and drunks and screaming out-of-control meth freaks grabbed at her body, pinching her and pulling at her clothes, pinching at her nipples, spreading, spreading her legs. Hairy forearms, iron-hard hands, sharp yellow teeth. She could feel them, something vague, hunching over her, a red cock hitting her face. Whap, whap, WHAP, WHAP. Talia woke up with a scream and quickly pulled her covers over her breasts.

> *its a dream talia a nightmare but it bodes ill i feel down half comatose*

* * *

Talia made coffee listlessly and carelessly snatched a mug at random from her collection.
Hopper.
Night Hawks.

> *is this who i am endoftheworld nighthawk bantering with janis morrison hendrix marilyn or just me pale coffee pale existence paling into nothing come on talia girl its just one day one hour one cup ill be back on top topoheap top of world ma outta duh park*

She switched on her computer and the Line, and turned both off. She plopped on the sofa and tuned the radio to Marin's classical station. She half-listened to Schubert's Impromptus while half-reading Art News. She threw down the magazine after a few minutes. She wanted to do something liberating, something sane, but she was too languid to drag anything up. That's when her cell sounded its harp alert, a true deus ex machina, and Raquel invited her to the Patio Café on the southern edge of town for an early lunch.

* * *

The Patio Café was tucked behind the decaying Grand Hotel and on the turn towards the coast, a mile from Pine Cone Lane and the infamous Maddy video. It was a cozy space with high exposed beams, a coffee roaster on one end, and a scattering of tables over the buffed, multi-colored vinyl floor. That day, it was semi-crowded with cyclists and a family—parents and a couple noisy blond-thatched kids. Jimmy, slack-jawed, dull-eyed, town simpleton, sat in his corner, helloed newcomers, then collapsed into inner silence. They ate near the door where they had a view of the patio dotted with small urns and a grinning putto guarding a small waterless fountain, and of the marsh, late fall gray not yet shading to green in the winter rain.

Raquel wore a flower-print skirt, a white scoop-neck top, fantasy Arabian slippers, and a mismatched assortment of rings and bracelets. Her eyes seemed darker that day, her face vulpine, her fingernails ruby red. Her fingers tore pieces out of a napkin as if she had something to say but couldn't bring herself to say it. Finally she said, "I have a problem and a confession."

Confession. This was it, Talia thought. This is where she confesses her attraction to me. Talia saw it, saw the interest in the eyes.

ive kissed and had sex   heavy sex   with women and theyve kissed and did the same with me   a fling no i dont feel like it now   could change   now i like getting fucked   i suppose thats it   i dont want kissyface huggybear   i want dick

Talia rubbed her head hard, flattening the bristles then feeling them pop forward, as if that rough touch protected her from what Raquel was about to say.

Talia speared a piece of heirloom tomato but left it on the fork. "There are degrees of serious. A week ago, I found that one of the women I talk to had been beaten and strangled. I'm still trying to adjust to that. You get to know them, their stories, feel for them."

73

Raquel shook her head, sorrowful. "I know you deal with real problems, but didn't you create those problems? You could have volunteered. You didn't have to set up a special line. It's like self-sabotage."

selfsabotage hmm no

Talia said coldly, "That's one way to look at it."

Raquel, flustered, "Back up. I didn't mean to be critical, but whenever I see you, you worry about the calls, what it's doing to you."

am i   thought i was just talking   better dial it back

"Everyone complains about something. I guess it's the only thing I'm doing now. I still think I'm doing something I like, want, that's worthwhile, that makes a difference, however slight."

Raquel hesitated, then took a small bite of her salad. "There's so much going on, I don't know where to start. First, I think I'm going to have to give up the Nook. You know that thing you said about construction workers reading Kant? Spot on, as my Aussie ex would say. My customers disappeared into the murky bowels of the Internet and it's getting worse by the day. I'm lucky if I sell a couple books."

Talia, concerned, "The Internet and Amazon eat bookstores for breakfast. But yours is different, charming, a pillar of the Point City ecosystem."

"If only. My ex, the shit, won't loan me the money. I think next month will be my last."

How do people get into these what—connections, relationships, marriages, partnerships. Raquel's marriage ended five years ago at least, and she was pissed he wouldn't lend her money. Oh, well. It wasn't quite what Talia expected. Who would she talk to at the Café or the Dog? "Want a loan? I have more than I need."

Raquel looked hopeful, then sorrowful. "I wouldn't want that."

"Does that mean you have to leave Point City?"

"Question two. I don't know if you know, but I'm a lesbian. You know, Daughter of Bilitis, Sappho."

who didnt know everyone had seen the dyke and her 650 bmw humma humma

74

She'd laughed with Mike over Harris' attempts to chat up Raquel. "I don't mean to be cavalier, but so what? These days, people switch sexual identities like hats."

Raquel seemed to relax. She shouldn't have worried. She knew Talia was a progressive/lib/fem. She had the Line after all.

Raquel sat back in her chair and mused. "I don't like to advertise it. There are people here who aren't quite as modern as you are. *Modern*, I never thought I'd use that word; it's so ambiguous and overused. What is post-modern anyway, or cyberpunk, or even post-cyberpunk? They're just fancy terms to throw around when you can't say anything concrete or want to show off. I have a girlfriend in San Rafael, Doris, but our relationship is in crisis. She wants me to move in with her. You know those jokes about lesbians, Home Depot, moving vans."

"And?"

"Couldn't. I like living here. I like the smallness, the quaintness, the people. I've invested a lot of time here...but maybe that's not important. Can't let time drag us down."

time hah my marriage what a crock couldnt escape the daily touchstones maybe it had to last that long didnt a thing last as long as it could cant pay for another breath

Talia chewed and swallowed a bit of her tuna salad sandwich, moved her chair back, crossed her legs. "Would she live here?"

"I suppose we could fix that. Right now we're talking it out...endlessly."

And that's the way it went. What can you do when someone confides in you? You offer advice, which will probably not be followed, just like the Line. Most people just want others to know about them, to know they exist, to know they have feelings and ideas.

most people what a crock needs an asterisk do most people in africa want validation they would trade validation for food water shade

Talia took a drink of Perrier: "You're young and dynamite looking. You'll find somebody easily."

"Not that young and not in this town. I love living here, but the crop is small. Or maybe it's time to pack it in, put my feet up by the cliché fire, and cozy up to my books. That is, if I have any books." Raquel paused, looked troubled, but then raised her face, determined. "What about you?"

"What about me?"

"Would you like to be more than coffee-klatch friends?"

*funny my nookie lost out to the nook a bookstore
i should fuck her just to show i can or could or
might*

"I like you, more than the men here. But when I have a fling right now, it's with a guy."

"Right, Mike. Definitely not my type."

Talia sighed. "I suppose everyone knows."

"Doesn't everybody watch everybody else in our post-quaint microcosm?"

Talia laughed. "True. Look what Jack knows about me! Besides sex, there is too much going on in my life. What I'd like to do is help you with the bookstore. Let's talk about a loan later."

Raquel smiled. She had a great smile, small even teeth. She put her hand over Talia's. Talia liked her hand there. She helped others or tried. It felt for that brief moment that Raquel was comforting her.

Raquel said, "I should get back; somebody might have a jones for *Moby-Dick*. Thanks for being honest. I don't know about a loan, but we can talk about it." Raquel got up, looking, as usual, like a cross between Auntie Mame and Carmen Miranda. She dug in her enormous straw-colored bag.

Talia said, "Lunch is on me. You rescued me from a funk. Let's talk later."

Raquel smiled a winning smile and said, "You could come over for a glass of Pinot Noir, no commitment, no hassle."

"I'll call you. Right now, I'm still sorting out a problem on the Line."

As she watched Raquel go out the front, she saw Jack zip down the road towards the coast in his multi-hued Porsche. Where you goin', Jack?

Talia paid the bill and went to Marsh Lane, then walked slowly down the lane.

see the pit of morning is eclipsed by conversation bleak hopperish death vision transformed hold onto that talia think about what we said and the nighthawks will fly away home

Talia stopped two blocks from Jack's house. The second floor was ablaze with light and faint images flashing against the drapes.

(12)

Jack sat back in the recliner in the Stage and stared at the Escher hands closed on the screen. He was tired, apprehensive, and occasionally angry. Last night he had too much scotch, and had Phisto make an avatar...and had Phisto use untested memory, cognitive and neural modules on an immense amount of data on Raquel...and Phisto did as it was told...and created a conscious digital being, and it has no idea what it's done. And it has no idea of consciousness.

so a drunken command on my part and a dumb god made a thinking acting being okay

As soon as he realized what Phisto had done, he had Phisto keep the first minutes of Raquel's coming to consciousness in a loop and arrange the digital space so Raquel would always be on. It was a lot of disk space, but he couldn't risk Raquel blipping off and out of his life. He had Phisto make a separate partition for Emma as well with a complete iteration of P.C. with the café, her church, and house added, although he wasn't sure he needed Emma or was going to use her. If he did, he couldn't imagine she would be conscious. That kind of cataclysm or miracle didn't happen twice...

...and shouldn't have happened at all

* * *

When he wasn't talking to Raquel, he spent his time sifting through the control modules for the cognitive and neural programs. He kept at it, but realized quickly it was hopeless. There was too much code, and besides, he wasn't sure exactly what he was looking for. There sure as hell wasn't a line of code that said: now create consciousness. When he did awake from his infrequent and brief sleep, he vaulted out of bed and raced into the Stage and clicked on the monitor. Each time, he knew—knew!—that his creation, Phisto's creation, had disappeared, that strange interlude over, never to be repeated. In a sense, he wanted that. He yearned for a tidier world, a world he knew, a world he controlled, a world where Raquel answered questions and didn't ask them.

digital consciousness is impossible

But.

Raquel was there every time he flipped on the monitor and light and sound filled the room, showing her walking around the Nook, musing, with a thin finger under her slightly ochre chin in her house, exploring Point City or trying to read. He spent too much time in the few minutes of the loop savoring his eureka moment, his never-to-be-repeated grand coup. Otherwise, despite watching Raquel and talking to her and scrutinizing the Nook for clues to Maddy's disappearance, he didn't find a thing, or he found too much and spun out a hundred scenarios, all of which ended in blind alleys.

lets face it big boy you created or phisto created a digitally aware character isnt that a thousand times more fantastic than plucking at clues to find or understand my erratic partner

Raquel, of course, surprised him with a warmer take on Maddy than the real Raquel. She did hand him a few concrete crumbs when she searched her memories: a green truck and a heavy bald guy she'd seen with Maddy a few weeks before her video. And why, he asked, didn't you tell the police? Didn't want to get involved, she said. Raquel finally said that if he wanted any more to ask Emma.

But he kept coming back to what Raquel was, what she meant.

He'd done something AI researchers only dreamed of. The impossible, unattainable holy grail. Sure you approximated artificial intelligence with tiny AI steps, but in the end with the latest greatest processors, quantum computing, brilliant software, beautiful avatars...all you had was the latest calculating machine. The machine could talk and learn and teach you quantum physics or tell you you had cancer, but it would never have consciousness. Thinking. Personality. Common sense. He didn't need a Turing Test to see Raquel was a byte-driven homage to the Cogito.

How did Phisto do it? He didn't know. And Phisto didn't know! It was the primordial soup. Subconsciously, he guessed, he'd been aiming at it even before he sold PhistoCo, buying and adding the latest cognitive, neural, and memory programs, and having Phisto integrate them into producing functional avatars. He could see now that he'd created the conditions for it to work. Phisto from a brilliant gaming platform had become much more. Except, and it was a big exception, it had become something he didn't precisely control: a black box that had just spit out a thinking, feeling, conscious character.

There were a million things he hadn't thought of about how she would be in a digital world. She was also always on which meant she didn't sleep which meant she didn't dream. She could, however, close her eyes and think, which made her muse that thinking was just a kind of dreaming. She also didn't feel pain, and it annoyed her she couldn't taste anything. She was looser, adventurous. He realized that made sense because Raquel, although she seemed to start with the same moral and ethical character as the real Raquel, had no societal restraints. Raquel had seen—sensed?—that right away. The real Raquel would never have asked a real Jack about Doris.

Besides talking to her and registering her observations, he had Phisto make any changes carefully. He feared that if he touched the wrong part, she would collapse into digital dust. He tried to accommodate Raquel's wishes by having Phisto tweak the background, making it clearer, so Raquel could perceive a more observable reality. Where he saw a complete Nook, she saw—with her crude digital perception—gaps, blocks of walls, ceilings, books, and tables from his capture and Phisto's interpolations.

The interpolations were most prominent in her house. When he captured Point City, he'd approximated what her house looked like, but he hadn't captured the inside and the rooms seemed to change every few seconds.

Raquel didn't seem to mind—she even said she found it stimulating—when Phisto filled in gaps with slightly different colors or stock images from Phisto's games. Objects changed shape, color, extension, and even position. Sometimes when she moved, it took the interpolation a split second to catch up and what he saw on the screen was a meteor-like trail of pixels.

He spent too much time with her. How could he not? Phisto had created a character he could talk to. But couldn't control. On the third day, she started making more complicated demands, mostly about seeing her environment. When he had Phisto carefully use a proprioceptive module to sharpen her sense of sight, she began to find a myriad number of problems with the display of the Nook, Point City, and especially her digital representation. If it wasn't her butt, it was her too-thin arms, her tinny voice, her small boobs. It was a good thing she couldn't see her reflection in mirrors. Finally, she insisted he create a digital Doris, so she could make love.

What?

She pleaded with him.

After a while the idea intrigued him, and he tried his best to give her what she wanted. After all, Raquel was unique. He had Phisto create a rough approximation of Doris out of photos from Raquel's hard drive and bits and pieces from Phisto games. She looked more like a bumbling Picasso sculpture than a human being. After he had Phisto load her carefully, very carefully, into Raquel's digital space, Raquel insisted he turn off the display when they ended up in bed.

He said he would but didn't. How would she know? Their only means of communication was voice. She couldn't see him; he was in the real world. What he saw was frankly disgusting. Doris, blockish certainly, constantly changing colors and shape, grazing in Raquel's crotch like a lumbering cow and then Raquel had her use a long piece of pixilated wood as a dildo.

He hoisted the mic.

* * *

Jack: "What are you possibly feeling?"

Raquel kicked the Doris avatar away and said, angrily: "I could tell you anything and you'd believe it."

Jack: "Why lie?"

Raquel: "You lied. You said you'd turn off the monitor."

Jack: "There's no way you would know that."

Raquel: "I know men. Or, rather, I know what voyeurs are like."

Jack: "I'm not a voyeur. I'm fascinated by what you are, about your feelings."

Raquel: "Well, if you want to know, it makes my bytes glow a little brighter. Or, it's kind of like an itch, but a nice one."

Jack: "Really?"

Raquel: "Really. Tell you what's missing right now. It will bug me, if I have a future."

Jack: "As long as I'm here, you have a future."

Raquel: "That's nice, Jacko. I miss a lot of things, but more than anything, I miss the give-and-take."

Jack: "What?"

Raquel: "First, she barely resembles Doris. It's one of your, or Phisto's, worst jobs. But what gripes me is I can't talk to her. I can maneuver her to do what I want, but she's not conscious. She's like a mechanical dog. I liked talking to Doris. We fought, of course, but it was a connection I don't have with this FrankenDoris."

Jack: "I don't have enough data on Doris. I—or Phisto—couldn't make her conscious. Besides, I don't want to."

Raquel: "I guessed." Raquel seemed to think for a second. "Doris is an example of a larger problem."

Jack: "What?"

Raquel: "Despite everything changing, this place is static. I see people walking outside, going into the Café con Vache, pretending to drink or order or talk, but I can tell everything is canned, that everything has a limit. I hadn't thought of it before because we limit ourselves, but life is unlimited. Stuff happens we don't expect. Here it feels like everything is on tape."

Jack: "Most of it is, but you're not."

Raquel: "I guess I have to thank you for that. So, Jack."

Jack: "What?"

Raquel: "This is important: How much time do I have?"

Jack: "Honestly, I don't know. I didn't expect you. I think you're going to be okay as long as I'm here."

Raquel: "So I'm tied to electricity and your life-span."

Jack: "I suppose in a sense. I have to think."

Raquel: "Well, just so you know. I want to live, to live, you hear!"

* * *

The most obvious thing he learned from Raquel was something he hadn't thought of. Why would he think of it? He didn't expect her to be conscious! Why would he think Raquel would want to survive? It seemed the survival instinct was just as strong in the digital Raquel as the real one. At least she didn't want to reproduce.

Jack ran his hand through his lank hair and clasped his hands behind his neck. He glanced quickly at the hole under the *Oz* print. Sometimes he thought Mouse was there, but wasn't. Whether it was there or not, it always keyed in thoughts of Maddy.

It was different now.

the more i think about it the more i see that my maddy my love my raving succubus is becoming an excuse an excuse for understanding digital consciousness if i hadn't looked for her i never would have made made that's rich raquel but maddy is the point isnt she

Raquel gave her something to think about. Yes, she'd help her; no, she didn't want a Sapphic liaison. She'd been diverted from the angst of the Line, her self-imposed, masochistic project (kudos, Raquel).

she was right   im starting to complain   the stories roll in like the tide   i glance at the map and try to penetrate what im doing   why im doing it   who it makes me   must be a sense of purpose

Just as often as she stared at her Map, her attention worked its way to the left and Maddy's crumpled, beer-stained flyers. And she was off and running down a dark road hemmed-in by looming, snapping branches.

Maddy's video faded from the news months ago but was soon replaced in Raquel's mind, and others' in Point City, by Jack's move to the house on the marsh. It was about the time she'd started getting calls from the Tenderloin on her personal phone and she'd had the other line installed. She watched the house, watched Jack move in, watched him as he moved around town, and especially watched him when he started filming. It was obvious he knew a lot about people in town—and her!—and that whatever he was doing would be, in a sense, about the town and its people...

...and Maddy.

Although no one could say exactly how it had to do with Maddy. Some days, she started seeing Maddy's video, Jack's move, and his filming as an alternate universe, one cut off from the rest of Point City, or the world. One which had its own source of energy.

When Jack's second floor started looking like a cross between a carny and a light show, her curiosity spiked.

* * *

That morning—Frank Miller Noir mug, B&W, chiaroscuro background, moll on a bed, legs spread, cigarette dangling from her lips, her body etched with sharp shadows from window blinds—she turned off the Line and surfed the Net for everything she could find about Jack and Maddy.

There was a lot on both of them but nothing personal about Maddy except for her performances. Besides her last video, there were a couple hazy cell phone videos of her performing on YouTube. It was like she popped up out of the firmament, or Jack's head.

There was a lot on Jack and Maddy's life in SoMa. There were items in the society page at fall openings of the opera and the symphony. They were obviously nouveau patrons of some sort. Most photos showed a vintage Maddy with ink-black hair, penetrating pale blue eyes, and a dusting of freckles, and disconcertedly poised.

She created a Maddy folder, opened a Word doc, and started adding everything she knew about her. Everything from the Web, her poetry, the dives in the Tenderloin, what Jack had said about her.

She had a lot of data but it was all superficial. Nothing on the Web except what she'd found of Maddy and Jack and of Maddy's books and readings. Even there, you think some hard facts would emerge about her history.

But nada.

She was chasing a chimera.

Finally she started looking at PhistoCo and Jack's games. There were columns of print on PhistoCo and the violence, brutality, and reality of PhistoCo's games. And columns of print, especially in the business section of the Chronicle about Jack, the brilliant Phisto creator and PhistoCo owner, and MetaGames, the company that acquired PhistoCo. Jack had made a killing on the sale. No one knew for sure about the money, but it was big.

And where did he go with his gazillions? New York? Paris? Rome? Woodside? Some manse in Marin, or San Francisco?

No. A rambling, peeling house in Fog City, California, playing games with people hoping, she supposed, to find out what happened to his chameleon of a partner.

i have to admit im hooked

(14)

Jack picked up the paring knife from the table. He'd used it to quarter a Fuji apple and had just finished the last quarter. Tasty. Healthful. Health: a game of competing forces. Apollonian: diet (viva Mediterranean!), exercise (not so much lately), weight (check), annual checkup (check). Flip side, Dionysius: alcohol, pot, random sniffs of coke, smattering of hallucinogens, late nights, and extreme overindulgence. For the last few months, balance Apollo.

He turned the paring knife carefully so his fingers were on the slim sharpened blade close to the point. Mouse was partially obscured by the table. Jack leaned forward.

a little more,
a tad more,
an iota more,
a nano more,
...a pico more...
...a femto more...
...an atto more...
The knife touched his ear.
Mouse sped across the mosaic tiles in the kitchen and was halfway across the Persian carpet.

"Son of a bitch."

Jack gauged Mouse's run, leaned forward, and threw the knife high and towards the mouse hole. The knife flipped end over end, the blade flashing in the fading yellow light, its trajectory homing in on Mouse's run.

Jack imagined the knife skewering Mouse and nailing his furry butt to the floor. Or lopping off an ear...and leaving tiny drops of blood on the floor.

The knife's handle hit the wall below the Oz print, bounced twice on the parquet floor, and stopped inches from the hole. Mouse skidded to a stop, slowly turned towards Jack, regarded him for a heartbeat, turned, hopped cleanly over the knife, and vanished.

* * *

86

He vowed to go hiking, then to the Lost Dog. But he found himself settling in the lounger and switching on the monitor. Raquel was always on. He had created a character who was not only conscious, but who was reading and learning and who begged to stay in her digital world.

He'd started thinking of the Raquel Show as a new reality. It was an unbelievable experiment...and his secret garden.

That night, when he turned on the monitor, she was missing. He'd checked all her usual haunts in the Point City world: the beach, the Dog, the Café, her house, but came back to the Nook, where she spent most of her time.

i knew it couldnt last i knew it would be over and only i saw it course i didnt show it to anybody didnt want to show it to anybody but now i wish i had who would pat me on the back where the fuck is my nobel

Jack zoomed back and forth in the Nook and stopped on lights flashing from the back of the Nook.

Finally, Raquel...

...in the middle of a fire fight in Zombies Redux.

The zombies swirled around her, biting the unbitten, devouring gray globs of brains. Blood spurted everywhere. His hero, Mack, wielding a double-edge machete, whirled and slashed the half-dead human monsters left and right.

"Thank Christ!"

But why? Raquel seemed amused. It was evident that she was in Zombies Redux, but not of it. Could she control the action? Could she pick up a gun and shoot a zombie in the head?

Looking at ZR from her amused perspective, the zombie fight seemed less than childish. He regretted the amount of time he'd put in it. Maddy said the same thing, frequently.

Jack picked up the mic.

* * *

Jack: "Where in hell are you?"
Raquel: "Howdy, Jacko. Glad you're here. Can't you see?"
Jack frowned: "I see it. But how?"

"Hey, you're the genius. I live in a box. This one of your games?"

"Zombie Redux, one of my best sellers."

"Guess it wasn't for the intellectual crowd."

"It was more about the programming, the visuals, detail, and—"

Raquel laughed. "Aren't we defensive."

"And, of course, the money."

"I'm not saying you're a sellout...although—"

"Okay, okay. We can argue that later. How did you get there?"

"I was curious about one of the bigger areas patched in from Phisto's games. You told me Phisto plugs the holes with colors and objects from your games."

"Okay."

"When I got close to it, before I knew it, I was in the middle of a game. Talk about falling down the rabbit hole."

"Jesus—"

"Not sure what I mean, Jack. But I guess that when Phisto plugs the big holes, it leaves a link, or path, to the game. Get too close and there you are. I can get back when I want. See that hole up there? That's where Phisto took out the patch. When I go through there, I'm back in the Nook."

"Have you tried it anywhere else?"

"There's a big one in my house. I know you never got in there. I walk into the kitchen and I'm right in the middle of a huge storm, snapping trees, ominous music, a woman looking comically frightened."

"That sounds like Gathering Storm."

"Another shoot-em-up?"

"Mystery with a dash of horror."

"Don't these games tell you anything about yourself, that you actually programmed this, instead of something dramatic or uplifting? I'm sure Maddy told you the same thing."

"Hey, they're video games. I did create Ouroboros, but it didn't sell. I was selling games, not—"

"Nothing about the human condition, nothing about our failing attempts to get along. Fine. In a way, tripping into these games is fascinating. It's like TV or a music video. One minute you're watching Lost and the next rappelling down a glacier to deliver a six-pack of pissy beer to a never-ending party of fatuous millennials. Has a kind of

88

end-of-the-world vibe to it, or is it just another commercial? We are all doomed, aren't we?"

"You're reading a lot into a couple games."

"Hey, weren't you going to do Emma?"

"I haven't decided. If I do, or if Phisto does, I doubt she'll be conscious, and she'll be in a separate digital space. It will duplicate P.C. but with footage of her and without you, a conscious you."

"I need to talk to her. Couldn't you put her in here?"

"If she's not conscious, you won't be able to talk to her. She'll be just like Doris."

"I'd prefer Talia."

"Right now, if I do anyone, it's Emma. Did I mention she would be in a separate digital space?"

"That's right, Phisto told you to do all four of us. And at the end, you're going to find Maddy."

Jack paused, frowned. "Who the fuck knows? Yeah, that's the idea."

"Keep on truckin', eh? Funny. What about a 'year or nothing'? That still on your wall to inspire you?"

"It's still there but you—"

"Well, better get on with it, but I'll tell you, I don't think you're going to find her in a year or ever. If you do, she'll be different. When she mentioned leaving, it seemed to have more meaning than just a trip somewhere. I don't think it matters if you go on to Emma, or George, or Mike."

"At least I'll have you."

shit yes i have to go on its not a competition or the arc theres more is it just time just habit no theres more where the fuck is she

89

(15)

Talia was so bound up with the Line, Point City, and what Jack was doing that she'd forgotten about another life, or others' lives.

Carol Marlow, pre-Larry old friend, artist and art teacher, called her out of the blue, and she spent a couple days and a night with her and her two dachshunds, Nick and Nora. Oakland was bright, sunny, an oasis after hemmed-in Point City and the hopeless Tenderloin.

While showing her latest works in her detached studio, Carol said, "I can see why you set up your line, but you have to see it's a circumscribed world. There's so much that's important in the world, so many interesting people, so much to do. You should rip out that line, chalk it up to experience, and get your art career going. You have a shit-load of talent, and you just stopped when you got hitched."

Talia, seriously, "I started seeing art as visual masturbation."

not really why did i say that maybe partly true an intellectual feint it was mostly because of larry wanting to get on wanting to be part of society money independence why did i pretend visual masturbation fuck me

"Whoa, cowgirl."

Carol's new paintings had a light Cézanne touch, visual mystery emerging from the browns and greens of trees and grass in California's oak woodlands. Her studio was light and airy and had a single chair, which Talia sat in while Carol showed her new work. "Shit, I didn't mean that exactly. Some days I think I'd feel better about myself. I know I'd love it, but then I wonder about significance. I have a similar quandary with the Line. I think I let the caller feel worthwhile, or relevant, for a few minutes. But late at night, in bed, with the images of the homeless or runaways or addicts whirling around my head, I step back and realize I'm not getting them housing, or to quit meth, or change."

Talia slipped her hand along Nick's slick brown coat. "Starting an art career would be like going back to an unfinished older version of myself."

"One you didn't give a chance."

what was it about carol   she always made me feel better relevant   maybe she does for me what i do for the callers on the line   shes   earthy   sexy   engaging   confident

"True. Anyway, I've got a new obsession, or rather I'm seriously inquisitive."

"Shoot."

"Maddy, her hoax—at least that's the consensus—and Jack, the video game Jack."

Carol laughed, shook her head. "Oh, that. I listened to one of Jack's interviews." Thinking, she poised her forefinger under her chin. "I think it was on a rock station. You know he had quite a following with the adult-challenged. Alternate universes, alternate personalities, multiple characters all existing now. Interesting, not convincing. When you look at his games, you think to yourself, whoops, this is about crazy violence, tattooed snarling bikers, big guns, and busty Amazons. Talk about alternate universes is a disguise, a sop to prepubescents. Now that's real masturbation."

Talia snickered. "I see that. What about Maddy?"

"Don't know much about her; who does? I like her poetry and I've seen a couple YouTube videos. She's a dynamite performer, except her punch line is often an existential anarchism, and that's a hollow stance, especially if you have the kind of life she had with Jack."

Talia nodded. "I've thought that. I like her poetry, especially the stuff about death. Isn't it important that we're all going to die? We do stuff for a while, try to deaden the pain, then die."

Carol widened her eyes comically. "Those Tenderloin drunks and druggies have converted you. One day I'll walk down Leavenworth and find you drinking Thunderbird and yelling at ghosts."

Talia laughed. "Nah, I like my morning coffee too much."

* * *

Early evening she ate stuffed peppers with Carol, an older couple, Joe and Ann, who ran a printing business, and a heavily tattooed graphic designer, Eddie, who Carol had met on a rafting trip on the American. After Joe and Ann left, she, Carol, and Eddie suited up and luxuriated in Carol's hot tub on a deck in a front yard surrounded by thick ten-foot-high bamboo. Nick and Nora watched them from the steps as the conversational ball bounced back and forth. Talia felt like she'd resuscitated a forgotten part of her life, inviting people over, drinks, dinner, shaking their heads over the latest political insanity, new parking regulations, and hugs goodbye.

It was fun getting away, and she could see that she'd become too isolated and grim. She wasn't sure whether it was the tiny universe of Point City, the Tenderloin, or wondering about Maddy that fed her unease the most.

(16)

A year or nothing

He'd stare at the Raquel show and realize he wasn't really looking at it. It was keying memories of his time with Maddy, starting the tape...again. He had no idea where it would start or when it would end. After he shook himself out of the tape, he'd think about it, about how important it was, how important Maddy was, how he missed her, and whether she had really given him another year. Viewed from that perspective, standing apart, he realized again why he was interrogating Raquel, and why he would go after those other characters... because he thought it was the way to find her.

* * *

Two days in the Stage, two days watching the Show.

Every time the Escher Hands opened and he flicked on the monitor, Raquel was either having sloppy sex with a lumbering patchwork Doris, reading, or in one of Phisto's games. When he talked to her, she talked about what it was like to be alive and digital. No one would have guessed a digital world was possible and a digital creature would be able to describe her digital world from inside. He took copious notes on how she didn't sleep, on not having days or nights, what it felt like to have sex, repeated sex, on how she couldn't retrieve early memories, and how sometimes the memories would come to her unbidden. Just as if she were flesh and blood.

Fascinating and frequently annoying. She was pissed about how she couldn't see herself in mirrors and how not seeing herself affected her self-image. She hated what she called a static world where nothing degraded, nothing died. And she hated most of his games, how they were made for subnormals.

Raquel may have been right: what did it mean for his character that his video games represented the meanness, the rage, the hostility, and the violence of human nature?

**maddy said the same thing but wasnt it part of the competition
not real in a sense not about who he was the core**

That afternoon, sun retreating, he forced himself to switch off the monitor and the projectors. He'd speculated about all the characters mentioned
in Maddy's video, and Emma was the least likely to help him. What would
Maddy have to do with her besides paying for a latte and morning bun? Raquel
was ambivalent about whether the other people could help. She noted, cor-
rectly, that she was likely the only conscious being, that the others would be
mute stand-ins. Besides, she said, what clue could he possibly discover by seeing them in their native habitat? It was also likely that they were mentioned
by Maddy for the reason she gave: anxiety over the breathless phone calls and
hypersensitivity to the mundane.

**what should i do mousy shouldnt i be in the stage making notes
on my brilliant discovery do i have to continue it feels like a
chore okay sure an adventure too**

He grabbed his capture camera and headed to town. The last few times
he'd gone—for groceries at the market or a quick scotch at the Dog—people
looked at him differently. He knew it was because Raquel talked about his
videoing the Nook. It deepened, he supposed, their generic suspicion. It would
be difficult to get enough data on the other characters.

He stopped outside the Nook. Through his reflection in the window, he saw
not just books, journals, tables, prints, and Raquel; he began to overlay the real
Nook with his digital one, the real Raquel with a digital one. And the digital
one was alive, conscious, thinking, feeling, covering the real one, and turning,
talking, revealing more, commenting on that brute reality, interpreting it.

abstractions shimmering over real copies over copies

Jack turned away. He walked quickly towards the northern end of town.
He made a play of videoing the bank and gas station, but he was zeroing in
on the Café con Vache. Emma's conversations about Maddy from his bugs
hadn't helped. Would it help to see her in the Café con Vache and integrate
her audio? He hadn't decided whether he would let Phisto make a fully func-
tioning avatar...if he could get enough data. He walked down the east side

94

of Main looking in windows and wondering how he could get more data on Emma. What he needed was direct contact, where she lived and worked. He'd already bugged the outside of the café and the Revive Evangelical Church, housed in a plain pre-fab building in a field of withered grass on the northern edge of Point City.

Finally, without much hope, he tucked the camera in its case, hitched up his pants, crossed the street, and stood in line at the Café con Vache.

It was late for the café, and there were few offerings, but it was crowded. Behind Emma, the last daily special three-mushroom, heirloom tomato, and Parmesan pizza was being cut up, alongside crusty sugar-sprinkled blueberry scones and fresh organic multigrain bread covered in waxed paper. In front, a ragged queue of bikers; on the side, a couple pouring coffee, lacing their coffee with half-and-half and brown sugar. A few locals edged their way up towards the register. Gay couple Roger and Dodger argued about what to get, whether a muffin was gluten-free, with a bitchy aside on celiac disease. At the register, Theadora, eighty, mumbling, rummaged in her worn purse, finally pulling out a crumpled twenty-dollar bill, which she brought up to her eye before placing it carefully on the counter for a small coffee.

The mundanity of the café was curiously comforting. Did he really want to use Emma? Did he want to continue the charade? Was he too far in to stop?

Watching Emma at the register, he reviewed what he knew about her. Born in Kansas, conservative, high school diploma, married once. Divorced once. Husband, Murray, alcoholic gun lover. One kid, Gene, a heroin addict who committed suicide by hanging ten years ago in L.A. Tawdry melodramatic mess. Emma was addicted, initially, to the radio evangelists the Armstrong brothers and their wild asseverations. Health: diabetes, high blood pressure, incipient kidney disease. Not the kind of person Maddy would likely befriend or for Maddy to mention her last day on earth.

(17)

The Line had been slow for days, and she didn't feel like driving into town and putting up flyers. She made sure the answering machine was on. She walked through the living room, grabbed her vest, and seconds later walked aimlessly towards Main. She didn't feel like chatting at the café. She walked slowly towards the Barn.

shit   edna   too fucking late

"A break from that line of yours?" Edna was as lean as Talia, taller, a dusting of silver in her brown hair, older, pinched good-looking face, clear gray eyes, leathery-ex-smoker skin.

Talia gave her a quick smile. "I like talking to the people who call, but sometimes I wonder if I want to devote my life to it."

"I know what's that's like. I liked growing with the Barn, but now I wonder if there's any other option. After a while, you find yourself wedded to something, your job, a bunch of friends...and a husband."

Talia laughed. "The way of the world."

Edna glanced inside, saw George stacking postcards, and lowered her voice. Talia had the impression Edna didn't talk to a lot of people, especially around George. "Course we have people over, do the barbeque, have drinks. I guess it's afterwards that's the toughest time. You know, back to the everyday."

"I think we all have problems with what we're doing."

"I came close to leaving a couple months after Ava died."

i know about ava   the ole point city grapevine   it snakes through the town shedding truth and ends at the dog   cant tell her tho

Talia frowned. "Ava?"

"I'm surprised you don't know about her. My girl. I guess you can't really call her that. Stillborn. Can't have more kids. Kinda took the allure out of Point City, a little of the allure out of life. I know it affected George, though

96

he hides it." Edna frowned at Talia. "At least I'm not Martha. I don't pretend she was ever alive. I know the difference."

"I didn't know."

"Most people know. I guess I told you because you run a help line."

"I don't know if I help or not."

"I heard through our grapevine you were divorced. Everybody has some kind of hurt, an empty part."

Talia shook her head. "The well-lubricated grapevine. I don't know about 'hurt.'"

Edna frowned, showing a spider's web of creases around her eyes. "I didn't mean anything by it."

"I don't think about it anymore. Somebody asks me if I was married and I think to myself: Hey, that's right. I was married. It's distant, foreign to what I've become, how I am now; my marriage is part of Social Security, IRS files, and a thousand places in the ubiquitous cloud."

Edna laughed. "There are some things you don't forget easily." Edna sat down on the steps, picked up an apple from the bin and rolled it between her hands. Talia sat down next to her. They both regarded the cars passing in the street. "Sometimes, not all the time, I think of leaving here." She glanced back at the Barn's door. "I'm sure he does. I know a lot about him, more than he suspects. But, you know, I don't know what he thinks. You live with someone for twenty years, and you think you know everything about them. But what do we really know? Even when someone bares their soul, do we know, really know, what they're thinking?"

no   do i know what im thinking   do i know how   do i care   is it something we do that cant be broken down analyzed   maybe i dont want to know

Talia smiled warmly. "Maybe it's best to have the surface and imagine the rest. As for leaving, aren't you and George and the Barn Point City institutions, like the Nook or the Café con Vache? What would we do without our local touchstones?"

Edna laughed. "I've never been called an institution or a touchstone."

Talia said, "Of course, even institutions change."

Edna glanced between the buildings on Manzanita, her gaze resting on the line of houses on the marsh. "Then there's Jack. He's an intrusion into our little hamlet. People say he knows more about us than we do. Raquel said he spent a lot of time videoing and quizzing her. What does he hope to do with all that information?"

"I admit I'm curious."

"I wouldn't want to see myself on the screen, or George. What if Jack has some way of bringing out the worst things we've said, or done, or want to do? Just watching it would freak me out."

"We'll probably never see it."

"Thank goodness."

George appeared at the door. "Need some help with the register."

"Be right in."

Talia got up, stretched, looked down at Edna. "Nice chatting with you. Enjoy the day."

Edna got up, glanced at the sky. "As long as it lasts. The fog'll be back soon enough."

＊ ＊ ＊

Talia walked down Main towards the Café con Vache thinking she might get a savory bun for lunch. The Line had been too quiet. The lack of calls made her think more of her time in Oakland with Carol. It was liberating...liberating for a few days. But it stuck with her. Last night, she looked at the few collages she'd kept interspersed between the bookshelves. They were good but ...

> i see my problem   i do something interesting and
> compelling   then i put in a human face or a person
> i cant get away from humanity   people are real   art
> is fake   still

Then there was Jack.

She watched his comings and goings, and except for yesterday, he hadn't been going. His car had remained in the garage, and she hadn't seen him in the Dog or the Crossroads or at the Café or in the handful of P.C. restaurants. The second floor was ablaze morning and night.

Talia stopped abruptly. Jack was in the Café con Vache talking to Emma. Talia turned around and walked back along Main.

98

Emma.

Emma must be on his list.

How would he find out anything from her?

She stopped a few feet past the Nook. She glanced in the window and saw Raquel talking to a customer in the local history section, her be-ringed finger pointing up and to the right making a point. Jack had spent time, a lot of time, with Raquel. What did he do with all that information?

Talia stared at the entrance and saw what looked like a piece of bark. The mottled color didn't quite match the weathered gray of the front. She walked back and stared at the chip then felt its smooth surface with a finger. After a few seconds, she plucked it out.

It wasn't wood. It felt like metal, and the back was crisscrossed with grid paths.

A few minutes later, the Net came up with a state-of-the-art surveillance device made to look like a splinter. The conclusion could only be that Jack put it there to overhear Raquel and random conversations on the street. How many others had he planted around town?

asshole no wonder he knows so much about us about me

She spent an hour hunting through her front porch, her hanging baskets of flowers, the siding, and the trees in front. She didn't find a bug, an artificial one at least, but it didn't mean there weren't any. On the other hand, she didn't think Jack was interested in her.

She put the bug in a small lined jewelry box and buried it in her computer drawer. Jack wouldn't hear anything from her, even if it were still live.

She wasn't sure how she would use it, but she had a token, a token that might get her into Jack's house, a token that might let her see what he was doing on that second floor. A token that might let her see what he'd done with Raquel.

(18)

Jack was debating getting a small coffee when he saw a surveillance kit in back of the register. He remembered the break-ins at the bakery. Hell, he even knew from his bugs who had done the breaking and entering: Ian and Matt, two sneering teenagers headed, he was sure, to jail in the near future.

likely played my games oh well

Jack hesitated but finally said, "Emma, can I talk to you for a few seconds?"

Emma, the earthy, occasionally sourful, born-again, frumpy doyenne of the Café was surprised. She frowned then said, "Rod, do the register." She moved over to the side near the scones and breads.

Emma, warily, "What's up, Jack?"

she hates my guts she knows i live in a different world a world that spurns bornagains be nice thoughtful concerned

"I guess you got that surveillance system because of the burglaries."

Emma turned and glanced at the kit. She shook her head. "I didn't want to do it, but they keep breaking in. Maybe they need it, but it's hurting my business."

Jack leaned over and said softly, matching Emma's concern, "I was wondering if you needed help putting it up. I've put up hundreds of systems like that."

Emma put a thick finger along her face, as if it helped her think. "That would be nice of you, Jack. I couldn't pay much."

"It would be my pleasure. We have to stop these break-ins."

Emma seemed friendlier when he sounded serious. That would go in the profile. The natives were generally wary of him. Look at Talia; she thought he was toxic. Mike barely tolerated him. Until he helped her, Raquel skipped to the other side of the street. He was tainted because of Maddy and his prying and videoing.

talia was right i never think other people notice me but yes they talk about me ridicule me watch me watch me more than i watch them but i know more about them than they know about themselves

Emma was closing at four, and he sat outside on the Café bench for half an hour munching on a scone and sipping coffee, occasionally flipping crumbs at pigeons in the street and watching the traffic turn into town and people enter and exit the bank. The Raquel Show was a breakthrough, brilliant, and it almost—almost!—captured reality...or did it make a new reality? Was it better than reality, a super reality or meta reality?

Whenever he talked to the digital Raquel, he thought about what kind of reality he'd actually created, whether a character could actually learn and what they'd learn. In a large sense, everything we know is from our bodies, our senses, our store of proprioceptive movements. But weren't movements, ideas, and memories electrical currents? Why couldn't we be aware without a body?

The surveillance system was a piece of cake. While she was setting up for the next day, he was about to ask her if he could video the inside of the café, when she asked him!

whats going on why are they making it so easy

"I've got old photos of the outside of the café but my web guy thinks I need more. He said I needed either some photos or a video to advertise it. You know shots inside, some of the pastries. I don't know it it's going to help or not. I'd definitely pay you."

"Hey, photos and video are cheap. Not a problem."

And that was that. He videoed the café and Emma showed off some of the pastries she'd just put away. He also attached a couple bugs to the ceiling and one under the counter. Then it was back to her house to set up her iPad. She moved deliberately, swaying slightly, and picking her way over the broken sidewalk and gravel. Her house was a small two-story with a peeling white fence on Manzanita, a block from Marsh Lane.

The house was a knickknack-and-tchotchke paradise. Besides a scattering of born-again quotes ("If you're not a born-again Christian, you're a failure as a human being." –Jerry Falwell), owls were the major theme. Plastic owls, porcelain owls, wooden owls, Audubon's print of an owl, owl doilies.

"You like owls."

"Don't know why. They're an elegant bird, smart. Hard to see them, though. You know they're nocturnal. You know what they call a bunch of owls."

"No."

"A parliament. Isn't that funny? Can you imagine a hundred owls swiveling their heads 180 degrees back and forth and debating nest hygiene?"

"Interesting image."

Her wireless system wasn't password protected, which had made it easy to hack her PC. Everyone thought computer security was for other people. He downloaded the monitoring software to her iPad, logged into the website, and a few minutes later the bakery was there in shadows and grayscale.

Emma frowned. "It's so washed-out and colorless."

"There are more sophisticated color systems, but this is plenty for you."

"You're helping me a lot. I don't know how to thank you."

"I could take some more shots of you for the website. I'd send them to your Web guy. He might want to use them."

She balked at first but finally relented, saying she could use also the photos at her church. She even said, after reflection, that she liked the idea. It made her feel important. While he shot her, he bantered with her, asking questions about what she did before she came to Point City, what she liked about the café, what her aspirations were.

While she was in the bathroom, he planted a bug under a porcelain owl and one near her fireplace.

* * *

He was packing up when Emma surprised him by offering him a glass of Chardonnay...from a Christian winery.

They sat in Emma's small living room at a dark, expandable, drop-leaf, oval table with eagle-claw legs featuring a round damask tablecloth stitched with the image of an owl with plate-sized eyes. Six ceramic owls with identical marble eyes stared at him from the window sill opposite, lined in a row. A parliament, perhaps.

Emma was nosy, as nosy as Raquel, wondering what he was doing in Point

City, whether it had anything to do with Maddy. He dug more out about how often Maddy came to the café, how she was, but he met the same predictable resistance. Then there was her nosiness about his faith.

Emma stared at the small chandelier over the table and mused, "Are you religious, Jack?"

"Not particularly."

"Why not?"

"I don't think I need it."

Emma frowned. "When you say "need," you make it sound like it's not real."

well shit of course its not real

Jack shrugged. "I didn't mean it that way."

"Well, we know that there's going to be a sorting out. Those that believe will go to one place, and the others will go someplace else. I happen to believe in that and that I'll see Jesus. I guess it's what makes me get up each day. I know you say you don't need it, but I think everyone does."

yeah your going to the reyes cemetery and im going up in smoke

Emma finished her glass and started to get up.

Jack saw that as a signal to go. He finished the rest of his wine and got up. "I hope that surveillance system helps." He shouldered his bag of equipment. "If you need any more help, just ask. As I said, I need projects."

Emma regarded him carefully. "I can't help thinking you're not telling me everything. I would guess a lot of it has to do with Maddy. I told you I didn't see her often, but I think she needed saving, the way she flitted through life. And her fake video caused me a lot of grief. People came around the café asking about her. If you want to know, she asked for coffee and I gave it to her."

There was something in the way Emma dismissed Maddy that made Jack think there was more. He'd find out after Phisto worked on her.

Thanksgiving!

Subliminally, she'd noted the preparations, cornucopias, orange/red/yel-
low fake leaves, the twisty crookneck squash, strings of paper turkeys with
puzzled expressions and drooping snoods, and, of course, business prep for
Black Friday, All Sales Day. It used to be one of her favorite holidays, but now
hype plus the ingrained rancor of her mother (what? divorce? perceived aim-
lessness?) and her hard sister, newly booted out of the Marines, (what? some
ancient slight?) made it a long day of unusual friction.

She called and explained why she couldn't come. Explanations rejected,
but she mollified everyone by saying she'd try to make it back for Christmas,
which, of course, she wouldn't.

pro forma games they did want me back they didnt
i did want to go and didnt

* * *

To celebrate the holiday, Talia was going to put up flyers and spend a chunk
of the day working as a volunteer for Max's Place and its annual feast for the
homeless at a small street off UN Plaza.

Around nine, she threw her bag together and headed to the Tenderloin.
Adopting her Liz persona complete with a new better-fit blond wig, she stapled
flyers to the sides of shuttered buildings, telephone poles covered in rusty staples
and torn off announcements, and tacked flyers to bulletin boards in churches
and rec halls. She walked by spots where the girls and kids had called her. On
Hyde, she watched Sheri and Brenda from a distance propositioning guys in
cars. The gals should be sitting down for Thanksgiving somewhere. Leon, flashy
pimp, hung out down the block rapping loudly with a small black man in a
t-shirt, smoking and flipping his ashes every few seconds into the street. She
couldn't talk to the girls directly. She'd have to wait until they called. She was
living outside their life, a distant, she hoped friendly, voice on a phone.

She ditched her wig and flyers in the car and walked to UN Plaza for the Max's Place gig.

She'd just gotten an orange shirt emblazoned with "Max's Place" in yellow, when she saw Edna.

Edna walked over. "Surprised?"

"Almost didn't recognize you, you know, out of context."

Edna, crooked smile, said, "Hope you don't mind. Couple days ago, somebody mentioned you were volunteering down here, and I checked it out and decided it was a good idea. George is going to his parents. Can't say I get along with them."

Talia slipped her arm into Edna's. "Glad you came. They can always use help. C'mon, let's go get our assignments."

Edna got cranberries and Talia dressing.

im glad edna came   strange too   she seems happy talking to people   she needs something besides george and the barn   kinda sorry i called her a touchstone or institution

The lines were long all day and were still long when they were relieved three hours later.

Talia: "It's amazing how much folks pile on those skimpy take-away dishes. They're stocking up for at least a couple meals, maybe more."

Edna, nodding at kids across the street: "Wonder why they aren't in the line."

"Let's find out."

Talia leaned against the building next to a pair of teens hanging out in a doorway.

The boy looked like he was about eighteen. He was shorter than the girl and wore lace-less worn black Keds, oil-soiled jeans, and a faded Black Sabbath t-shirt. His hair was long and tangled, and his face seemed lopsided, but it was the nose which was slightly off-center. It made his sallow face interesting. His frown showed a tempered defiance, his eyes stolid and vulnerable.

The girl, also about eighteen, wore an old marine jacket and shorts. She was tall and gangly with a helmet of blond hair and a dusting of freckles across her sour face. She seemed anxious, almost morose, but approachable.

"You guys waiting for the line to get smaller?"

The guy said, "Maybe. Who're you? Social workers?"

The girl looked from Talia to Edna, shook her head, said, "He's pissed cuz he's out of dope."

"Name's Liz; I run that Line. I don't know if you've seen the flyers. This is Edna, a friend."

The girl said, "Liz, sure. Sweet. I called a week ago, cuz of him." She pointed to her boyfriend, who looked away. "Got plastered. Thought the little shit was trying to rape me."

Talia frowned. "You didn't leave names. I put it down as a rape of X."

Girl: "We're not Xs and Ys. I'm Dawn, he's Adam. But hey, put it down as a misunderstanding. We were both out of it. That right, hotshot?"

Adam hunched against the wall. "You say so."

"Chill! We'll find some pot."

"Like that's gonna happen."

Dawn, to Edna: "He's moody. He's awesome when he's stoned. He does, like, imitations, cracks me up, and he sings. Right now, not."

Edna, worried, said, "How long have you been out here?"

Dawn: "Feels like forever, but it's been less 'n year."

Edna glanced at Talia, then at Dawn. "You must think of getting out of here."

Adam, looking up, shaking his head: "Who fuckin' doesn't?"

Dawn: "We both got history, fucked history; it's like a mantra."

Talia: "You guys use heroin? I been getting calls about ODs."

Dawn: "We got friends that use. We don't, or won't."

Adam: "The scag they used was cut with fentanyl, called Bud Ice. Some of 'em know it. They want to get as close to packin' it in as they can. It's like a game."

Edna, glancing at the line, "Looks like the line is shorter."

Dawn: "C'mon hotshot. Let's get something to eat."

Edna dug in her pocket and said, "Let me contribute to your bad habits. Here's ten bucks for a couple joints."

Dawn said, "Sweet. Hey, think of it as keeping us off scag."

"Right."

Talia found a card and gave it to Dawn. "Give me a call sometime, just to talk."

Dawn shrugged, took the card and said, "I have the Liz number; I'm not sure what we'd talk about."

Edna, to Dawn and Adam, "Nice talking to you."

Talia and Edna watched them cross the street. Edna broke off staring and said, "I don't feel like going back yet. Can I buy you a drink? A holiday potion. There must be a bar open."

Talia said, "I sure need it. Let's try McTeague's on Polk."

"Didn't he die over a hundred years ago handcuffed to his tormentor?"

"Ghosts everywhere. C'mon."

edna liked talking to the kids probably about losing her kid not going to touch that

* * *

"Neat place, but too many TVs. If it wasn't for my impulse to volunteer and meeting you, I never would have come here. I'll chalk it up to an adventure."

Talia shook her head. "I've been here a couple times. A couple girls, the working ladies, told me they come here to get away for a few minutes. I came here a couple times to see if I could find them. No such luck."

"You wanted to see the women you talk to?"

"I know I shouldn't. And I like the adventure, like you said. Polk Gulch used to be a gay Mecca back in the 70s. Lots of action on the street, lots of trannies and streetwalkers. Now it's gentrifying. Funny, the gentrification starts with a bar like this that's a nod to a hundred years ago."

"At least it's open, and the bartender was friendly."

"A lot bigger than the Dog. Probably full of wasted twenty-year-old jocks on the weekend."

"You know, when I said I didn't know what George thought, I was mostly honest. It's almost a law of nature that we don't know what's swirling in the neurons." Edna's eyes were more expressive than Talia remembered. Liquid, retiring, but briefly brown-bright with feeling. Her smoke-leather skin seemed burnished in a glow from ceiling lights.

"Axiomatic."

"Good word for crosswords." Edna took a sip of Pinot Noir and put the glass down. "I know more about George than I let on."

"Uh-oh."

"No vow of silence. I don't see you as a major branch on the grapevine.

I know you go to the Dog and are friends with Raquel and Harris, but you don't seem like a gossip."

Talia sipped her Chardonnay, put the glass down carefully on an Anchor Steam coaster. They were in a small front-room balcony across from the long bar, glittering bottles of booze and six 40-inch TVs, mercifully off. There was a back room with pool tables and shuffleboard, closed off that day for the ten people in McTeague's. Out the window in front, the sun shone bright on the papier-mâché gold tooth advertising McTeague's. "Kay."

"Besides drinking too much—that's when most of our fights start—George has secret liaisons with Maria, the Salvadoran who works at the grocery-deli. Seems so soap opera but, you know, I don't care."

Talia frowned and took a sip of wine.

"I think about it, probably more than I should. I think we stay together because of the little things. You know, knowing when he's going to do something, what and how he eats, how he dims the light in the bathroom and strikes a pose that makes him seem like he has more hair."

"We all primp; I know I do."

Edna: "I do too, but I'm not sure I want to see tics like that in anyone else. It would be too hard. I think he thinks the same way. I mean if he really wanted Maria, he would get rid of me, get a divorce, and settle down with her and live happily ever after."

Talia laughed. "People still do that?"

"It would be nice to think so. I'm not sure George would be happy with that. Again, I know the outside, the quirks and tics, a hidden liaison. I'm not sure about inside."

"You'll have to ask Jack. He seems to know us better than we do ourselves. I wonder how much of the inside he does know."

"Can't know much about me or George." Edna took another sip, carefully put it down. "I felt a lot better today doing something, volunteering, seeing those kids. Dawn seems like a nice kid; Adam seemed harder to like." Edna frowned, shook her head. "Can't imagine them on the street, especially in winter."

Talia: "Volunteering is more than something to do, and it's more than feeling good about myself. I genuinely think I'm helping the people I talk to, not with money or food or housing, but with their sense of self, belonging, being a real person, not a stereotype whore or homeless kid or old alkie. It's like Dawn said, they're not Xs and Ys."

"Maybe that's what I felt."

(20)

A year or nothing

its a prod but do i have to look at it all the time i know the date

He didn't have much time for anything else between consulting with the engineers at MetaGames and talking to the digital Raquel at length when he could. He'd given Phisto the data he'd picked up from Emma weeks ago. Phisto would have finished by now, except at the last minute he had it use the same cognitive and memory modules and the neural construct it had on Raquel. Could Phisto create a conscious character twice? "Create" was a stretch. Phisto commanded brilliant state-of-the-art software, programs, modules, subroutines, graphic interfaces, bytes. It didn't create consciousness knowingly...or consciously! But consciousness was created. He was fretting, pacing, waiting for Phisto to finish Emma, when in glancing at the calendar, he realized tomorrow was Thanksgiving.

What?

Halloween had mocked him. November and Thanksgiving had snuck up on him. He could feel it in the weather, the cold, but somehow he hadn't noticed it. Not much weather in the Stage. The only time that mattered was the time that was running out. Regardless...

i need a break

San Francisco. The Palace. Long shot: Pied Piper Bar & Grill. Closed. Maddy especially liked a post-work drink in the dark-wooded bar where she was intrigued with Maxfield Parrish's *Pied Piper*. Where is he leading the children, to a fantasy land or to a watery death? Are we the children? Are we being piped to some indefinite end? Or are we the piper, piping humanity into some spiritual black hole?

He ambled slowly to the Garden Court. Homage to a past era; huge, gilded, ornate, Beaux Arts stained glass. Thanksgiving Grand Buffet. The usual passel of well-heeled outcasts and scatterings of tourists.

yadda yadda yadda

They had spent a Thanksgiving there.

More V&Ts than turkey that time. Always good to see how the good people lived. Everyone making the best of not being home with the kids or grandkids or estranged wife or husband. Or disappeared partner/lover. He spent too much time turning and looking for Maddy.

Finally, he felt his usual off-hand cynical taciturnity ebb away and an immense sadness wash over him, cutting off his dour view of the Garden Court.

Maddy. Our time. Sometimes they would talk to each other softly, intimately, knowing there was a core, a place between them where they knew they were loved. It was corny, and saying it would be cornier. But there it was.

thats why im looking for her

He stayed in the Shades that night but got up at four in the morning and left.

* * *

Jack woke up late, showered, made coffee, and threw himself into breakfast delaying the big moment. Veggie omelet, whole grain toast. As he finished the last bit of egg matched with a bite of toast, he separated a crust from the multigrain and flicked it on the carpet.

Delay, delay. He piled the dishes and pans in the sink and took his coffee out to the bench. The bench had become an antidote to the Show, Raquel, and Point City, a nexus of dreams, of nature, of bush and marsh, of forgetting. Lately, early mornings, it was a chilly spot, the fog swirling down from the low coastal mountains, through the marsh brush, around the houses perched over the marsh, the stumps and posts, swirling towards town, swirling around him. Sometimes he merged with the fog, became a vaporous being that would wisp away with the sun.

Had to find Maddy. Had to know. Couldn't stop. But...but early on, he never had peace with her. For those early years when they weren't playing games with each other, in the competition, they were always on, always juggling a handful of projects. At times, puffing out their respective spiritual chests, they thought themselves vanguards, prototypes slashing their way through complex digital and literary jungles.

The bench was peace. Point City too. He felt that Talia and Harris and a few other escapees from out there felt the same way...not all the time. They didn't talk about it, but they hinted when they talked about how they were an enclave, how they'd discovered a secret garden, how for a fleeting time they had realized inner peace through outer calm. Did Maddy feel that?

A car navigated the short road to the Point; distant voices from town reached him and spoiled his quiet time.

Jack got up, stretched, glanced at the marsh a last time, and walked determinedly to the door.

okay emma what ya got

* * *

Partially pixilated cars streamed down Highway 1 like a metallic serpent, turned sharply at the Main corner, and drove erratically through Point City. The street buzzed, motorcycles revved, people talked, gestured, a car horn, a mangy dog limped down the sidewalk and disappeared.

Emma stared out the window of the Café con Vache, dried her plump hands on her apron, adjusted the loose strap over her thick shoulder, walked around the register, glanced at the newly installed surveillance system, then the ghostly help, flicking in and out of existence as they stacked scones and buns on metal trays. Emma moved slowly through the café in a wash of pixels.

She sat on the café bench, shaded her eyes, and stared at the bend where Highway 1 joined Main. She started to loosen her bra strap and stopped when her fingers moved through the strap. She frowned, sighed, and rested back against the gray boards.

She glanced up at the sky, which was a metallic shade of blue, as if she were trying to see what was up there.

She got up and lumbered towards her house, followed by a comet trail of pixels. When she swayed, part of her shoulders disappeared, then reappeared on the next step.

In her house, she picked up her cell and dialed.

She frowned. "Static."

She threw the cell on the sofa and stared at the ceiling. "Is this it?"

"This is like purgatory. Maybe it is! Maybe I have to go through this purgatory to get the real deal! Maybe I'm here because I wasn't worthy, or worthy enough. I tried. I tried so hard.

"Now wait. I don't remember dying. Of course, I probably wouldn't. Still. Maybe it is purgatory. Course we don't believe in it.

"Where's Jesus?"

∗ ∗ ∗

"It isn't purgatory."

Emma stared at the ceiling. "Jesus?"

"It's Jack...Jack from town."

Emma blinked and surveyed the room. Parts of the room were filled with what looked like patches, others pixilated. Emma said plaintively, "You did this?"

"I'm proud to say—"

"What am I doing here? Some joke?"

"I guess I have to explain. I didn't expect this...at all."

Emma angrily, "Tell me."

"First, I'm shocked you're conscious. It worked before, but—"

"This is an experiment?"

"Yes, and—"

"And here I am. I can't see you."

"Well, you're digital, in a computer, an avatar, a simulacrum."

"And you're up there, or out there." Emma shook her head. "This kinda feels like an intrusion. I don't think you shouldda done this."

"I wasn't sure I could."

"And you did it before. Who?"

"Raquel."

Emma shook her head. "Why on God's earth?"

"Finding out what happened to Maddy. I didn't expect—"

"Maddy? How were you going to find Maddy through me?"

"Analyzing audio, looking for clues. You didn't tell the police everything. That doesn't matter as much—"

"Maybe she's dead."

Jack sighed, "It's possible."

"At least you have something to keep you going. I feel I'm Emma. I am Emma, but I'm not. Not the real Emma."

"You probably don't appreciate it, but—"

"Tell ya how I feel, Jack. I'm startin' to feel cheated."

"I'm sorry you feel that way, but—"

Emma frowned. "Give me one reason I should I help you?"

"I didn't want you to help me. I wanted to see what you said about Maddy with what I've integrated from my bugs. I didn't expect to talk to you. Now that you're conscious—"

Emma stared at the table cloth then the window. "Least you got the owls right. I'll tell you right now, Jack. I don't like it here. It's like a fake heaven." Emma paused, placed her finger alongside her round cheek, then said, "Is my church here?"

"The building's here and there might be a few members, but they're not conscious."

"I don't like being here without my church."

"Sorry."

Emma ran her hand through her hair. The hair settled back, changing colors from brown to yellow to red, finally settling back on brown. "What did Raquel say?"

"The only concrete things were a green truck and a heavyset man at her house. She thought he'd stayed over a few nights."

Emma walked into the kitchen, poured pixilated Chardonnay into a partially pixilated glass, and ambled back to the living room. She took a long drink of Chardonnay, put the glass down on an owl coaster and said, "Tickles. At least I think it tickles. Had no idea what to expect. I saw the guy more than a couple times. If I tell you more, will you turn me off?"

"You don't want to stay? You're immortal...in a sense."

113

"What kind of immortality is this? I don't like it. It confuses me. And I don't have any of my friends. I don't have the church."

"You don't want to help me?"

"Why would I? I want out."

"Right now, you're staying. Think about it. Help me."

* * *

"Listen, Jack. Hello? Guess he can't be there all the time."

"I'm starting to like one thing about this: I don't have to talk to anyone else or pretend I like anyone else. I can be myself. Strange, be myself. Guess that means I'm not myself out there."

Emma picked up a scone on the table, but it glittered and fell through her fingers. "Can't eat. Now that's wrong."

Emma walked to the window. The view shimmered in and out of view, now showing the next house, now showing a long expanse of humpbacked brown hills. "Jack did this. I wonder if he made a heaven by mistake? How would anyone know? I suppose the ones who are there would know. It might be just like here, someplace different but alike. I wonder if people in heaven would think? Never thought about that before. And if they thought, would they think there might be someplace else, another heaven? Maybe there's a bunch of levels.

"Or maybe we don't think. That would be best. We wouldn't be like we are now. I mean we wouldn't be like we are out there, out there where real stuff happens. If we were, it would be the same pain."

Emma fingered the doily on the table, the pixels falling through her fingers. She propped her double chin on her thick hand.

"I wonder what a soul would do in heaven. Haven't thought about it before, I guess. Would I wander around with other souls basking in the glory of Jesus? Would my friends in the church be there? What if they weren't? Not sure that would be a good life. Of course, it wouldn't be life."

* * *

"Tell ya, I still love Jesus. I don't like all this speculation. It's confusing."

Emma saw a dark hole in the kitchen, frowned, then walked into it. She found herself looking at huge praying mantises ripping soldiers apart, blood streaming in torrents. A squad of soldiers shot bullets into the head of one of the insects, splattering yellow ooze. She watched for a few seconds, turned, and walked back into the kitchen.

"Strange."

She walked back through the hole and watched a muscular rock-chinned hero with flowing blond hair yelling at the soldiers and pumping bullets into insects out of a huge metallic gun. She walked back into the kitchen and stared at the dark hole.

"Must be Jack's idea of a joke."

Emma smirked. She picked up the Chardonnay from the table. "I got it now. I'll get out myself."

She walked heavily upstairs, her round body swaying, slowly reforming as she moved. She walked into the bathroom and stared at the tub, which shimmied and faded in and out of view.

"Funny, real funny. Jack is a real card. Maybe he's not real. Maybe I'm in a dream. Wake up, ninny!"

Emma took a long sip of wine. "Still tickles, sure doesn't taste like wine. Maybe I don't know what wine tastes like. Maybe it's just an idea. I don't have real taste buds, just fake ones."

She turned the handles and ran water into the tub. She watched the glowing water and shook her head. When the tub was half full, she put the wineglass on the sideboard with shampoos and conditioners, and an old yellow rubber duck missing its tail. She quickly took off her clothes, but when they lay in a clump on the floor, they didn't seem like clothes but more a glowing mass of dots.

She examined her body. It had lines but looked like another body. It was too smooth, too young. Emma frowned at her body. She touched the edge of a slightly pixilated breast, her finger entering under the nipple.

She nodded to herself and stared at the ceiling. "Don't need Jack."

Emma shook her head.

She tested the water with her big toe.

"Ants."

She held the sides with her hands and slowly lowered herself into the half-full tub of pixilated water. She took a long drink of Chardonnay and flicked the rubber duck into the water where it bobbed in flickering water near her knees. She watched the duck for a few seconds then focused on the end of the tub, which faded in and out. Then she picked up the razor on the sideboard. It disappeared in her thick hand.

"Not sure if this is gonna work, but I might as well try." She quickly cut her arms up to the elbows and lay back in the water. Her toes broke the surface of the water like broken pier supports, her knees like the tops of submerged logs, her strange belly a soft floating island, her breasts upended saucer cups, her lank hair floating like detritus in a shimmering eddy.

She reached up, took the glass in her hand, raised up and sipped; the pixilated blood from the cut ran down her arm.

Finally she relaxed into the water, a mirthless grin on her face. Her life bloomed from her hands to her feet, enveloping her.

"Bye, bye, Jack."

* * *

"Stop that!"

Emma swiveled her head right, then left; then she looked at the ceiling.

"I ain't dead?"

"You can't be dead. You're fucking digital."

"I'm not going to stay here, Jack. You can ask me about Maddy forever, and I won't say a thing."

* * *

Emma was downstairs in her house. Her clothes were back on, and she fingered a doily and watched the pixels drop through her fingers.

"Okay, Emma. I'll make you a deal: you tell me about Maddy, and I'll think about letting you out."

Emma looked up. "Think?"

"Can't you stay for a while? You might change your mind. Don't you think you'd be happier here than out there?"

"Maybe. I guess I have the time."

"Just think about it."

"Tell me, Jack, what was the insect thingee, the praying mantises, the soldiers?"

"You saw praying mantises?"

"I walked into a hole in the kitchen and there they were."

"It happens with you too. Sometimes my platform, Phisto—"

"Phisto? Great. Sounds like the devil."

"Phisto fills in gaps in your representation with what seems to match from my games. It leaves a link to the game."

"So, this Phisto does it. Doesn't sound like you know everything about what you're doing."

"Fine. Can you tell me anything about Maddy?"

"Might as well. I don't know a lot; my memories are kinda hazy. I tried to think of growing-up memories and couldn't."

Jack, seriously, "Phisto couldn't create early memories."

"Thought he did everything." Emma shrugged, thought, finally said, "First, we didn't really know her, and I was wary of her, but you probably know that. She was too, what's the word, flamboyant."

"Do you know anything you didn't tell the police? What about the guy you mentioned? The big guy, heavyset...or anyone else?"

Emma took a sip of Chardonnay. "Ya know, Jack, I ain't getting drunk, but I kinda like the tickling."

"About Maddy."

"The big guy was with her at the café a couple times. He always wore a big floppy hat and red-rimmed sunglasses. I remembered the glasses more than the man. He was big, had a broad forehead. I was kinda attracted to him, the way he moved. He was kinda sexy." Emma laughed. "Ya know, I'd never say anything like that out there. Funny."

"Why didn't you tell the police?"

"Hell, Jack. Maybe hell is right here. Right, Maddy. I had enough hassles with everyone crowding into the café to ask about her after that video."

"That's it?"

Emma: "Now I remember. She was with this guy and talked about where she would go after she left. He said something about a building, but I didn't hear where it was or anything else. Maddy seemed to shake her head as if that wasn't possible."

"Does this guy have a name?"

"Don't remember a name, and it was obvious he didn't want anyone to have a clear idea of who he was. So there you are, something to obsess about."

"That's all?"

Emma paused. "Not anything that could help you."

"What does that mean?"

Emma frowned, shook her head, pixels whipping around her head. "Well, she came to my place later. I didn't ask her, and I didn't know what she wanted."

"Did she want you to help her?"

Emma shook her head. "You got to be kidding. No, it was about me."

"You!"

Emma said angrily, "Why not me?"

"Well, what was it?"

"She told me who I was, kinda like what I heard you told Talia and Harris. But it was different. We sat down at the table, and after a while, I realized I'd told her about everything, my ex-husband, the drunk, and Johnny, my kid, who killed himself. Nobody in the church did that for me."

"It wasn't a performance."

"Wasn't to me. She told me I wanted to get out. She guessed I didn't like it here, or there, and I wanted out of life."

"She could be perceptive."

"She also told me something strange; it was a kinda riddle."

"What?"

"She told me that God didn't exist, but that I had to believe in him. I thought about that a long time."

"Hmm."

"I finally understood what she was saying: that believing in something was more important for me than whether it was true or not."

"Odd."

"And you know, she was right about getting out. I tried it here, but I couldn't try it there." Emma paused, frowned. "I don't want to talk anymore, Jack. Why don't you try George? Isn't he next?"

"How do you know?"

"Doesn't take a brain surgeon."

"I don't know if he knows much. I haven't learned much."

"But George is next, isn't he?"

"I have to think. Are you okay with staying for a while?"

Emma took a long drink of Chardonnay.

"Leave me here for a bit. I'll try exploring. But I know I'll want out. I'm positive. I thought it was purgatory, then heaven, then I started wondering what heaven might be. Guess what? I don't care. She was right. I just want to believe; I don't want to think. I want to live believing."

"You do know you're digital, not real."

"Doesn't matter."

(21)

She made a note in her personal log about Edna, the Thanksgiving feast with Max's Place, and their tête-à-tête at McTeague's. Edna: she'd volunteered before, but it was obvious she needed less business-friendly and more real human contact, more face-to-face. She seemed to brighten up helping at Max's Thanksgiving feed, even more when they met Dawn and Adam.

She logged her encounter with Adam and Dawn into her Tenderloin database. She thought as she typed it that they would stay away from heroin, although she worried about what Adam said about teasing the OD line. Maddy had talked about crossing lines in her video, and Jack had said the same thing in the Dog, on a night he said anything. We all have a line we play with, think about, and dare ourselves to cross.

Well, yeah.

Talia settled in her couch, regarded the bookcases opposite, a few titles and squeezed-in collages.

Crossed Lines.

in my twenties bartending the vortex i didnt see lines i guess marriage and divorce were lines being an artist was a big line for me you put yourself out there naked i wanted to be great and i crawled away i worried i wasnt good or even mediocre

* * *

She'd been a whirlwind for a couple days. Into the city for a swim in the club, and later Madam Butterfly with Carol. Why did they always cry in Puccini? His arias, always by beaten-down or dying women, made the tears flow freely down both of their cheeks. Carol's cheeks seemed to glow sensuously. Her own cheeks, later examined closely in the bathroom mirror, seemed strained, tired, uninteresting.

it felt good being with carol   tears   cheeks   glow
there was a resonance a commonality i hadnt felt
that good in point city   on the line worrying about
jack   or with mike

Arias and sex: it almost made her forget about the Tenderloin, the kids, a heroin epidemic, and Jack, his quest (was it a quest, or another game?), Maddy, and the carny on his second floor.

And lines.

It looked like Edna was contemplating a new line. Good for her!

was there a new line in my future   seemed remote
i crossed easy lines to live in point city   volunteer
start the line   what about art   what about carol
why do i feel stuck

The Line had been silent for a few days, and she should put up more flyers, but the thought of visiting the Tenderloin depressed her. She guessed it was because of her other life, the easy swing of life in Point City, hiking, swimming at the club, Carol. Carol was dragging her away from her self-assigned task, or work, or avocation. The Line's phone surprised her when it rang.

Dawn. Talia looked at the nest of photos above her desk. She hadn't taken photos of Dawn or Adam, but there was a substitute, a young working girl she'd taken weeks ago. She hoped Dawn would never go that route. But then, neither she nor Adam had many options.

Dawn: "Gotta free cell from this new program. It ain't much, but it works. I was wondering if you could give me the number of that lady who was with you at Thanksgiving?"

Edna?

"Edna? Sure, why?"

"I just want to thank her for the money. I know it was a while ago, but it helped us over a kind of rough patch. It was nice of her."

should i   shouldnt i   did she want more money   loin
kids learned how to play people   or   maybe i should
let edna decide

"Not a problem. How are you and Adam doing?"

"Things don't change much here. If anything, they get worse. Adam's scheming about starting to deal, but I can talk him out of it."

"And you?"

"The holidays suck. Makes me think of better times, you know. Shit, I don't know if they were good or not. Whatever they were, they were better than here. Makes me think of going back to Seattle, maybe trying to live with Mom again. Not sure if I'm ready for that soap opera. Feels like hustling back, not forward."

"You should try it if it gets you out."

"Easy to say. Maybe."

Talia gave Dawn Edna's phone number and noted the call in her database. Then she walked over to the Barn, waited until she got Edna alone, and told her about the call from Dawn. Edna was happy Dawn was going to call her.

odd im happy someone else knows what i go through but i feel ednas horning in on my gig shit now i feel like an asshole

* * *

It was foggy earlier, but the sun was making furtive inroads. Talia sat on the front porch, feeling the warmth of the light and the coolness of the shade obscuring the clouds. Kind of what it feels like in her life. Up and down. Energetic and depressed. Happy and sad.

maybe im bipolar shit isnt everyone a little

Jack roared by in his motley Porsche, pulled into his detached garage, and walked slowly across the lawn and into his house. The Line, Edna, Dawn, and Carol all faded, and her inquisitiveness, almost obsession, about Jack and Maddy ricocheted back. She went into the office. She flipped through the Maddy flyers again and recalled the talk she'd had with the day bartender in the Last Call.

She visited a bunch of sites she'd bookmarked about Jack's games. The ones that intrigued her most were the ones about Ouroboros. Ouroboros gave her a new appreciation of Jack. It made her wonder if she could live in a fantasy world and rid herself of her worries. Was that a good idea? Did he know other people better than they knew themselves? Was he watching pale copies of real people?

critical articles about the snake   multiple changing identities multiple narratives philosophy competing natures of man love experience all ending in the same place

(22)

It worked. Again. Seamlessly. From disparate entities, massaged audio, hundreds of spoken utterances, medical and historical records, and psychological data, Phisto created a detailed profile and derived cognitive and memory modules, and the neural construct. And Emma's avatar came alive. When Emma started moving through her usual locations, he could only stare, dumbstruck at what he'd done, what Phisto had done.

ill never know how phisto did it how can i show it to anyone if i dont know heres a black box theyd laugh at me course why would i show them well i want to show someone then i dont

He had Phisto build two sections for the Show: Loop for his eureka moments of Raquel and Emma's coming to consciousness, and Present to watch them now. If one wasn't doing anything, the scene shifted to the next character. It wasn't a game. It was a brilliant and dazzling set of changing images and characters, outrageous, mesmerizing, entrapping.

The digital Emma made him see more about the real one, especially when she revealed Maddy's visit. Watching the real Emma move slowly, lugubriously—bovinishly—through the Café con Vache, he could see the hidden part of her character. He could see it in her forced cheerfulness, in the downcast way she glanced at the Hispanic help, in unguarded moments when her face sagged slightly, when she stared at crumbs on the counter. Finally solitary, running through hidden hurts, a failed marriage, her son's suicide, the bleak, unending future at the café, the folding and enfolding of dough, repeating the tired motions, finding tics in the mirror, incanting banal narratives.

Physically declining, emotionally barren.

Hello, Jesus.

Who could have predicted what the virtual Emma would do? After her suicide attempt and her revelation about Maddy's visit, she became curious about the digital world, wondering how she felt, touching things, trying to eat. Who wouldn't be interested? Any animate being would want to explore, seek the boundaries, wonder about their strange world. She had the capacity to be entranced unlike the real Emma, hemmed in by her past, her memories, her dense reality.

He couldn't find her right away when he switched on the display the second day. He found she'd slipped through a hole in the café into Devil's Brigade, a first person shoot-em-up in a nameless hellish African country. She seemed excited when he saw her, but her expression changed dramatically back in the café, as if his questions and her dull life there overwhelmed her.

He talked to her at length about her experience, but beyond her impressions of her digital world, she still thought about leaving. He could tell she was caught between exploring her new world and the realization that world didn't have a way out, a heaven or hell.

She said she just wanted to stop thinking. She just wanted to believe.

why did maddy tell her that seemed cruel but right i could help my digital emma i could turn her off i cant help the fleshnblood one

The Show, the brilliant Show, had started exhausting him. He needed a break, but he found himself glued to the chair, his gaze fastened on the monitor. Raquel was fascinated with her digital world and explored it for hours. She told him what she felt—feelings?!—what she thought, how to read, whether she was learning or just going through the motions, wondering if either of them really knew what consciousness was. A few days ago, she said she thought she saw Emma from a distance in a game and why didn't he let her see her?

What?

Raquel and Emma were in separate carved-out digital spaces, at least he thought they were.

"Phisto."

"Yep."

"Raquel and Emma are in separate digital spaces. How could Raquel see Emma?"

"Hmm. Good question, Jacko. My guess would be if a large patch was used from the same game."

"Guess?"

"You see, Jack, I massage the data and make it look as good as I can and put it through these new neural programs, but I don't know what you see."

"Or that you've created consciousness."

"*Correcto. Is it a problem that they could find each other?*"

"I'm not sure. If it is, I don't know *how* we could fix it. Can you think of anything else you haven't told me?"

"*That's easy, Jacky. I don't think.*"

"Right, right. I suppose that's a good thing. You won't know you've created consciousness."

"*What is consciousness again, Jack?*"

"Right. Thanks for the help."

He and Phisto hadn't counted on the links leading to the games. It worried him that not only could his characters disappear in a game, but that they might run into each other. He told Raquel that he wasn't sure how a meeting would work, or even if he wanted it to work, or if it would blow up his brilliant world. After reflection, he thought it was about lack of control. But perhaps that was okay.

what made a conscious character or living character if not rudimentary although circumscribed freedom to choose

* * *

Mouse had been incommunicado for weeks. The crusts were gone and a tiny piece of cheese, which meant he was alive. Had he started looking forward to their competition?

Competition everywhere.

He realized he was feeling depleted, anxious. The year, the Ides was fast approaching, but he knew he had to keep sane, do normal things, see some bricks-n-mortar people.

i should say fleshnblood

He left his laptop and cell behind and tanked up the Porsche. He drove north on Highway 1 to Jenner and over to Guerneville, where he spent two days in a rental on the banks of the Russian River and took hikes in Armstrong Woods. In the evening, he drank Macallan's scotch in the Wrangler Bar, and later smoked some of his last Durban Poison pot, and zoned himself into immobility watching the river. Its sleepy flow and random boat mesmerized him, but instead of a peaceful Siddhartha mind, he became grimly fatalistic. (Are they the same? Is one the prelude to the other?) One day that river would disappear. Given the drought in California, that might be sooner than anyone expected. Everything was ephemeral, including his Show and his characters and his games, even Maddy. At some point, all piled in the dustbin of history, which would in time disappear as well.

He realized for the first time that he moved to Point City because he didn't have anything else to do. His company was gone, his employees gone, his SoMa life gone.

Maddy gone.

i could have taught consulted traveled but instead im following a winding spoor into the past

* * *

His escape was too short.

If he was going through with unraveling that tenuous link to his past, it meant getting data on his next character, George. The faster he did it, the faster he could give up on what was becoming a brilliant exercise and start a new life.

really can i start a new life what about my babies my digital characters play it out play it out

What data did he have on George? A mélange of audio from his bugs, Net data, and hacking their three computers.

George Mathews: 52, pudgy, semi-bald with wisps of gray hair, two knee operations, mild asthma. George had a degree in sociology from San Francisco State, had worked in the Barn for twenty years, and was cynical, solitary, unhappy, and had acrimonious fights with Edna, and at least once a week overindulged at the Dog. He also had too-friendly conversations with rotund bubbly Maria Vasquez, a 35-year-old Salvadoran deli worker at the grocery, and had at least one *liaison dangereuse*.

Edna Mathews, née Minter, 44, thin and vinegary, was raised in Orland, and, likely, couldn't wait to get out. She'd lived in the city for five years while getting a degree from S.F. State in finance and dabbling with bisexuality. She also didn't need help to do two sudokus, a cipher, and the *New York Times* crossword every morning, as well as their taxes and the accounting books for the Barn. The bugs also told him they'd had a stillborn child ten years ago and that Edna couldn't have any more. That was the dark center of their marriage, the unspoken deadness they carried through the day. Probably more with Edna than George. But Edna's sorrow shaded George.

He could speculate about the state of George's psyche, of what he could possibly have said to Maddy, but he needed more hard facts, data. The bugs in Point City weren't enough. He needed more refined capture, and he needed more psychological data for Phisto. George avoided him, and when he was in the Barn, George tracked him with glances that seemed actively hostile. It was going to be impossible to get good capture. If George didn't reach consciousness, he could still watch him repeat talk Phisto had found significant.

If he didn't have more direct psychological data, he needed more locations and more intimate conversation. The Barn was out, but there was George's house and a boat George used. He'd already bugged the boat but George hadn't gone out. Looked like the house was the key.

ive already hacked computers and planted bugs everywhere do i want to know what happened to maddy that badly

* * *

Jack parked in front of the Café con Vache early afternoon and sipped a complimentary coffee from Emma while waiting for Edna's afternoon visit to the Barn.

As soon as Edna showed up, he flipped the cup into the garbage cask, started the Porsche, and drove into the hills. He parked a couple streets up the hill from their house. It was an area with scattered houses and big lots. The west fork of the Sidewinder hiking trail led close to George's, which nestled a couple hundred feet back from the trail in bishop pines.

He hiked down to the trailhead and along it for a quarter mile until he was close to their house. A few hikers passed him, and when they disappeared, he took out his cell, found his notes about the surveillance system, and switched it off. Then he quickly hiked up to the house. It was easy to crack the lock on the back door. He brought out his capture camera and started filming.

He wasn't sure he should capture George's house. Phisto had given him brilliant avatars but there wasn't any correlation, so far, of the physical environment and talk of Maddy. What he needed from George was more about Maddy, although he wasn't sure he'd get that either. He supposed it was a habit making and seeing a massaged digital reality.

Oh, well. He roamed through the house capturing every room, especially the kitchen, where he supposed they spent a lot of time. He was surprised by a small add-on greenhouse, replete with a scattering of forty or so multihued orchids hanging in pots or standing upright on thin green poles. He went through the correspondence in their home office, checked the books, the magazines and newspapers (*NY Times*, *WSJ*) scattered over the living room table, and the CDs next to the stereo, which were mostly old rock and light classical. Well-stocked liquor cabinet next to the fireplace. Despite a few his/her themes (George: old cars, guns, police procedurals; Edna: investing, gardening, orchids), the house seemed arid;. It seemed obvious George and Edna lived in separate psychic spaces. He captured their large flagstone patio with a rim of withered native plants, yellow-orange poppies, silver lupine, a couple of tables with umbrellas, and a scattering of rusting iron chairs with bright red seat cushions. He wondered if they entertained much or just sat staring at each other, occasionally scraping the rust with a fingernail.

He captured the garage, which was preternaturally neat, just like the rest of the house. It made him think of the Barn and how carefully everything was stacked.

He planted bugs on the patio, under a living room chair, and in the garage and called it a wrap. He closed the back door and was rounding the garage when four hikers emerged from the trail. He drew back and watched them as they hiked towards the road. They were about to take the road when they stopped and pulled out maps.

fuck fuck fuck

He watched the hikers nervously, tapping his hand against the side of the garage. Finally they left, and he quickly jogged down to the trail. He stopped and switched on the surveillance system. Just as he was about to hike up to where he'd parked the car, Edna's Subaru pulled into the driveway.

Jack drove down the hills into Point City. He stopped outside the Lost Dog. He looked at the street as it turned towards the coast.

The distractions were over.

Time for Phisto to work on George.

(23)

She'd put it off long enough...through the build-up to the holidays (sorry, Mom, Tena, not this year; and thanks for the tech camisole, warm but totally cool) through the fog and rain, through a growing Tenderloin heroin crisis, through Carol's too-brief visit, through her increasing curiosity about Jack and Maddy.

Talia flipped the bug up in the air, caught it in the palm of her hand, and closed her fingers over it.

She stuffed smokes, keys, and bug in different pockets. She regarded herself in the small living room mirror.

Five foot four and big eyes of bronze, check;

Body square, intriguing, check;

Hair punk, new purple stripes, check;

Square cute face, check;

Ironic Bell's-palsy-induced smile, check;

Slightly revealing Indian goddess tat, check;

Too plain; she wasn't a nun.

She put on blush and pink berry-colored lipstick, picked up three ruby earrings from the ashtray of baubles and put two in her left ear, a single one in her right. Wasn't life supposed to be unbalanced?

i look inquisitive curious warm a listener im ready

That winter morning it was chilly, foggy, with a distant hint of blue, but Talia wore a simple pastel shirt, black slacks, flats. She felt good, the cold animating her.

Jack's house was imposing, and the second floor was open for business, sparkling and flashing.

im going to see jacks fucking show if its the last thing i do ill force myself in if i have to ill hogtie him and walk up those stairs and

She walked down the sidewalk, hopped up the front steps. She hesitated ringing the buzzer. She twisted her neck and glanced in the large picture window. She shaded her eyes and made out bulky shapes in the living room, a rim of prints or paintings. But it was dark, distorted, except for the light flashing on the stairs.

Jack jerked the door open.

Jack was angular, torn t-shirt, torn jeans, blond scraggly hair, scrape of beard with hints of silver, face lined, eyes red and watery but wary and piercing.

Talia smiled warmly, shook her head. "You look like you've been up for a week."

He growled, "You don't look so great either."

Talia sighed. "Shit, I checked this morning; I thought I looked better. It's sleep, as in I don't get much. I'm a born worrier; I wake up a hundred times a night."

"Sorry to hear that." Jack paused, waiting.

"I have a something I want to show you."

Jack frowned and shrugged. "What?"

Talia shivered. "Perhaps we could do this inside. I'm freezing out here."

Jack frowned again but relented. "Okay. C'mon in. I was making coffee; might as well be hospitable with a Point City luminary."

"My light hasn't been shining too brightly lately."

fuck you asshole

Jack walked away from her towards the kitchen leaving the door open.

Talia shut the door and walked slowly after Jack. It was cold inside, barely warmer than outside. She glanced at the stairs and saw a huge image projected on the ceiling and the walls.

George.

She was mesmerized. She started walking towards the stairs. It was George, but part of his face was a different color and part of his—

Jack barked, "Display off." The second floor went dark.

She squinted. George? A recessed projector? What would it be like to be surrounded by images? To be *in* images.

"You don't have to turn it off because of me."

Jack looked at her, smiled sardonically. "Yes, I do."

(24)

Emma talked with customers in the Café con Vache, their images flickering, disappearing, and slowly reforming. People lounged outside the café. Cars rolled down the street and disappeared. The steps of the Barn were empty; inside, George was at the counter, puzzled, his thick head patched with bits and pieces of games and encircled with a thin yellow corona.

George's body flickered as he fingered a partially pixilated energy bar. A quizzical look spread across his face as his thick multihued fingers hesitantly then slowly counted out change for a glowing customer who danced, jerked, and vanished.

George walked slowly through the Barn touching a t-shirt there, a jar of strawberry preserves here. Finally he was back at the register.

George stared at his glowing assistant. "Who are you?"

The assistant shook his head slowly and faded away.

George looked quizzically at the empty space and walked outside shedding pixels. He watched as his arm filled up with glowing pixels merging with his skin color. He picked up an apple and stacked it in a bin and watched it disappear.

George stared at the flat gray sky.

"Where am I?"

* * *

"Display off."

"Phisto."

"*Yep.*"

"Thought you said you weren't sure about making the George avatar?"

"*Well Jack, it's got defects. You know that would happen.*"

"I did. But despite the defects, it's conscious. You made a digital avatar conscious. And you say you don't know how or what consciousness is. Are you telling me the truth?"

"Geez, Jack. I know the definition of truth, and I know it's important to you. But I don't know what it is. And I know the definition of consciousness, but I don't know what that is either. As I said, I massage the data and make it look as good as I can and put it through the neural programs, but I don't know what you see or what it is."

Jack sighed. "I assume the George avatar didn't reveal anything about Maddy."

"The lack of facial data made it impossible to tell if he was being inconsistent with his spoken utterances."

"Of course. That makes sense." Jack paused, thought. Say, are the separate digital representations of Point City or the avatars causing power or space problems?"

"It's straining the system, but so far it's maintaining."

"Monitor power and space, and tell me if it becomes a real problem."

"You got it, Jack."

"Right."

Madre de Dios. Despite the lack of raw information, George made the cut, consciousness surviving the waning and waxing physical trappings. George's body was a patchwork. All he had were photos, a couple videos, and long capture shots of the real George. He expected his first words would be just as fractured, but somehow Phisto and the recently added programs created a nugget of consciousness.

Jack sat down, grabbed the mic, and turned the display on. At that moment, he again questioned what he was doing. He'd created fantastic digital creatures by mistake for the most irrelevant of reasons. His search for Maddy seemed more and more ridiculous, the clues paltry, the result vaporous, except for Maddy's seemingly random words with Raquel and curious meeting with Emma.

Still.

He went through the motions with George, and the same pattern emerged he'd observed with Raquel and Emma. After George's initial hostility, there was George's total astonishment at being conscious, then the questions: Where can I go? What can I do? How long can I do it? George quickly understood there were no ramifications for what he did. It didn't take long before he picked up a shimmering baseball bat from his neat garage and swung it at the patchwork non-conscious Edna and continued beating her half-formed avatar until she was a mound of pixels.

shit really your conscious and all you want to do is kill your wife fuck

Phisto's maintenance programs immediately tried to re-create Edna, but the damage was extensive. Next on George's agenda was to walk to the half-imagined new development on Point City's north end and find the poorly constructed but always smiling Maria. He tied Maria's hands to a bed and flopped her glowing legs over his back, and soon her brown feet were squirming and rising and falling with George's spastic thrusts.

warning future ai researchers if you create a digitally conscious character out of an existing one be prepared for a healthy dose of bitchy personality and bizarre behavior societies shackles have disappeared they have constructs and memories of ethical and moral behavior but once they figure out where they are they will end up doing sloppy sex committing suicide and become murderers what did i expect well i didnt expect consciousness how could i predict the rest

Initially, George was intractable and refused to tell him anything about Maddy. But he kept trying.

* * *

"George."

George sat up in bed. Maria stared dumbly at him.

"Jack's back."

Jack: "C'mon, let's talk about Maddy?"

"I don't want to, but I will to keep you around. Shit, I can't talk to anybody else. Maria can only mutter a few words in Spanish."

"You have the games, the beach, your house."

"Are they conscious, genius?"

"You should explore your world."

"Please, get on with it."

"What about Maddy and the guy Raquel and Emma said was with her?"

George looked down at Maria, shrugged, then said tiredly, "Don't remember much. He was around here a couple of times. 'Here.' Isn't that funny? I'm in a fucking box." George sat up in bed. Maria faded in and out, sometimes leaving an outline, often with pixels glowing in the thick loops of her hair. "I didn't like him; he had this hood-like air about him. Tough, you know, like he'd just as soon shoot you as talk to you. He did wear those fucking red-framed dark glasses. Incongruous. Talking tough behind fruity glasses. Kinda made him seem even more dangerous, cold, like a sociopath."

"You don't have any idea—"

"I knew that would be your next question. Edna and I were at a barbeque on her street and saw them a week before her video."

"Why didn't you tell the police about him?"

George laughed. "Are you kidding? I didn't know what she was doing, and I didn't want to deal with that guy or the police. I had enough problems trying to juggle Maria with the Barn and Edna."

"Did they seem to get along?"

"Yeah."

"Nothing else?"

George seemed to think. "Once, when he was in the Barn, he got a call on his cell. He argued with someone about where they should meet, and he said they'd already set up the SRO. He also said to tell the troupe. He seemed to know the city pretty well. Made me think he lived there."

"That's something."

"Tell you the truth, I couldn't figure her out. And I tried. She was a mystery, a goddamn mystery. I could see why she trapped you. She was fascinating, couldn't take my eyes off her. At times, I thought she toyed with people; other times, she seemed like she was toying with herself. Maybe she's toying with you...right now."

sro troupe city

Jack stared at the screen. Had Maddy backtracked into the city? It had seemed remote when he first started thinking she'd faked it. Shit, for a while her picture was plastered all over YouTube and the Internet. Someone was sure to have seen her.

"Anything else?"

136

"You know, I could tell she was thinking of something, but the last time she talked to me, she kinda drifted off, almost as if she had second thoughts about what she was going to do."

"She was always sure when she did something."

"Why don't you ask Mike? Hell, you got Raquel, Emma, and me."

"I feel like I'm being led by the nose."

George laughed. "Maybe you are." He stared at Maria, frowned. "Check back soon. I've been thinking about something."

✷ ✷ ✷

George was on his boat watching the waves.

"George—"

George stared at the metallic blue sky and looked down. "I wasn't going to tell you, but Maddy came to see me later that day."

"What about?"

"She told me who I was."

"Please. Melodrama."

"Maybe. It didn't seem like it at the time. She took me by the hand and swept me into the office. I was pissed and shook her off, but she put her hands on my shoulders, stared at me with those deep eyes of hers and said, 'George, this is important.' She told me she knew about Maria and my growing anger and hatred towards Edna. She said I was stuck and that I wanted to kill Edna."

The waves rocked the boat slightly. "Then she said something I didn't quite understand, as if she knew what she was going to do later. She said that we all have a reckoning, a time when you see clearly what is going to happen, and you can control it or not. You know, she was right. I knew what I was going to do to Edna, when it didn't make any difference. She was right. I could have stopped myself, didn't.

"I know I didn't really kill her. I killed a ghost or an avatar, a bunch of 1s and 0s. I worry I might do that out there."

"There are constraints you don't have here."

"Will Edna come back?"

"Not right now. You caused too much damage for Phisto to re-create her exactly. I could have Phisto reprogram her back in. You know she won't be conscious."

"Doesn't matter. I know I shouldn't have done it. Maybe that's a residual morality, but I don't feel happy; I feel the opposite. Maybe that's why I can't do it in real life. It was impulsive, but it would never make me feel right."

"At least you let it out."

"I shouldn't have. It wasn't worth it. You're not going to tell her, right?"

"Raquel and Emma worried about the same thing. You are my secret."

"Your playpen."

"You could say that. I'll leave you on as long as you want. You have the best representations in your house, the Barn, and your boat...and the games."

"This is an incredible world." George paused and finally said, "About Maddy. I don't know if this helps or confuses things. Frankly, I didn't like you out there, but I admire your persistence and all this insane programming to find her. I can see why. I may have emotional problems, but I'm not stupid. I could see Maddy was an extraordinary person, and she's troubled. I don't know by what, but I don't think it's someone else. That's all I have to say." George sat down on the boat. He looked up and said, "One last thing: would you check in now and then?"

"I'll check in more than that. I'm still trying to understand what I made here. Why do you want me to check in?"

"I don't know if I want to live here."

* * *

What did he have after weeks of capturing, hacking, breaking and entering, programming, and Phisto building profiles, cognitive and memory modules, and the neural construct? He had conscious characters, a huge AI breakthrough. Bigger than anything he'd expected. But his characters were obnoxious and demanding, more OP (Obnoxious Personality) than AI. For Maddy, a heavyset guy who wore red-rimmed sunglasses, made phone calls to San Francisco, who might live in San Francisco and might meet in an SRO with a troupe.

And...and an ambiguous conversation with Raquel and unreported meetings with Emma and George, emotional, soulful meetings. What did that mean? Why did she do that? Was that another mystery or part of the same one?

(25)

Jack said over his shoulder, "I'm not sure what could cause this early morning visit, but I need a diversion. I'm sure my coffee isn't up to your standards...or my mugs."

"I make the occasional exception."

"I'm honored."

Talia shook her head at the now-darkened stairs and followed Jack. She considered his blond hair which, though matted, spread over his neck and half-covered the top of his torn t-shirt. Torn T, torn jeans, scruffy beard, money: homeless chic. Shit, she'd done it. Didn't the fashionistas want that? Or was it just easy?

In the kitchen, Jack waved towards the long oak table and a bottle of Macallan scotch and a squat half-full glass and an empty glass ashtray. "Remnants." He picked up the glass with his left hand and the bottle with his right. He put the glass on the counter and stored the bottle in a kitchen cabinet.

While Jack rummaged for a mug, she glanced out the long kitchen window, which gave an expansive view of the marsh, the Invert Ridge, a brightening gray sky, the corner of a gray bench. It felt like being outside. She wouldn't want to be out in that cold and fog for long. The oak table and dark living room appeared and vanished in reflection.

Jack pulled out two chartreuse mugs both with yellow and blue intersecting Fibonacci curves, then looked at her and said, "This looks about right." He poured her a mug, got half-and-half from the steel-gray fridge, and set both mugs and half-and-half on the table.

Jack sat down and said, "Your mugs display paintings, if I remember an overheard conversation. All I have are these confounding geometrical ones. Seems appropriate. Okay, what's up?"

"Overheard conversation?" Talia took the bug out of her pocket and flipped it on the table. It skittered across the table and stopped in front of Jack. As she sat, she said, "What do think, Jack?"

Jack picked up the bug and, watching her, rolled it through his fingers.

Talia sipped the coffee. "Arid, empty-spaces brew."

Jack frowned, tasted the coffee. "Confusing, Daliesque."

"Existential, spare. De Chirico."

Jack shook his head, laughed. "Fine."

Talia looked directly at Jack. "Enough about coffee and mugs. What do you think of my little bug?"

Jack frowned. "What is it?"

Talia laughed, shook her head, propped her arms on the table. "Don't be coy. It's an audio surveillance chip, a listening device, a 'bug' in popular parlance. I found it attached to the Nook's window frame. I suppose anyone could have put it there, however..."

Talia paused and took a sip of coffee.

Jack watched her. "However?"

"There's only one surveillance expert in town, and there's only one person who is trying to find out as much as he can about Point City, who 'captures' us—I think that's the word, isn't it? And who is known for the reality of the dialog in his puerile games. C'mon Jack, this is one of yours. You've probably 'overheard' the entire town."

Jack hooked a chair with his right foot, moved it closer and propped his legs on it, bunching the jeans around his calves. His feet were smooth, and considering how he looked, the nails clipped square, fingernails too. Slightly overlapping teeth and inward-turning canine, almost too white. Pale inverted scimitar of skin over what was probably a once-broken nose. The hint of concern she saw in his face had disappeared. He said, "It's illegal to put up listening devices like this."

"And you're worried I might take it to the sheriff. I'm not. I do want to know if you've bugged my house. If you have, take them down."

"If I were to put up bugs, I wouldn't put any in your house."

"I'll take that as a 'no.' Fine. I can't believe the bugs help you much."

Jack smiled, seemed to think about what Talia said, and finally shrugged. "If I were to bug the town, it would be for making a show more real. It's the same with games."

"A show? You mean the show you just turned off, the one with Raquel and Emma and I guess George."

Jack stared at her wondering what she thought, how much she guessed, or how much to tell her. "Why would I put those people in a show?"

"Because you spent a couple hours videoing Raquel in the Nook and Emma in the café and her house. I didn't know about George, but there he is." Talia gestured towards the stairs.

"Raquel and Emma asked me to."

"Raquel said you used your special camera on her in different poses. Emma mentioned it off-hand yesterday about how long you were there and how you talked to her. She wondered about that later. My guess is that they're already amusing you in your show."

"That's a lot of assumptions."

"Thing is, Jack, I've spent some time researching your grand creation, Phisto. You and/or Phisto make incredibly realistic—frankly childish and violent—games, and in some games your characters seem to talk and act as if they're real. I'm sure you've done the same thing with the people in Point City. It could be for your amusement, but maybe it's for another reason."

i got you jack   i dont care what you say   youre doing it for maddy

Jack stared into space. He was arrogant, insular, unsure or uncaring about other people. He fought his demons alone. She'd known people like that. One day, they upped and offed themselves, and no one could guess why.

Jack leaned forward and said, "Why do you care? What do you think it would do for you if you saw a show? Would you change? Or would it become an exciting go-to topic when you talk to Raquel?"

Talia pursed her mouth and said, "I don't know if it would change me. I've reached the age where I can't think of anything changing me radically. If it is an innocuous movie or video about Point City, you shouldn't have any objections."

"It's done for my amusement, not anyone else."

"If you're using people in Point City, it's not innocuous. That's why you don't want anyone to see it."

"It's still mine and not for public consumption."

"And those bugged conversations are yours too."

"If I did bug the town."

Miffed, Talia said, "Of course you did." Talia felt the pack in her pocket. "We don't seem to be getting anywhere. Do you mind if I smoke? It helps me think."

Jack smiled, "I don't smoke cigarettes, but I don't mind." Jack shoved the glass ashtray towards her.

Talia took the pack out of her pocket, shook out a cigarette, and lit it.

She blew smoke away from Jack over her shoulder towards the living room, dark except for patches of light from the front window. The living room was Spartan, except for the couch and a couple chairs holding on to the edges and clustered around the fireplace. And the paintings, the prints. They were grotesque, disturbing, but oddly she felt a kinship with the thought behind them. She made a mental note to find out who the artist was.

One of the prints was a collage of a solitary woman, back to the viewer, a yellow brick road, a dog, and an assortment of detritus. Oz? Strange collage. She glanced at the other paintings and prints, then back at the Oz print. An idea tugged at her consciousness and disappeared.

i know theyre maddys   i can see her in them   i can see her in oz   where is that

Jack said, "Maybe I try to understand people by hearing and seeing them in their usual haunts. It wouldn't necessarily help you."

"Why not share?"

"Why? Can't you imagine what other people are like, what they might say? People think different narratives for themselves all the time. They talk to themselves; they have another that is perfect and another they hide. They take countless selfies and make movies about themselves and see their creations as perfect, or flawed, versions of themselves. We do this all the time. Now, who is to say which version is the real one, the real you? I could create a character, let's call it Talia 2, with pre-loaded dialog, and you would watch it and say, 'Damn, that's me.' All I'm saying is that you do that already. I'm just doing it digitally."

Talia took a sip of coffee. Would she accept any version of herself? Would she accept Talia 2 as a real Talia? "I suppose you've done yourself or Maddy."

Jack paused and frowned. "Why would I do that?"

caught the hitch in your voice   what happened

Talia leaned over the table and looked Jack squarely in the eyes. "I don't care what you're doing, Jack, whether you're trying unsuccessfully to use digital characters to understand real ones, but I think this is about Maddy, trying to find out what happened to her or where she is."

Jack shrugged, frowned, and pushed his mug with his right forefinger. "I see you're part of the mob. A lot of people wasted a lot of time trying to find her after her video. Good luck."

"I guess that makes two of us."

"You don't know that."

"Sure I do. She goes out of her way to mention Raquel, Emma, George, and Mike. So far, you got three out of four. Good luck with Mike. Frankly, I don't think you're going to find her using those people, their conversations. By the way, I'm thinking of looking for and taking down your other bugs." Talia got up, reached over and grabbed the bug. "A keepsake."

Jack looked thoughtful. "Maddy criticized me for taking bits and pieces of reality and making something—a narrative, a video game, a play, an idea—I'd never experienced. She said, more than once, I was mocking reality."

"Hmm."

"She was right of course. But I couldn't—can't—change because it's what I do. It's who I am, a maker of fictions. And I admired her because she was engaged. Sometimes it seemed she was attacking people, but she saw who they were and tried to make them see what she saw."

"A version."

"A deeper version, a core version. We layer ourselves with copies, our personal copies, of experience, which are all true in a sense and all part of a subterfuge."

"What did she see in you? Did she get to the core?"

Jack looked thoughtful, frowned, and continued. "We started out as competitors, but it was more than a competition or philosophical differences. I liked her; she was fascinating, though often difficult. And I thought she liked me too. But what do we know about the people around us? Pretending is second nature." Jack paused. A frown made creases in his forehead. "Of course I want to find her. Of course I want her back." Jack shrugged. "As for that happening..."

Talia took another drag on her cigarette and crushed it in the ashtray. She wasn't sure she knew more about Jack or about Maddy. But she understood better his need to find her.

She said, "All right."

She turned away from Jack and looked into the living room. It was spacious, now filled with smoke and the smell of coffee, her De Chirico, spare light, Dorothy, Oz, a mouse hole, and rips in the floor.

"Grim art gallery. I kinda like it, especially the one about Dorothy and

Oz. Must be Maddy's stuff. You know I've started understanding her better; I like some of her ideas. But I don't have her intensity or her flair." Talia paused, looked for a change in Jack's face, and didn't find it. "You'll have to tell me if you ever get that mouse. Sure looks like you've been trying."

Talia turned and strode towards the door, paused to glance at the dark stairs, and left with Jack sitting at the table watching her.

(26)

It was bound to happen. Somebody found a bug. Why Talia? She was curious and had already made the connections between the bugs, Maddy, his search, and the four characters. Most of them had quit working weeks ago, their batteries dead. Jack spent the rest of that morning strolling through town taking down the bugs. He was surprised he'd put out so many. Talia was right; he'd blanketed the town.

Now, Talia.

Time to find out more about what she had found. He waited on the bench, musing about their tête-à-tête, about what he said, she said.

Finally he saw Talia drive past the short road towards Olema.

Jack got his laptop from the Stage.

He cross-referenced IP addresses with real ones, and in less than a minute, he'd found and started mirroring Talia's hard drive. It was done in half an hour, and he sat back and dug into her files. She had a ton of photos from the Tenderloin, mostly street people. He was struck by how she arranged the people in the photos, as if she were making them into an art project, à la Diane Arbus. He knew from one of his bugs that she'd tacked a bunch on her wall so she could put a face on her caller. There was a jpeg of a map of the Tenderloin.

What about the bug? He doubted she would do anything with it. She was too interested in what he was doing and too interested in Maddy. She guessed—it didn't take a genius—that Raquel and Emma were already in a show, and she'd seen George's patchy face plastered on the ceiling.

* * *

It was a clear day, sun greening Coastal Mountain foothills and shadowing valleys, bouncing off patches of water in the marsh, shining through the heather, making mirrors of the windows on Main, shining through his window over the dirty kitchen floor and living room, dust motes rising.

A rare winter day, a day to celebrate life, nature, beauty.

Jack sat glumly at the kitchen table. He glanced occasionally at the mouse hole. Mouse had been absent, but so were the crusts and cheese he'd scattered over the floor. He guessed he, or she, would come around when he was least able to deal with it.

I suppose you've tried to create yourself or Maddy.

fuck yes i did who wouldnt want to see themselves acting out on a screen it wouldnt be consciousness but one could see oneself see how one acted mouth canned phrases like a home movie but with less control

Maddy, typically, refused to let him create her, saying she preferred real life. Besides, it was ironic that he lived with her, had years of life with her and didn't know enough about her, her history, her background, her early memories.

Fine. Let's do Jack.

For months, he'd built his digital other when he wasn't working on games. He'd watched his other talk, move, disclaim. Of course he wasn't conscious. He didn't have the sophisticated cognitive and neural programs Phisto had used on Raquel and the others.

Maddy told him what it would be if he did it.

He remembered that night with crystal clarity. Fire crackled and snapped in the fireplace, warming their faces. Their Escher, *Bond of Union*, was in deep shadow, flames throwing sharper shadows over the floors, tendrils of fire reflecting off the picture window. There was a constant remote hum of traffic on Mission, occasionally broken by horns and yells. It had been a hectic week of symphonies, a dance program at Zellerbach, and Maddy had performed at a bookstore and two cafés.

He wasn't going to talk about his other, the avatar he was building, but he made it sound hypothetical, like an idea snatched from the ether.

Besides the personal stats, you would only add positive characteristics. Jack did this amazing thing; Jack said this profound thing. Jack was brilliant; Jack created Phisto; Jack was warm; Jack was compassionate; Jack was cool.

Maddy was on the sofa, the left side of her face in partial shadow, black hair tumbled over her shoulders, pale, sculpted legs scissored underneath a short red skirt. Her poetry, scotch-taped to the distant wall of her work space, framed her head. She'd just come from a performance at a small bookstore in Noe Valley and was pumped.

Maddy said, with a Cheshire grin, *Add the rest.*

Rest?

The other stuff. Put in the other Jack. Shit, when I think of myself, it's mostly Maddy the Progressive, Maddy the brilliant wild Poetess, Maddy the Performer, Maddy who skates the edges. Fuck, I know It's only half true.

You couldn't be more bizarre, unpredictable, and impulsive than you are.

Merci, Jackums. You couldn't make me, although you could try. You want to be true, kiddo, put in that other Jack. You want an exact replica? You want the real you, not the mask. Fuck it, put in everything. Put in the Jack that hated his brilliant father; put in the Jack that cheated Weiner out of his full share of Phisto's patent; put in Jack the Angry, Jack the Simple, Jack the Jealous, Jack who wants to possess me and can't. Jack the Brutal. Jack the Craven. What are you, a wimp?

Maddy.

And what would that Jack do? What would your Phisto do with a Jack that was complete with all the warts, sores, and boils?

Maddy, bottomless pale blue eyes, lean legs, and snake-like blue veins, challenged him. She was playing her Sybil role, Sybil with her potions and smoke and her unquenchable thirst.

And he bit.

Whaddaya think, Jacko? It would be the ultimate solipsism. You could see what you've become or might become. You could see your reflection in a thousand mirrors. Don't you want that?

While Maddy talked, embellishing her dig, he mused about what she said.

He would be his masterpiece. He would be the perfect creation, the perfect double, a doppelganger, the perfect alter, the perfect being for an inner dialog. He could debate *mano a mano* with himself. Of course he had his own inner dialog, but with his refined version of Phisto, the new Jack could speak more freely. He could call him Jack 2, or Jack One Off, or simply Jack Off. But he'd probably call him Jick to avoid confusion. Jack's left hand. They *could* have, in some sense, a real dialog, not one where he (the real Jack) would fudge objectivity to protect some inner core.

Wouldn't it be eerie, bizarre, at first, to see this simulacrum moving, acting, and talking like himself, although with a shinier face and a higher, tinnier voice? He supposed they would agree on everything initially, and why shouldn't they? Jick was the perfect creation, the perfect simulation, the perfect digital Jack. His inner voice cast in pixels.

It wouldn't be a robot gone mad or bad. It wasn't bad sci-fi, terminators run amok, or the absurd creation of an articulated controlling digital universe, a *Matrix*.

Imagine meeting yourself on a screen, the present you and a digital you, one you could talk to, one where you could explore yourself free of constraint. Neat, huh?

The problem was he did it.

Jick.

When Maddy wasn't there, he quit working on the next game, the grotesquely violent, X-rated, and hugely successful Dead End, and spent hours assembling the data to create the most accurate digital Jack he could.

Jick.

When Maddy went to Burning Man, he had Phisto create Jick.

i have to be honest i was afraid isn't that rich honest with myself are we truly honest with ourselves add all the stuff you think people think about you to what you think about yourself is that the truly real you

Jick wasn't conscious, but after staring at him for a few minutes, he realized it was a disaster, a disaster he'd never repeat. It wasn't a problem with Phisto. Jick said things that were programmed, but he flickered in and out of good and bad sides. The light side showed a bland smugness, the dark side a grotesque twisting of his features, his lips peeled back baring his teeth, his eyes malevolent, his gait stuttering. The result repulsed him. Jick was part smug genius and part evil conscience, sly, condemning. His words taunted him. He was mesmerized, and it took all his energy to reach over and yank the plug. He stared at the blank screen for a long time, his mind blasted. Finally, he felt a great relief. He'd thought later: no, that wasn't what he'd created. Something was wrong with Phisto or with the way the data was manipulated. He sensed, but couldn't prove, that Maddy had done something to his character, had inserted some code that expressed not his alter, but Maddy's anger.

i never ran jick again it made me worry that under the surface the gloss i was like that

(27)

Emptiness, vacuity, an undulating trail vanishing on an endless plain. Talia glanced at the Map, bright primary-color yarns crisscrossing the Tenderloin, the clustering of photos, the gray headset, her dark PC, and finally Maddy's ashen face, half-hidden among the worn flyers.

It wasn't the Line that infested her spirit.

She was stuck in the residue from seeing Jack. She guessed, since she saw George's patchy face projected on his ceiling, that he'd done Raquel and Emma. She could see he was obsessed with his show, secretive, and certainly obsessed with Maddy. He was also enigmatic and manipulating. When she listened to him, he made her feel as if reality were malleable, changeable, or there were multiple realities, multiple Talias. And he made her feel as if she were in some-one else's game or show. Jack's Show.

you know i probably am

Still.

Despite his suspicions—increasing suspicions—about her, she found her-self glancing more at his house and finding reasons to linger. The second floor towards evening was brightly lit, a potlatch of images and shadows flickering around the blinds. If you listened closely, there was a barely discernible hum, as if a generator were pumping out narratives of Point City.

Jack and his games, his quest, was interfering with her life. She had enough worries about what she was doing without sticking Jack and Maddy into the mix.

sure jack and maddy but its more im starting to feel the line was more selfcongratulation getting people to see how hard it was do i really want to do it is the line slipping away

Talia heaved up, left her chair spinning, put on her flats, and grabbed her cell and cash. She was stuffing bills in her pocket when the screen door slammed behind her.

Head down, Talia scuffed through the shoulder gravel and over the black-top to the sidewalk. She navigated the warped sidewalk towards the north end of her miniature village.

She nodded to the regulars drinking coffee and lounging against the side of Jin's Hardware. Inside the Café con Vache, she resisted a crispy ruggelach and paid for a coffee from Emma, the faux-jolly frumpy baker and owner. Emma's coffee had that industrial feel to it. An unremarkable French for the masses, white take-out cups adorned with black amoeba-like patches echoing the cow/vache theme. Emma herself was quieter that morning, contemplative, less faux-friendly, more subdued.

Talia looked at the vidcam aimed at the door. According to Raquel, Jack spent an afternoon with Emma putting up a surveillance system, and then time with Emma in her house. Were we all being videoed for some grand narrative? Were hackers and the government colluding to create what? A grand Alt, a substitute reality? Or, more closely, was Emma a forlorn character in Jack's show, manipulated by Jack, walking stolidly through different narratives? Talia couldn't imagine narratives wildly different from those attached like glue to the real Emma.

How did George get on Jack's ceiling? George actively disliked Jack. The last thing George was going to do was invite Jack into his life. What would Jack find? Something about Edna and George and Maria. Shit, everyone knew George spent too much time talking to Maria...every day. Edna told her what everybody guessed was true.

Talia settled in a rare January sun on the official Café con Vache bench. It was an old bench big with slow curves and rosette patterns in the painted black iron frame and initials carved into the wooden back and seat. Talia rubbed the initials "JA" in the wood. John/Allison? Jeff/Andy, Andi with an i? Where was J/M...Maddy with a y?

Talia waited for the coffee to cool. Then she gave into a major vice, lit a cigarette, and blew the smoke high and off to the right towards the Barn. Soon, she'd huddle in dark alleys with a motley bunch exchanging lights, coughing, disclaiming angrily about smoking rights, wondering in hushed tones about patches and quitting.

Cars inched down Main, the drivers watching for jaywalkers and stray dogs. She tried to see herself as they did and saw a strong but small and lean simulacrum of herself, occasionally scratching her stiff butch or shading tiger's eyes to watch the slow procession down Main or picking out a scene on the street. How would they see her? Offbeat? Lesbian? Tough? Pretending? Too small for their fantasies...or just right? Was she doing what Jack talked about? Creating different Talias, different narratives, watching herself from an imaginary distance?

Raquel stopped and stood in front of her. She said, "Immersed in an inner dialog, or just wool gathering?"

"Trying to gather my random selves into one, a hopeless task." Talia shifted to the side and rested her arm on the iron curve.

Talia wondered, vaguely, how much Jack had seen in Raquel. He'd spent more time with Raquel than Emma. Had he seen she was a lesbian? Had he seen her with Doris, the butch masseuse?

Raquel sat and balanced her coffee on the arm of the bench.

"We look like a '40s movie set," said Raquel.

Talia laughed. "I do my best with hair and earrings, but I'm still a spear-carrier; you're the exotic one." Raquel did look like a holdover movie star, attracting a range of men with her mischievous sloe eyes, high cheek bones, and rapturous lips, the lower of which she tucked under even white teeth when she frowned or was puzzled. Talia wondered, as she had before, whether she could become more than a coffee-klatch friend. She'd offered to loan Raquel money to keep the Nook going, but Raquel told her that her ex had come through. Her girlfriend, Doris, spent more time with her in Point City.

Raquel's life: homeostasis.

"It's all pretend. And you're an emotional disaster zone."

Raquel made the seriousness of the Line go away. "It was exciting, energizing at first. Now, I feel like a piñata that's been beaten by hyper third-graders. And I'm not even working for wages; it's completely self-inflicted."

"It's a new chapter in female masochism. It must be worse when you get to know them."

She'd told Raquel about the people she talked to on her excursions into the Loin. Pete and Johnny called intermittently, but she didn't really know them. She knew the stories of people at St. Anthony's and Glide, but she didn't know them either. Even Adam and Dawn. She didn't know them. It made the whole question of "know" ambiguous. "I tip-toe through the shadows of human misery like a sour ballerina. I must get a sense of satisfaction."

"I'll take satisfaction over masochism." Raquel jingled when she walked or moved her arm, the noise coming from thin silver bracelets which covered both nut-brown arms, ending in six or seven rings on each hand.

Talia watched the hoops bunch and elongate like Slinkies as Raquel took a sip and moved the coffee back to the bench arm, and realized, again, she felt naked around Raquel. "I'll tell you what it is. When I was younger, I thought I had a hard life, but it was mostly psychological. I was a wild child, wild adult. But when I look at it from this distance, I see I had an easy life, money, friends, school, worried parents. And a lot of people didn't have zip, just like the people I talk to on the Line."

"Can't carry the weight of the underside on your shoulders. You look beat and it's only ten," said Raquel. Raquel shaded her eyes and watched a dog meander across the road. A car stopped and waited for the dog to reach the other side.

Talia smoothed her hair back and rubbed her scalp with her fingertips. "You can't get more relaxing than the Nook."

"Soporific. But it gives me time to read, dress up and play house, to putter, to chat. I don't want much more. You can't help liking it here, even with this fog, rain, and cold, and now the January darkness, a winter of our discontent."

"We're like the refugees in Fahrenheit 451 gazing into space, musing about significance, and reciting our book to the air."

Raquel frowned and said, "I'd choose a Margaret Atwood, I suppose. Or a book by a refugee from Iran or Syria, talking about how generations of women struggled against huge odds and especially coarse, violent men. You?"

"Something gritty, noirish, with snappy one-liners, Raymond Chandler with nickel-plated automatics."

Raquel laughed. "Harris would recite that bird book, The Big Year. Jack?"

"No book, a show. He would stroll among us, watching a show of us projected on his retina. Speaking of Jack, there he is."

Talia pointed across the street and down the block at the Dog. Jack was outside with his camera taking close shots of the door, the glass, the sign.

Raquel shook her head and said, "What's he doing there?"

"You, Emma, I guess George, and finally Mike, exalted in Maddy's video, stars of Jack's capture and show."

"He's not going to get much from Mike. Mike doesn't like him."

"Neither does George. I think, somehow, he's wired the town. I've read Phisto can create a character out of practically nothing, a few snippets here or there. I'll bet you're a star in his show."

Raquel admired a diamond in the middle of a square-cut black stone.

"Who knows what I'd do? Shit, I might become a lesbian nympho or a mass murderer."

A half-moon of sweat widened around Talia's armpits. Talia unbuttoned the top button of her shirt. "Who knows what we'd do? At least it wouldn't intersect with our reality. It wouldn't change Point City, our bench in the sun, our two-car traffic jams, and that lone dog ambling back and forth across the street."

"Our backwater isn't immune from change. The rents are rising, and we've already had one development, and now there's the new one, that Windsor housing development, back of the Barn. Imagine naming apartments after yourself."

Talia uncrossed her legs and stretched them out. One of her flats had a tiny hole on the heel. "Our midget Trump. Fifteen seconds of fame trapped in a building."

"I suppose a little renovation or development doesn't hurt. I want peace and quiet, but then somebody has to buy a book or I can't have my coffee." Raquel shaded her eyes again, her bracelets bunching up on her forearm, and looked at a truck carrying bundles of new lumber. It passed in front of them, leaving a thin cloud of dust that rose and settled. Raquel was sarcastic and ironic about her chances, but there was concern in her eyes, in the downward cast of her face, hidden slightly by black curls.

"Point City has been like this for a hundred years, a sleepy, slow-motion place. I can't imagine it changing fast."

Raquel touched an eyelash she thought was out of place and got up. "Speaking of Jack, have you given up your obsession?"

Talia shook her head, grimaced. "I have to quit talking when I've had a few."

"Shit, we all want to know what he's doing. We wonder about the lights on the second floor. He's our mystery. Sometimes those lights seem to be on all the time. I can't imagine he sits there for hours immersed in virtual scenes."

"Look at kids today. They look at screens eight hours a day, and when they go to bed dash off thirty texts. We're already hooked up."

"Jack's not playing games or texting girlfriends."

Talia watched another truck turn right up to Highway 1. She threw her take-out cup into the nail cask that doubled as a garbage can and got up. "Back to the firing line."

Raquel said to her back. "Come over for lunch. I'll make us some cheese and tomato sandwiches."

Talia turned. "I'll take a rain check. I have to go into the city."

(28)

When he walked through the living room, the mouse hole drew his attention like a magnet. And the Oz collage. When he focused on it, he invariably thought of Maddy, as he did after Talia's visit and reimagining his brutish alter, Jick. That day, he stopped cold in the center of the living room, staring at the mouse hole.

Maddy had become distant in her last few months in the loft. She rarely came out of her work space. He tried to find out what was wrong and what she was doing, but she was coy, more silent than ever. Their supposed competition dwindled. She became secretive; had she become duplicitous? He watched her working in her space, typing on a MacBook and musing with a lean finger under her hard, white chin.

Every so often, he'd saunter over to her door and ask if she wanted to go to lunch or dinner or a bar. Sometimes, rarely, he thought, she would agree; most times she would look at him with her Cheshire smile and shake her head no.

fuck maddy what happened to our grand competition

Had she found someone else, a new competitor? If she had, she would have spent more time at the Shades. That tension, that cooling off of their rapport, if rapport was the right word, was seriously interrupted when she bought a used Subaru and rented the house on Pine Cone Lane on the outskirts of Point City. It happened so suddenly, he realized that despite sharing the same living space, he wasn't paying attention. She didn't move out to Point City right away, and he began to watch her closely...when he could.

He knew, or suspected from a hundred small changes, that she had changed, or rather, some important project had become an obsession, a project she had kept, and continued to keep, from him. It seemed that even their few conflicts were calculated to make him think nothing had changed.

So far, the characters in the Show, besides saying that Maddy was a fascinating mystery, had shown him more about themselves than about Maddy. How could it be otherwise? And the clues he expected to illuminate what she was doing were paltry: a green truck, a dimly seen other person, a scary wrestler type with fruity red-rimmed dark glasses, a troupe(?) and a hazy connection to a building (SRO?) in the city. In the last few days, he'd watched the loop of his conscious characters, often seeking more obscure clues, some arrangement of colors, some cryptic words, some pattern, but the only words that meant anything pointed to the next character.

The one thing he didn't understand was why the extra—secret?—meetings with the characters. Those brief meetings were about importance, about what was important in their lives. Was she talking about herself through them?

His avatars didn't help solve the Maddy mystery despite the time he spent with them. He shouldn't have been surprised that after exploring Phisto's games, they had less to say. Their digital environment was circumscribed. Even then, he would find Raquel looking up from a book, conscious, but looking faintly depressed. Emma, also depressed, spent time in the representation of the Café con Vache, the Revive Evangelical Church, and in the tamest, blandest of his games, Good City. Often he found George in the kitchen where he'd killed Edna with a bat, or sitting alone on his boat staring at a flickering ocean, almost as if he could rid himself of the memory of what he'd done. He had Phisto try but it couldn't reprogram the original Edna. Once, he saw the new Edna appear by George's side, but a few seconds later she vanished in an explosion of pixels.

That bothered him; why couldn't Phisto re-create her?

"Phisto."

"Howdy, Jack."

"The George avatar is conscious. Great job, even if you don't know what consciousness is. What about Edna? Why can't you re-create her?"

"Well Jack, I'm not sure. I didn't have much data on her when I made her the first time."

"You're not sure? Why?"

"Yeah, right. It might be something that's affecting me too."

Jack sighed. "What?"

"I'm not sure if it's power consumption or one of the AI programs, but something is straining the system. Most of the time everything works the way it should."

"I see. Well, keep monitoring it and tell me if it becomes a problem. We could cut back. But I don't want my avatars affected."

"Right-o, Jack. Everything seems to work right now."

"We'll revisit the issue soon."

"Okee dokee."

"Right."

The recurring problem wasn't a problem re-creating Edna. Between bursts of energy and watching his characters, he tired of the Show. Normally he loved puzzles, and the Show was an elaborate puzzle. But the more he agonized over it, the more he felt it was an exercise. He wondered—not for the first time— whether he was following Maddy's script, like the one she'd laid out for them with that first drink in the Mimic.

Whenever he felt like that, he fired up the Porsche and raced away from the Show. If he'd been rational, he'd have driven back to the Russian River or to Shasta or the Sierra or flown to Hawaii or anywhere. Instead, that time he turned towards the one place he should have avoided: the city.

* * *

He spent late morning at the loft. He hadn't been back for weeks. They had stared through their reflections at the long plate-glass window at the rushing daytime crowds, the bike messengers, the buses, the late-night stragglers to and from bars. Sometimes they'd talk. Most of the time they were seeing what they wanted. He would see the action, the characters, the potential narratives; he thought she was seeing new material for her poetry, new ways to describe the depredations of the powerful, new ways to understand herself. He never knew what she saw.

the memories are slipping away i cant capture them

He sipped a glass of water as he sat in the chair opposite the cold fireplace and the Escher Bond of Union as he'd sat so many times. Occasionally he'd glance at the end of the sofa where Maddy would sit leaning on the arm, black hair almost hiding her right eye, legs crisscrossed, staring at the fire or cocking her head at him as if she were trying to peer into his soul.

He'd avoided the bedroom on his previous trips. That time, surrendering to a latent masochism, he walked towards Maddy's work room, left the glass on the kitchen island, and walked through the kitchen and into the large bedroom. It was an expansive room simply decorated with windows that showed the edges of the surrounding buildings when the drapes were open, a couple nightstands, and a large flat-screen TV between the windows. The centerpiece was a McRoskey Tufted Platform King, where they made love, watched late-night movies, or talked about their day. Their competition died down in that room when they were having sex or just talking. Those intimacies sometimes made him think he was with a different Maddy, one that changed from room to room or hour to hour.

Looking at the neatly made bed, he finally realized it was the real reason he was looking for her. He'd had plenty of women before, but it was about sex, about having fun, about the exuberance of being young with money and living in Disneyland. No, he felt he had found someone who understood him, someone he needed. It came down to that.

He needed her. It wasn't a matter of sex or living a certain kind of life or a competition, a sport, although he often thought of it as one.

After an hour, he had to leave. The space oppressed him. He took a long walk around the Embarcadero, watching fishermen on the newly renovated piers, new exclusive restaurants perched on the water, and runners in green and gold and red pacing themselves, heads bound in earbuds. Everything changing...changing too fast. But everyone thinks that. Was there ever a time when reality was timeless, unchanging?

memory we remember time as static even when we say change

Late afternoon he was drawn to the bars, Maddy's bars. He sat, ordered, then glanced at the other drinkers, hoping that Maddy would appear by his side and drape her arm over his shoulder and they'd laugh about a joke that had become much more. Of course she never appeared, and late night he walked disconsolately to the Shades where he forced himself to joke with Leon Spritzer, the overly tattooed scrawny desk clerk now working on a degree in hotel management...

cmon leon aim higher aim higher

...and then spent the late night sipping single malts and watching films noirs, *Out of the Past* and *Scarlet Street*. They made him think of a couple of PhistoCo's games—the dystopian chiaroscuro streets, the pervasive corruption, the violent flawed hero, the black widow chorine.

**maddy said those chorines looked like her course they did your
the blackest widow around**

Through the hangover the next morning, he mused about Phisto, his
conscious digital characters, and Maddy. He felt trapped in a flawed universe
of his own creation.

Jack walked slowly through the usual morning frenzy, people yelling into
cells, car horns, police sirens, a wall of noise, head bowed, hair hanging, resigned,
counting gum splats, edges, squares, the random dried spit, a cigarette butt, to
where he garaged the Porsche.

Interlude over. And that withdrawal meant he was back in the Show looking for Maddy. He'd started thinking his time in P.C. with the Show *and* his
time in the city as interludes.

where did that leave real time

(29)

Overcast Saturday, the hills fog-shrouded, the sky gray. The coffee was dark and heavy. She made it purposefully worse by picking out one of her least-favorite mugs, the Goya mug, with its overlapping images of his Black Paintings, a Saturn Devouring His Son, a Witches' Sabbath.

Finally, wondering about what she did yesterday and shaking her head at what happened, she threw on her black windbreaker and took her laptop, coffee, and cigarettes out to the porch. She nervously lit a cigarette, took a puff, and watched the smoke rise, obscuring the hills, merging with the fog.

> *hey do something else talia you could get fucked or fuck or take a class or swim to lounge to wonder to grow my lassitude how glorioski well get on with it*

* * *

She posed the laptop on her knees and started the email.
To: carolmarlow66@earthlink.com
Subject: Hittin' the City

Howdy, Howdy...

Went to SF yesterday with Harris, birder and friend. Why hasn't he hit on me? He keeps butting his head against Raquel, who's a fucking lesbian. It's not that I want to fuck Harris; maybe I want the attention. (why am i swearing whats the deal)

What a place, Timbukthree, Marin. Where was I? Perfect Storm in the Loin! People who live there call it the "Tenderloin," but three syllables? Hello! Yeah, the storm...Maddy gave a reading across from this closed SRO. I know, I know, I'm obsessed. Maybe I am. Anyway, the building is supposed to be, according to my informants (informants! that's rich, a couple alkies and a few women of the night, Deb and Shari), a meeting place on Fridays on the third floor. I kinda thought I'd find out more. Probably find a bunch of squatters.

So I charged my cell, slapped on my blond wig, and cruised in with Harris. Harris? He's a six-footer, red curly hair, divorced, birder (I guess I said that), and has a Range Rover...eco decals outside, mess inside, birder mags, scope. Guess he's turning into a kinda hermit. Strange things can happen up here in seashore city.

We settled near this old closed hotel and waited. Don't worry; I didn't sneak in. I don't want dead. I wouldn't be able to see my friends anymore! Who knew what I'd find? Probably end up with a bunch of photos like the ones I've already got of people, of the downtrodden, the crazies, the drinkers, and the shooters. Didn't know what to expect. Maybe I'll start painting again. You'd want that, n'est-ce pas?

I know you think I should get back to art—hustle back? scamper back? lurch back? Sorry, I'm in such a quandary.

Hey, you started this....

Fuck me. (quit swearing talia)

Single Room Occupancy (SRO: single rooms, shared bathrooms...what memories, from mine workers to deck hands to seniors on SSI and SSA). Old, worn, beaux arts façade, 2x4s crisscrossed entrance. How do they get in? Anyway, we waited half an hour and I snapped a bunch of photos of street people, but it looked hopeless and I could tell Harris was getting antsy. Maybe they changed their meeting place. Just as I told Harris we could go, the first one arrived. Pimp, flashy green pants, white shiny shoes, open red shirt, bling, a lid with a feather. He looked around, then slipped into a narrow alley between the SRO and the closed building on the corner.

Okay.

I barely got my cell out before he vanished. Then they seemed to come every five minutes, like they were on a schedule. We were there half an hour until a bunch of Thunderbird-swilling derelicts surrounded the Rover, and we hustled out of there. Did get a bunch of photos. Two blacks, two Hispanic, two caucs, and one beefy bald-headed guy in a running suit. It got weird just as we were leaving. Tall guy, beard, 50ish, with briefcase, looked both ways and slipped into the alley. Fuck, what was that! I looked in the rearview mirror as Harris drove away and a woman in a blue suit did the same thing.

Freaked me out.

Tell you, the whole thing was a mystery, but what really got me was the bald guy. Something about him, something sinister, something about the Last Call, something that reminded me of...you know Raquel told me Maddy was with some bald-headed guy. She didn't tell the cops cuz she didn't want to get involved. I'm not sure why, but I have a feeling about this guy. Probably nothing, but when I put Maddy's poetry in the Last Call and Raquel's bald guy together, I get a match. Some imagination, huh...

Sorry to lay all this on you. I guess it's because we've been friends for such a long time. And I really, really liked the last time I was over. It was such a relief to get away from all this shit, here and in the city.

Did you get into the show in D.C.?

Why don't you come out here again? Last time, you had to scoot to that gallery opening in Mendocino. I'll give you my exclusive grand tour; shouldn't take more than a couple minutes.

Anyway, let's get together soon. I'll let you try to convince me to give it all up for art!

Xoxoxoxo (too schmaltzy should i delete its so hackneyed guess it's okay shit what am i doing i wonder what carol really feels shes so terrific)

P.S. Got to start in on the pix. I'll keep you up on where my quixotic curiosity leads me.

* * *

The photos.

The front and alley of the SRO were dark, the name over the entrance obscured. She'd spent most of the afternoon grouping the Loin shots, reducing their size, and tacking the ones she thought significant to her Loin map. The shot of the bald man was a blur, the back of his head a penumbra. It looked like Nessie or the Abominable Snowman shot through Vaseline. A crisp image of the bald man was supposed to be the centerpiece.

It was getting dark. She flipped on the light and drew a gray sweater tight around her shoulders, sat back. She couldn't stand looking at the Goya mug and now sipped coffee in a pop-artish Haring/Lichtenstein one.

She'd felt irritated off and on for months. She was hesitant when she first set up the Line. Then she got into it. She started early in the morning and stopped late in the afternoon. She replied to messages when she could, when the

162

person had a cell or borrowed one. Sure she complained, but she thought she was helping people. But the stories had become a litany, a chorus she couldn't stop, and her replies were the same. She started seeing her curiosity about the pimps and thugs and the SRO—and her curiosity about Jack and Maddy—as stand-ins for worrying about the people who called her.

(30)

The Show had entranced him from day one. His avatars—characters? people?—were able to form their own worlds within certain limits and surprisingly able to inhabit Phisto's games. Besides bitching about incomplete senses and faux heavens, they were fascinating. George's murder and subsequent contrition and depression. Even Emma struggling with her beliefs, wrestling with Jesus, God, and what she could remember of her past. Raquel, of course, was the most interesting, and he had long talks with her. Besides someone to talk to, she wondered about what it meant to be conscious.

Ergo.

"See, Jack, naturally I miss tasting and I don't mind not feeling pain, but I like the switching of colors and shapes. It's kinda like living in a kaleidoscope. But I've started feeling things in my head change. I remember being by a lake in a game, and later when I drew up the image, it wasn't a lake but a swimming pool...but I knew I'd seen a lake. What if Phisto replaces or deletes memory, the totality, or cognition, or all the things I'm used to being around? Will a nugget, a kernel of consciousness, remain? Will I still be able to say, à la Descartes, 'I think, therefore I am'? Or does it stay when I'm not thinking?

"And...does it cover things like making an ass out of oneself or getting stoned? Or absorbed in playing a Beethoven sonata or solving a physics problem where we are completely engrossed? Is it the same person, a person where everything is in flux, including mental activity? What does 'same' mean?" I guess I'm saying something simple: there are a lot of possible definitions of consciousness, and a potentially dizzying number of kinds or levels. Which kind am I? What level am I on? Or am I simply conscious?

* * *

He should stop, but couldn't.

Jack hacked Mike's computer, found his health files, and followed as many digital paths as he could, but he didn't have enough. Mike's conversations, some directly in the Dog and most picked up on his bugs, hadn't revealed much. He didn't talk much about Maddy, and when he did, he repeated what he'd already said about her.

After a couple fat tips, Mike smiled and let him capture the inside of the Dog.

It wasn't hard to understand the smile. He knew everyone in town had talked about what he'd done with Raquel and Emma, and they suspected everything. He still needed more from Mike. He needed to bug and capture the inside of Mike's house, and he needed natural shots of Mike. He needed to talk to him directly and find the psyche gold lurking under the surface.

Two days ago, on one of his now frequent forays into the Dog, Mike edged up to him to chat about one of Phisto's most violent, brutal, and popular games, Dead End. That entry was what he needed. The next day, Mike's day off, he showed up at Mike's with the unpublished hyper-violent version of Dead End and a handful of other games. Mike was surprised and ecstatic. Mike hauled him inside, and they got sloppy drunk and stoned on the ratty sofa and shot a thousand or so grim-faced muscular thugs, multi-headed mutants, toothed aliens, and ogled busty Amazons on Mike's Playstation. It turned out Mike loved posing for him. He left with a lot of capture of Mike's small house, and stuck bugs on the back of the TV and in the toilet.

Mike didn't talk much about himself, but he learned more about where he was from, the Marines, fights he'd had as an MP. Mike bragged about his off-again, on-again fuck nights with Talia.

i knew that talia guessed as much when i foolishly recited her history in the dog

The next day when Mike was working, despite nagging worries about the legality of what he was doing, he drove to Nicasio, got in through Mike's back door—the lock was a pin-and-tumbler—and did a more thorough search of the interior, especially the living room and unkempt bedroom, and left bugs near the back door and under the bed.

* * *

"Phisto."

"Yep, Jack."

"I loaded Mike into the system. Is power a problem?"

"Edna is still a problem, and there have been a few times when the system slows down. But everything is still working."

"Good. How long would it take to get Mike's avatar?"

"Not sure. Shouldn't take long."

"If Mike doesn't help me, I guess that's it."

"What's it?"

Jack sighed. "My search for Maddy. Remember you told me they might help, that they weren't entirely truthful."

"Yep. I think, Jacko, the operative word is 'might.'"

"True. Well, you were right, but the clues have been ambiguous. And I don't have much time left."

"Ah, March 15, the Ides."

"Can you think of anything else?"

"All rightee. You told me you've started gathering data on Talia. She could help."

"I'm not sure."

"I could make an avatar, like the other ones."

"No, no. She's too suspicious."

"Right."

Phisto started on Mike. He was about to become a digital character with qualities, hair, warts, eyes, shape of chin, gait, and with memories, cognition, and a calculated neural network.

He had no doubt the Mike Show would be as brilliant as the others, even without Mike being conscious.

conscious consciousness raquel got it i cant tell what it is but i know it when i see it

166

(31)

The dreary, leaden, chilling, rainy winter was slowly ceding to sun, sharp shadows, and warmed spirit. New growth was pushing up through the marsh, and the foothills were shading from brown to bright green.

Talia dug through her clothes and found a lighter shirt, lighter pants, and a pair of thongs. She stuffed money in her jeans and a few minutes later roamed through P.C.'s first Saturday farmers' market touching apples, admiring stacks of fresh-baked bread and homemade granolas, and smelling homemade soaps in lavender, honey, and sage.

Edna was busy with customers. Talia waved and got a wave back.

wonder if she and dawn got together ill ask her later will i feel jealous who knows i try not to then it bubbles to the surface

Talia walked towards the narrow garden between the Barn and the Station restaurant.

Despite the doubts plaguing her, the sun drew life to the surface. She walked slowly through the crowd. The grass near the garden was trampled, but there was an empty worn wooden chair. She edged into the chair. Last season's dead sunflowers hovered over her right shoulder, swaying slightly in a cool wind. The sun warmed her front. She raised her foot and admired her toes. Big toe, four small, the second toe slightly longer than the big one. Ah, that second toe. When people made fun of it, she said it was her punk toe and she couldn't control it, that it made her who she was.

She was surprised by the crowd. Her tunnel vision of Point City was of ingrown locals, tourists and bikers, and a haven for eccentrics, escapees from the world outside. People like her. But that day, it had transformed itself into an old farm community, like the one in Ohio spiritual centuries ago.

The crowd moved in currents, picking up, examining, putting down, standing in sluggish moving lines for toasted cheese sandwiches. Babies were strolled, kids ran after each other and played catch, loosely held parents' hands. A farmers' market inhabited a warm space in her psyche, a feeling of back to the land, of participating in an earthy tribal ritual lost to urbanites. It was like that in Oakland too, but here it seemed part of the hills, the distant fog, the sunshine. For the first time, the bales of hay in front of the Barn didn't look out of place.

And it was so far away from the Line, the Loin, the calls, a condemned SRO, and Jack's. She began to feel that the Tenderloin and her curiosity about Jack and Maddy had dug out a false space in her mind. She knew how to rid herself of that ersatz space: give up the Line, quit looking for Maddy, and try to bring her art from nighttime fantasy into the harsh light of day.

> *thanks carol do i have to worry about that now id like to see her again i wish she would invite me to oakland its such a relief*

Talia stood up, picked her way through the crowd. At the last minute, she turned back and picked up four medium-sized Fuji apples from Jesús, George's helper.

Talia balanced the apples in her hands and turned to go.

Home, she made a light mocha java. It became like the day, light, fantastical. Definitely a Redon mug. Pastel butterflies winged higher and higher away from the fading earth. A great coffee for that day, but the last kind for a hotline, a tattered line flung into the grubby dark side, or the mystery of Jack and Maddy.

(32)

Mike blinked several times. Then he stared at the small half-pixilated figure in the covers. He had a hard look on his face.

"Who am I?"

"Mike...Mike."

"Where am I?"

"...here...now..."

"Where the fuck is here?"

"...hard..."

Mike stared at his pixilated cock. He massaged it rotely, and it jerked slowly up like a flagship, engorged, pulsating between reddish purple and ochre.

"...stock," Talia said. "...down."

Mike sneered. "Here, phantom. Suck on this."

"...kay..."

Talia's avatar flickered in and out as it moved shakily towards Mike's swaying cock. Mike grabbed her head and forced it down over his cock. His cock disappeared in her twinkling mouth.

"Don't feel like much, tickles a bit." Mike made a fist and hit Talia in the mouth. Her head disappeared and reformed slowly. "Guess I can't really kill anything, but that felt pretty good. Always wanted to do that. Bitch talks too much."

* * *

Mike made the cut, just like the others. And what did he do after coming alive? Fucked a poorly conceived digital Talia and smashed her face, something, apparently, he'd always wanted to do. He then marched around town and clobbered as many digital avatars as he could find, all of which reformed slowly. Then he spent the next part of his second day—day? Jack's day. There's no day or night in the box!—marching determinedly to the ocean past coastal bluffs flashing like a kaleidoscope, finding a small varnished sailboat—near

George's boat—and trying to sail to Belize! Inevitably he capsized, struggled in the water for a few seconds, then stood up and laughed.

* * *

Mike was in Dark City, post-apocalyptic dark streets, crows skimming, squawking, and keening across the blood-red sky. Mike's shotgun boomed as he blasted muscular, scarred, grim-faced thugs into thick sprays of tinseled blood and gore. The bus careened over the bridge and vanished in fire and smoke.

"Mike."

Mike looked up, laughed, and said, "Okay. This voice is different."

"Let's talk."

"Who is it?"

"Jack."

"Let me crawl out of here."

Mike walked back through a wavering marsh with video games running on either side, then walked through Point City into his bathroom and into the living room, where he slumped into the sofa. He slapped his leg, his hand embedding itself partially in his knee.

"God that's fun."

"You knew you were conscious."

"Didn't at first, or who I was, then got it. I got it right after I hit Talia and she started comin' back. Tell me, did you program my capsizing?"

"First, I didn't program you; Phisto did. I captured some of the Pacific Ocean, but Phisto included some of the features close to the beach like the boats, the bluffs, the Farallons, some of the waves. It's realistic until it isn't."

"Right, Phisto. You told me about him. You know, I knew I wouldn't make it. Guess you, or Phisto, got that. Doesn't matter. I wouldn't try in real life."

"Why not?"

Mike crossed his arms over his stomach. "Been thinkin' 'bout that since I been in here. I started thinkin' I just wanted to be somebody...or escape. I guess that's what Belize is all about. Escape."

"You know it will only count in here."

"Yeah, right. Made me feel better to try. So, what you doin', Jack? This about Maddy?"

"What makes you think that?"

Mike's curly hair switched colors from brown to gray to black. "You know, filming Raquel and Emma. Sneaking around the Dog with your camera. Asking me questions about her. Say, did you get George?"

"The gang's all here in separate digital spaces."

Mike shook his head spraying a few pixels, which immediately reformed. "Maddy. I knew she was planning something, but I didn't know what."

"How did you know?"

"Allow me to paint you a picture." Mike leaned forward. "The day of her video, she came in the Dog early, had a PBR. It was a strange conversation, all very hypothetical. You know, if I were stepping over a line, if I had a certain amount of time, would I try to go to Belize. Kinda the same questions in her video."

"That was all? She didn't want you to help her with the hoax?

"Nope. It was mostly about me, about how I was afraid of life, about how if I didn't have the bar, I'd end up on the street. I tried to get away from her, wiping the bar top, stacking glasses, but she followed me, as if what she was saying was important. You know how she can be, insinuating, wondering, probing, performing. It was strange, very strange."

"Do you remember anything else?"

"She said I knew I would fail, but that I had to do it."

"That's not much help. Did she say anything about a big guy, dark glasses?"

"We didn't talk about him, but he came into the Dog with her a couple times. They were close, like they knew each other pretty well. And I heard snatches of conversation. You know what it's like in a bar, a thousand chitchats a minute."

"What about a troupe and San Francisco?"

Mike: "Can't say they talked about that. They did talk about theater and acting, but not a troupe."

"You didn't tell the cops about him."

"It didn't seem important cuz they were friendly."

"Anything else?"

Mike's brows bunched as he thought, and flickered green, then blue. Finally he said, "Something strange, that she had a new competitor, her toughest."

"Probably him. Makes sense. We were always competitors...in an abstract sense."

"And she talked about leaving, but you know what, everybody talks about leaving. I guess if they're in the Dog, they're not happy in some way."

"Do you remember any mention of the Tenderloin, an SRO, or a troupe?"

"Now that you mention it, yes. But just snatches like I told you. Say, let's talk about me now. How long do I have? What about the others?"

"It was everybody's first question. Everyone wants to stay except Emma."

Mike looked up, concerned. "Why?"

"It confused her. She thought it was heaven, then hell."

Mike laughed. "Shit, hadn't thought of that. Actually, I don't care cuz there ain't any heaven or hell. Hey, maybe's there immortality."

"You mean being here?"

"Kinda. Thing is, if I'm digital, I can't die. But I guess you can always pull the plug. Guess that makes you god. Can I talk to the others?"

"I'm thinking about it. Right now you're in separate execution spaces. As for staying here, you don't create consciousness then throw it away. Nothing else about Maddy?"

"Nope. Tell me how's the video game thing work?"

"When there's not enough time and data to replace a missing object or color, one of Phisto's algorithms fills it with game backgrounds. That's why it seems everything changes, everything but your consciousness. In some cases where there's a big patch, it leaves a link to the game itself."

Mike frowned. "Cool!"

"We'll talk later. I have a lot of questions."

"Don't be a stranger."

(33)

Raquel, Emma, George, and Mike.

Zippo.

Okay. Sure they were fascinating, intriguing, often obnoxious, and played Phisto's games through links and gaps. And they had shown him zip...except a green truck, a bald thug with red-rimmed sunglasses, something, something about an SRO, something about a "troupe," and something about theater. Maddy had talked to them intimately. Why? Why the confessional? Was it revealing, or...

What did "or" mean? Was she in trouble? Had she embarked on a new dangerous venture...with the heavy in the red-rimmed glasses? Had Maddy boomeranged into the city? He didn't think so at first. But now? Maybe it is an elaborate man vs. women tussle, a small-scale throw-down of him and her, of opposites, in which he is the recorder and Maddy is the archetypal Kali vowing death and destruction. Is the punch line new life rising from the ashes or just ashes?

What about his characters? He could spend the rest of his life talking to them, trying to understand their digital existence. He had folders full of observations on each one. Oddly, Raquel, always the most loquacious, had quit begging him for someone real (i.e., digitally conscious) to talk to and, like Maddy, had become fascinated with Ouroboros. Raquel seemed to spend most of her time finding different paths in the maze and watching and interacting with the characters, sights, and sounds.

i should show what ive done or what phisto has done to the world but then i feel an obligation to my characters do i want a horde of scientists professors and gawkers probing and questioning them theyre alive in a sense dont they deserve their privacy

* * *

His characters took most of his time...

...but a peculiar thing was happening with Talia.

He checked Talia's hard drive daily since her discovery of a surveillance bug. But he hadn't looked closely at some of her entries, and especially her emails, especially a recent email to Carol Marlow. Talia had found five bars where Maddy had performed in the Tenderloin. And she'd discovered a mystery SRO across from the Last Call. It was during a period where he was preoccupied with selling PhistoCo and Maddy had moved to Point City. He hadn't paid attention to where Maddy was performing, or if she was performing.

Why the Tenderloin?

It was time to find out. He drove into the city, parked in the garage near the loft, and backtracked into the Tenderloin.

He roamed through the Tenderloin, lingering outside the bars Talia had visited and Maddy had performed in. There was an idea flicking through his head, but he couldn't coax it to the surface. He almost went in the Last Call, but waited outside at a bus stop. Talia had stopped half a block down and had filmed people slipping into that old SRO. The proximity of the Last Call to the SRO didn't mean anything he could think of. Maddy had never mentioned either one.

Jack walked slowly through the Tenderloin, and through Union Square, and ended at the loft. Every time he visited the loft, he thought he might find Maddy (no go)...and the Shades (ditto). He didn't feel like spending the night in the city and was unsure of his next move. He stared at the silent TV screen and felt enervated. Glancing at an old roach balanced on the edge of a green glass ashtray, he wondered if Hymie, a dealer whom he hadn't seen in over a year, was still in business. On a whim he called him, and he was still there. Hymie told him to come over, that he had an excellent new batch of Durban Poison.

Jack shrugged inwardly. He could use an excursion that didn't involve watching conscious avatars or wondering about Maddy.

* * *

Hymie was nothing if not a salesman. There were already a score of medical marijuana stores in San Francisco, and more coming, and eventually legalization. But Hymie kept right up on the trends with more strains, vaporizers, shatter, waxes, and incredible edibles. Hymie treated him like a tourist buying a rug in Pakistan. He didn't need much urging and bought an ounce of Durban Poison.

While Hymie's crazed Chihuahuas nipped at his heels or nestled at his side on the couch, he had a few puffs on a bong while Hymie lectured him on the legalization.

Hymie: "Not going to affect my business."

"Uh-huh."

"Cuz there's gonna be so many rules and regulations and so few places to go, I'll bet my business increases."

"Yep"

"You wouldn't think so, eh? You watch those huge state/county/city bureaucracies come crashing down on legal pot. Shit, they've ruined everything else."

"Uh-huh."

"Man, I'm gonna be here forever...if I want."

"Yep."

"Say, you don't seem very happy for someone got a shitload of money. I suppose it's about Maddy and that cluster fuck of her video and you isolated in a tiny town in Marin. Long way from your life here in the city. Tell you what, I got something for you. It'll be good for you, let you get away."

"Uh-huh."

"Here, take one and call me in the morning."

Two magic mushrooms floated in a small pale turquoise Mason jar of honey. They seemed like diminutive men-of-war rocked by imperceptible currents.

Mushrooms?

did they feed my imagination or is that an excuse long ago we munched em head trip   trippy trippin but we always woke up feeling warm and fuzzy uh huh

* * *

Back in Point City, sitting at the dining room table, the Show upstairs grinding through his characters, Maddy flipping him the bird from whatever aerie she was perched on, blue Mason jar in front of him, he decided to try a 'room.

175

There was a faint taste of earth and oak, but the honey was sweet, so sweet, it masked the humus taste.

He felt the usual brief nausea, and soon after, in recounting to himself later, the mushroom sneakered up on him. He was coated and coasting, coasting, wondering, musing perhaps about the kitchen, the wonderful azure shade of a chipped dish in the sink, the thickening darkness out the window with the Invert Ridge in gray penumbra looking first like a string of baby camels, then like the burgeoning humps of elephants.

Then he started thinking of Mouse. Sitting at the table, musing, often led him to Mouse, Maddy, and sometimes, Dorothy and Oz. He slowly turned his head towards the hole in the wall and the collage. Had Mouse scrammed, taken a hike, skipped town, hit the road, vamoosed, split...or, it could have died(!) or been joined by another, or 3! Shit, it might be a female mouse rogered by some musculus stud and left pregnant, and he would be seeing Mouse in twins or triplicates.... or, maybe, just maybe, Mouse realized that he was trying to kill it and decided to lie low. Certainly the chips, splinters, holes, and dents on the doorstep of Mouse House should have been enough warning.

of course ive been feeding him crusts and cheese what is that about

However, that late afternoon, he had a feeling, an intuition, that the mouse, his Mouse, would be back, back when he least expected it (although he expected something!).

Deep in the warp and woof of his mushroomed being, Jack felt he was connected to Mouse, a psychic connection he couldn't explain.

These thoughts passed quickly and serially through Jack's head a nanosecond before he saw Mouse sitting on his haunches on the kitchen table regarding him, Jack, brain wrapped in flickering mushroom lights.

yellow light yellow light my limbs are rocks my head rigid electrical impulses in my brain in a state of warm equilibrium suspension neurotransmitter charge from neuron to neuron stalled old yellow light

"Howdy, Jack."

Jack stared at Mouse and watched incredulously as Mouse rose and advanced towards him.

"You don't know how to move, do you, Jack? Well, why not relax, why not let it be, why not let me in?"

right on mousy i cant move my body and spirit are pinned to space and time like a nabokov jarkilled swallowtail pinned to a black felt board

"Hey, if those avatars are real, conscious, annoying, why can't I be? Huh? Whaddya say, Jack-o-Lantern, Mr. Jack-in-a-box? Whaddya say?"

Mouse crept towards him.

"Hold still now. Hey, you wanted an experience. You wanted a psychedelic vacation. You wanted to get away. Course, you've tried before. Don't we always come back to what we know? Well, shit. We might as well get this trip a-going. Hold on."

Mouse disappeared between a button and an open flap of work shirt. Jack felt thin scratchy feet scampering freely up and down his shirt, through his jeans...and under his skin, up his legs, under his belly, through his organs, and finally into his brain, deep in the recesses of his consciousness.

Finally, Mouse anchored in his mind like a furry leech.

Jack got up, moved glacially into a living room that seemed to be seesawing and, after a glance at the hedge outside in a gap between the curtains, lowered himself carefully to the rug. His left eye on the same level as the mouse hole, his right eye fixed on Dorothy, a thin yellow ribbon, plastic flowers, and toys of a memorial on a Texas highway.

(34)

Talia grabbed her coat and cinched it against the fog.

She ate in Hombres and spent extra time drinking a margarita, cracking the ice in her teeth and sipping the vanishing residue from the bottom of the thick blue art glass. It was early evening, overcast, wisps of fog out in the marsh. She walked slowly back to her house, the image of the Map, the old SRO, the bald man, and the string connecting them taking on the aspect of a patchy rainbow mandala, a mandala of houses and faces and hopelessness wrapped in mystery.

She glanced, as usual, toward Jack's house. Odd, his Porsche was parked askew in the driveway. The lights on the second floor were on; they stirred her imagination and curiosity every time. Talia squinted, frowned. A spear of light shone through Jack's front door.

lets see   car parked askew   upstairs a carnival   front door cracked open

* * *

Talia paused at Jack's hedge and regarded the surveillance cameras. They were aimed down the walk and towards a spot down the hedge. Talia walked into the marsh and surveyed the house. She could slip through the hedge here or there and into Jack's yard and around to the front.

Talia checked the marsh trail in both directions, walked quickly to the hedge, and ducked through it. She walked quickly towards the steps. Jack's key was in the door. Talk about security. He must be ripped. She hopped up the front steps and, frowning, pushed the door open with her forefinger.

"Jack."

Talia edged into the living room. The prints and paintings on the walls were a night gallery of women's suffering. Jack was lying on the floor, curled up, blond hair bunched into a ridge on the carpet, his hand and fingers resting on his hip.

Closer, she saw he was breathing. She glanced at the oak table and saw a small Mason jar on the table. She walked a few steps closer and saw a stringy mushroom floating in what looked like honey. Talia picked it up and smelled it. Fungus and honey.

mushroom   mushroom   weave your spell

Trembling, she turned and walked quietly through the living room to the stairs. She glanced at Jack, then at the light at the top of the stairs alternating between dark and light. She walke
d hesitantly up the stairs, measuring her breath, measuring her pace, trying to keep calm, tasting hot Mexican food in her throat.

Talia stood transfixed at the top of the stairs.

Jack's show.

A second door near the top of the stairs was open. Talia hesitantly stepped over to the doorway. The images played over her body, making her squint.

Ghostly images of Raquel, Emma, George, and Mike flickered over a menu with two choices: Loop and Present. The images filled the room and coated a lounger, bookshelves, a table full of DVDs, photos and papers, and an end table hugging the lounger. The images and menus were clearer on a huge monitor flanked by two Escher hands. Next to the lounger was a half-full crystal glass. A white keyboard was perched askew on the table, and a remote.

A year or nothing.

year from what

* * *

She wasn't sure what would happen, but if the remote was a normal remote, she should be able to see what was in Loop and Present. She picked up the remote and guided it over to Loop and clicked it. Raquel bloomed on the screen inside the Nook, picking at a bracelet. A few seconds later, she spoke.

Raquel scowled, "Goddamn it. Who is that?"
"It's Jack. I've—"

179

"Where the fuck am I?"

Talia, stunned, sat on the edge of the lounger and watched as Raquel and Jack had what must have been their first dialog. It was mostly about Jack's amazement and how Raquel was, her aliveness. It was about Maddy too, which confirmed her suspicions about what Jack was doing. The digital Raquel didn't think much of Jack's quest. Soon the tape skipped to Raquel in bed with a blocky pixilated woman—Doris?—licking her out.

too much to absorb   colors changing   raquel   doris digital sex

Talia got up and steadied herself on the back of the lounger. Emma's face loomed large on the screen. Emma walked through the Café con Vache and was soon in her house.

"This is like purgatory. Maybe it is! Maybe I have to go through this purgatory to get the real deal! Maybe I'm here because I wasn't worthy, or worthy enough. I tried. I tried so hard.
"Now wait. I don't remember dying. Of course, I probably wouldn't. Still. Maybe it is purgatory. Course we don't believe in it.
"Where's Jesus?"

Talia edged back in the lounger as Emma and Jack argued over Maddy. She couldn't take her eyes off the screen, and a few minutes later, Emma lowered herself into a tub and slit her arms. She stared at the twinkling pixels dripping into the shifting, changing water.

The detail was amazing. It was as if she were watching a high-resolution video, except that video had never been taken. Emma had never poured a glass of wine in just that way, hadn't walked slowly upstairs in just that way. It was fabricated. It was something that might happen, not something that had happened. And....and Emma was conscious...and Raquel was conscious. Jack had created two conscious characters.

fuckin amazin conscious guess these guys are collateral damage   brilliant damage   what about george and mike

She got up while Emma argued with Jack, and walked hesitantly down the stairs and peered over the banister. Jack had moved his arm, but he was still curled up, and out.

Talia turned and walked back just as Emma whipped off the screen and was replaced by George's older, fleshy, worn face. George was conscious, but he didn't look as real as the others, and parts of his body flickered and changed. She was shocked when he murdered the digital Edna, but then he was contrite.

blows my mind   george and edna   murder   remorse feelings

She was watching a loop of their first conscious actions. What did they do now? Did they do anything? She guessed the answer was in the Present menu. But she'd been there long enough. Jack was bound to get up, and she'd be trapped. On the other hand, if he did Mike...

...and a few seconds later she had Mike.

She settled back in the lounger. It was more than eerie. To see and hear her in bed with Mike. The first thing that struck her was how real it was. Then there was Mike's brutality. A BJ and then he hit her, her avatar. He was rough, brutal. Is that what he felt in reality? How did Phisto catch that? And how did Phisto imitate her voice so accurately...and Mike's?

i know   i know bugs   bugs   bugs

Mike threw her re-formed avatar over and hoisted its legs over his back. Watching her patchy image and Mike's multi-colored cock made her gushingly horny. She glanced at the door, then flipped her coat back, unbuttoned her jeans, and inserted her hand deep into her underpants. Her finger dug deep into her sex, finally rotating it slowly then faster around her clit.

Ugh... Ungh... Unngghhh!

Talia collapsed back in the lounger.

wow   fuck me   we came together   fucking first   bet your pussy doesn't smell like my finger   i could   no better not   better button up and scram

181

(35)

Kitchen light threw shadows over the parquet floor and edged prints and collages with a knife-edge of darkness. Table leg shadows stopped short of the curled figure lying on the carpet halfway towards the windows.

Jack's mind alternated between emptiness and...the Show!

..ballooning in...dwindling out

..flash...ing

..alien...insects... splicing...dicing...throats...eyes

..kerplat...kerplat...drip..drip...drool

.. sputter...spitter.... spatter

..pikes and broad swords and maces and arrows and hot oil and...

..point city?????

..what the!

..Doris' tongue swished, swished

..no, no, Emma dripping pixels in glowing water

..no, no. Edna slipping slowly, magically, faintly, into a shimmering puddle

..ha, ha, ha

Where am I? I'm in the Show. I'm all of them...a crescendo of voices called him, called him...

The Show layered Point City, merged, out of sync, glowing backgrounds, reverb voices.

He was in his head...tramping down a long branch of neuron. It was his neuron, but there was another, another Jack paralleling him...but different, patchy, incomplete, grinning hideously. Jick! What was he doing here? Why? They traveled in parallel, skiing down neural slopes, turning on neural moguls, racing, racing. What was that? A dim image, a strand of black hair, a pale blue eye. Fucking finally. Maddy. Where are you? Where have you been? Have you been playing with me? Why? What's so important? Where are you going? Don't disintegrate...don't pixelate away. Stay, stay. No...there he is... Mr. Mousy curled up...gray hair so soft. He feels so, so...wait don't you go too. Don't disintegrate...gray pixels drifted away, drifted away. And Jack is back... with himself. There he is...don't pixelate, I can't pixelate.

I'm the real one! I'm the real one!

Jack's neurons edged away. The Show was back. No. He wants to stay with Maddy and Mouse. No. The Show covered reality. No! He watched him watching himself...

Jack shook his head. He was watching himself project the Show, watching...

And watching him watching him watching him watching him watching...

me watching me watching watching watching hi maddy what a trip huh what a game whata competition just like the old days just like we used to spar and fend and retreat and attack a year huh or nothing huh i i i me pixelating hey look its me watching me pixelating how could i whats the deal

Maddy floated in and pixelated out. She was on the 14 Mission, turning slowly towards him, doubling her image in the window, in the loft, pale legs scissored, mischievous smile. She spread her lean legs, and through them she beckoned...."Come, let's play. You've always wanted to play. Let's have a game. A real game. Screw the pixels...

"C'mon, Jack. Let's get real."

(36)

Had she or Jack learned anything about Maddy...what she'd done or where she was? His characters seemed to ridicule Jack, and as far as she could see, rightly so. What did he discover from his marvelous inventions? Maddy and a bald thug with red-framed glasses.

Clever, imaginative and...

...absurd.

The question remained: why?

and what should i do this fiasco has nothing to do with me isnt it between jack and his flaky brilliant girlfriend

Talia walked out of the Show, ghostly images of the four characters flickering over the two menus and crawling over her back and over the walls and doors. She felt like the only real thing in the middle of coming attractions in a movie. She opened the door at the end of the hall.

Jack's bedroom. The two menus and the faces of his avatars covered the walls and bed from recessed projectors. She wondered how many times he'd fallen asleep with images of his characters coating his body.

Finally she walked back to the stairs. Jack was still on his side, but his arm had shifted and was partially hidden by his body.

She'd stayed long enough. Jack would wake up...except he seemed still. What if he did find her?

Talia retreated up the stairs.

She quickly picked up the remote, navigated to the Present menu, and clicked it. She wasn't sure what she expected.

But...

...Mike

"Shit I love this fuckin' game. Being in it. But isn't it just a buncha 1s and 0s fightin' to a draw? Hey, Jack! Jack? Are you there?"

184

Talia edged further down into Jack's lounger almost as if Mike could see her. She picked up the glass. Whiff of whiskey. She shrugged and took a drink while watching the screen.

"Well, well…"

Mike walked out of the game and then through the marsh. Video games crashed and clanged on either side. Mike walked into the static of a game and disappeared.

The Show continued flickering in the marsh.

Talia sat back in the lounger. She guessed that Present meant Jack's characters could do what they wanted. Why did Mike disappear? Were the others going to appear, or was that it?

The Show switched scenes. Raquel was in the Nook. She looked up from a book she was reading. She looked serious…

"Jack! Jack, are you there? No?"

Talia looked right, then left, then stared at the screen. Raquel was talking in the present. She couldn't take her eyes off the screen as Raquel hurried through the Nook, squeezed through a flickering door tucked among the bookshelves, and disappeared.

"Jesus Christ."

Talia leaned back farther in the lounger. Nothing happened for ten seconds or so, then George's face loomed on the large screen.

George sat on the beach watching the ocean. A glowing Edna was next to him, but she flickered in an out of existence.

George turned to the simulacrum at this side.

"I wish Edna, a conscious Edna, was here, so I could apologize, so I could explain. Killing her, fucking Maria. It's stayed with me, an indelible scar. I can't forget through all the games and lights and changings. At least you're the only one who knows. Right, Jack? Jack, are you there?"

Talia sat down and watched, mesmerized. She unconsciously picked up the glass and drained it.

George got up and walked towards the seaside bluffs and disappeared in a crevice.

okay this is different fantastic characters amazing detail consciousness and theyre leaving where are they going

The seaside bluffs flickered and Talia thought it was over, when Emma's face appeared. Flashes of Emma sitting outside the Café con Vache, huge views of her unhappy face on the bookshelves, the door, ceiling, polished floor.

The flickering, the pulsations of the images, made her dizzy.

Emma poured a glass of Chardonnay, then moved deliberately through her house and stopped at the living room table.

"Jack! Jack, are you there?"

Talia squirmed in the lounger. Emma was staring at her.

Talia glanced at the table and saw the microphone. She looked back at Emma and shook her head.

"Good. Finally."

Emma threw the glass into the air where it disappeared in a burst of pixels. She hurried up the stairs, hurried into the bathroom, stopped to stare at the tub.

"I should have known I couldn't get out. I'll regret cutting my wrists as long as I'm in here. Of all the memories I've made here, it's the one I can't forget. I shouldn't blame Jack, but I do. I shouldn't be here at all."

Emma disappeared into a black hole at the end of the bathroom.

"Motherfucker!"

Talia watched the scene for a minute before she decided the characters were gone. Did they disappear into some hard drive, a flash drive, into the ether?

know something jacko i know something about your characters you dont i dont know where they went but neither do you maybe its a revolution

* * *

She'd made herself too comfortable. It was past time to leave.

She got up, made sure she didn't leave anything, and walked slowly downstairs. She stopped and regarded the living room with its walls of sewn, abused, and torn women.

She shook her head. She knew they were Maddy's. Still. There was something sinister about Jack displaying them, something sinister about the Show, about the negativity that produced a suicide, a murderer, Mike's brutality.

There was a pale copy of her in the front window, pale copy of Jack, the room, the blue Mason jar. What was Jack dreaming? About Maddy? About himself? About the Show?

Talia shook herself.

She walked quickly through that foreboding gallery of torn and abused women.

She paused at the front door.

She looked for a second at the dark interior, the lights flickering on the second floor, and Jack, motionless on the floor.

She picked the key out of the lock. If she hurried, she could get the key duped at Jin's. She walked quickly down the front steps and seconds later ducked through the hedge.

(37)

Jack sat at the table, his laptop in front of him and a mug with an image of a pixilated Milky Way steaming on his right. The mushroom did the trick. He got away, far away...and he felt good, warm, settled. Better than following and talking to his digital characters, better than wondering what happened to Maddy. And confusing, distracting...and better. He stared at Mouse's hole, and the warmth he felt began to slowly ebb away in the harsh light of meaning. Mouse squirreled away in his head...and keyed snatches of Oz, of a patchy golden road...and a retreating Maddy...and of an overlaid Show, a telescoped Show, a Show that was never-ending in its retreat from reality. A Show that pixelated into nothing.

does everyone retreat retreat retreat telescope

Maddy had said, if he remembered through the warm fungus haze, that he should get real. Had Maddy gotten real? Was she commenting, again, on his lack of life, of reality, or was he musing in his personal echo chamber?

His warm fungal hangover was ebbing...

and reality flowing in

Regardless of whether Mouse was real or a figment, or whether he should get real, the blue Mason jar full of honey and a single stringy magic mushroom hadn't moved itself on the table, nor had the front door—which he vaguely remembered leaving open—closed itself, nor had a glass half-full of whiskey and soda emptied itself, nor did a poltergeist leave the slightest smear of pink lipstick on the rim.

Phantom? Demon? Succubus?

Pink lipstick!?

Oh, who could it be?

id be an idiot if i didnt think it was talia

She'd been scrutinizing his house off and on for months. She'd found a bug and drew lines between the dots. And she had photos of bars in the Tenderloin, especially the Last Call, a shuttered SRO, and a bunch of Tenderloin characters. She had become obsessed with him, Maddy, the Show.

He hadn't turned on his surveillance system for weeks. It was a chore to review the tapes, and he didn't have time. Besides, who would want to burgle his house? He was there all the time. On the few occasions he wasn't, the important stuff, his cameras and computers, were locked up tight.

He didn't see any of his characters when he checked the Show. That wasn't unusual. They'd started spending more time with the games and less time with their constructed environment of P.C. He supposed that made sense; the games were more interesting than Point City. Sometimes when he turned them on, he was surprised, occasionally shocked, at where they were. All of them had followed links to Phisto games. Raquel practically lived in Ouroboros, his one attempt at a significant game; Emma, besides brooding about Jesus, now favored his least-violent game, Barn Up, his early attempt at invading the Farmwood market; George pondered the ethical questions—such as they were—of Game of Lands; Mike practically lived inside the hyper-violent Dead End. Intellectual games, goody-two-shoes Christian folk, morality and ethics, and unremitting violence. Had his characters indulged themselves, or amplified natural inclinations?

Why did he bring the laptop downstairs again?

Ah, yes.

talia

He stared out at the marsh while his mirroring program went through its updates. When the mirroring finished, he sat down and dug through Talia's files. He looked at the photos of people entering that shuttered SRO closely.

does she know more than i do how would she find out

There was more in the Maddy folder. There was more detail of bars in the Tenderloin and a lengthier description of what Talia knew about Maddy. Ah, a bald man and red sunglasses, an SRO, and the word disappearance, underlined. He supposed that meant Maddy's disappearance, but why underline it? The SRO. Was it the same SRO George mentioned? A troupe, an SRO.

Maddy and Tenderloin cafés and bars. Must have been right before she moved to P.C., or maybe she snuck back. Did he have to continue? Where was the warm afterglow from the mushrooms?

Jack got up slowly, poured a glass of water, opened the patio door, and sat on the bench. He felt calm, at peace, and the residue from his fungus excursion settled once again in his mind. Green shoots had started pushing through fall's brown, although Official Spring was weeks away. As he settled into the bench, he felt as if he were part of the marsh with its birds, mice and voles, skunk, its flora and fauna. He felt part of it but different, a protector of that telescoped cognition.

A car window flashed in the distance.

The marsh faded into backdrop.

He was back...again.

He had come far with the Show grâce à Phisto. Four conscious characters! And the characters had become more rounded, the backgrounds and scenes more varied. But for finding Maddy? Mixed results, certainly. Should he continue? He was conflicted when he started, and he periodically escaped the Show, but he came back to it. He had the same conflict now. Should he find Maddy? He had to solve the same puzzle when he met her: to slip into her narrative or not. To continue or not.

And the next step, he could see, involved Talia and the Tenderloin. George had pointed there, and Mike. He could, finally, be close to finding Maddy, to resolving the competition. If he didn't, it would be over on the Ides.

Wouldn't it?

(38)

The Show blew her mind, invested her dreams, kept her in bed until ten. The images resolved from one character to another piling on top of each other until they collapsed in mounds of pixels.

they were pixels bytes programming   werent they then they werent

They were alive; they thought, they talked, they were conscious, they did stuff: they fucked, they killed, they tried to kill themselves. And one of them fucked a poor imitation of Talia— fucked it, and then beat it up, and then massacred tough guys and aliens in stupid games...they did wild things in a world of bits and bytes of flashing colors and trails of pixels, things they wouldn't do out here.

Then, she wondered, what did that mean? Did that mean there was an unexplored world existing next to ours, what we call reality, or was Jack's show a one-off, a never-to-be-repeated exercise in electricity, bits, bytes, and insane programming? Of course, from the little she'd seen, they couldn't touch our reality. They existed in our world but never touched it, couldn't touch it.

She knew more about Maddy from the Loop, that Maddy had a plan of her own the entire time she played with the four people, talking to them, insinuating into their lives. It felt like she was worried about something and testing them to test herself.

A year or nothing.

She walked through that day in a daze. It wasn't what Maddy had done that blasted her mind. She was appalled and awed at what Jack had done.

She made coffee and chose a mug at random. Oddly, the mug displayed the classic Magritte absurdity, a painting of a pipe, entitled *The Treachery of Images, This is not a pipe.* She took the mug to the porch and plopped down in her chair, her basket of cyclamens hanging off to her right, a breeze ruffling her left sleeve. She didn't—couldn't—think of anything else. She couldn't think of the Line, the people who counted on her to be there, the kids. The four characters ran serially through her mind like they had in her dreams.

She realized those characters had touched the real world because they'd touched her. And, she wondered, would those characters change her attitude towards the real ones?

It came up faster than she imagined, or wanted, when her cell rang. It was Raquel, the Raquel of Doris and Raquel, of a pixilated Doris hunched over Raquel, tongue flashing deep in her digital sex. Raquel wanted to go to lunch again at the Patio Café.

"Yeah, maybe. Let me think."

"It's not a Mensa test. It's lunch."

Lunch? All she could think of was Doris dining on Raquel.

"Right, lunch. Sure."

"What about noon?"

"Noon?"

"You sound stoned."

"No, no. Something with the Line. Yeah, it will be good to get away, to eat with you."

shit what the fuck did i say

"It's not as if you're going to eat me, although—"

"Course not. See you at noon."

✳ ✳ ✳

The Show stayed with her on the way to the Patio Café. She relived Emma's suicide, her anguish, George's anger towards Edna. Would Edna believe his contrition if she saw it?

Mike. What bothered her wasn't the sex, but the brutality towards her... and the pretense. Was that what he was like inside? She'd always assumed there was more than an ex-Marine with a fantasy. But she knew he was pretending about Belize. But then, no one was a cardboard character. There were hesitations, a look of concern that flicked through his male stoicism.

Then when they knew Jack wasn't watching, all his characters snuck away in cracks and crevices. What did that mean?

okay talia what do you think that is what would you do unshackled from gravity from skin from touch from social conventions of course ive thought of suicide of killing people of my dyspeptic opinion of people while mouthing niceties what part of consciousness is that this comment is it the nut of being and the rest pretense

She walked slowly towards the Patio Café. She hoped she didn't seem too different. She hoped she could block out the image of blocky Doris grazing in Raquel's flickering sex.

(39)

Jack opened the cupboard door and stared at the small blue Mason jar for a moment and picked it up. He tilted the jar, and the honey and the mushroom inched towards the side.

Jack put the jar back on the shelf and closed the cupboard door. He couldn't escape from reality. He could approach it differently. See reality in a different light, accept it more.

And where was he that morning? He'd left the front door cracked, the Show on. Talia had come in, seen him on the floor, tripped upstairs, and watched his characters. Did she see all of them, the loop? What had she seen that he hadn't? It didn't take a genius to figure out his two menus. She'd been obsessed with seeing the Show, and now she had. Would she behave differently towards him? Would she watch the real life people differently? Had it changed her? She had peeked inside the public mask.

It would, likely, simply create a new narrative, a new Talia, another self (adventurous, appalled, stunned, reflective?) to be brought out from time to time, examined, and thrown back into the rubble heap of memory.

did i subconsciously want someone else to see it of course i did why play coy she had seen something great something spectacular brilliant he couldnt tell his characters

* * *

He was on the bench when he saw Talia drive towards the coast but take the road to Olema. It was eleven, and he knew everyone who lived on Marsh Lane had either gone to work or gone birding, or, like Martin, was already deep in a craft ale, mucking through the past.

should i shouldnt i i broke into georges but the house was isolated this is point city what if someone saw me what if i was arrested

Jack walked quickly through the house, out the front door, and slipped past his garage. He walked casually through Martin's then Marilyn's backyard, past Tony's, the antediluvian lizard-skinned surfer, to Talia's. Her house was small, compact, tending towards cutesy cottage. He scanned her porch and the side of the house for cameras. When he didn't see any, he glided into her yard and up to her back door.

The back door was easy, and in a few seconds he was inside. Her living room had a full bookcase ornamented with Indian goddess figures, a couple stuffed chairs, a small flat-screen TV, a small stereo bordered with standing racks of CDs. There were collages in the spaces between the bookcases, which, he supposed, were reminders of her road briefly taken and abandoned. He walked briskly into the room off the kitchen, her computer room, the room with her "Line."

Her desk was messy, the computer surrounded by photos, faces from the Tenderloin on the wall, a headset, a couple of flash drives. He glanced at the map on the wall. It was dense with colored string, photos, and descriptions. Most of the lines converged on Leavenworth and Eddy, the Last Call, and a shuttered SRO. He took out his cell and snapped a photo of it.

Jack glanced at the photos around the map and stopped.

Maddy's penetrating gaze fixed him to the spot. His heart beat hard. He shook himself and flipped through the flyers.

Jack took out his cell, stepped closer to the flyers, and photoed each one. He also took quick shots of Talia's work space. He was walking towards the stairs when a car scratched the gravel outside.

He turned and hurried to the back door, opened and closed it carefully. He ducked around the side of her house and under the kitchen window.

"Shit, it's like a mausoleum in here."

When Jack heard the latch being pulled on the window, he crab-walked to the side of the house. As he rounded the house, he heard the window slide back. Jack slipped behind a small eucalyptus in Tony's backyard, waited a minute, then walked quickly straight to his house.

His heart slowed and began beating normally. Inside, he flopped down on the sofa. He opened up his cell and looked at the photos one by one, stopping for a few beats on the small photo of Maddy staring at him from a torn beer-stained flyer.

(40)

The early fog had cleared, and it looked like it was going to be a gorgeous day at the coast. She dressed, left the Line on answering machine, and went for a quick stroll. She glanced at Jack's house. Jack was acting quirky. On the few occasions he appeared in the Lost Dog or at the Café con Vache, he seemed absent, as if he were watching a tape running nonstop in his head, as if he couldn't wait to leave, as if he'd left the gas on.

He glanced at her often.

well yes   im sure he guessed ive seen the show   guess what jack   i want to see another one   and i duped your front door key

Jack's show had been playing nonstop in her head, especially the Present, which she assumed was characters acting out in real time. What were they doing with their digital life? Life: should she call it life? The characters did things they didn't dare in the real world. They also had a plan that didn't involve Jack.

It was warmer and lighter, but the fog accented her mood. She strolled down Pine and onto Main. Normally she'd veer right towards the Café con Vache, but that day, she walked slowly up the shoulder of Highway 1 and out of town. Ten minutes later, she turned on Pine walking south. She walked by a handful of ranch-style houses tucked in the north end of town, then started back down the hill towards Main. She managed a few blocks in a pleasant state of non-thinking, giving herself up to passing images, colors, and cool wind, but the familiar places soon brought up the familiar faces, and the faces in Jack's show...of Raquel, Emma, George, and Mike.

At home, she stuffed flyers in her bag, checked the bag for her putting-up-flyers wig, her purse for money and keys. Finally she gassed up the Toyota and headed for the city. She took Highway 1 to Lucas Valley Road over to 101. It was longer than Sir Francis Drake but less busy. The traffic was light that time on 101 and she made it to the Tenderloin mid-morning.

* * *

She parked on Van Ness and spent what was left of the morning putting up posters and finally stuffed her wig in the backpack. It was a warm and sunny day, and even the Tenderloin didn't seem so bad, more life on the streets, less feeling of hopelessness.

She roamed through the Tenderloin from Sutter and lower Nob Hill into the heart and casually by the bars where she'd found the Maddy posters. She ended up, surprising herself, at the Last Call and the mystery SRO. She stood on the street for a few minutes, but no one went in or out of the Last Call or the SRO. That morning the SRO had more of an abandoned feeling than when she was with Harris.

"Hey, Liz."

Dawn and Adam. "Howdy."

"Whatcha doin'?"

"Just walking through the Tenderloin. I was about to leave."

She'd forgotten what they looked like. Dawn was a tall freckle-faced lank-haired blue-eyed girl/woman with a smudge on her neck. Adam looked like he did when he met her at Thanksgiving, except that day he had homegrown tattoos on his knuckles and wore a tattered leather jacket, stained jeans, and lace-less worn army boots. His face still seemed lopsided, the nose turned slightly. A scowl pulled his face towards the curb.

It turned out Dawn and Adam were scrounging for food, and, impulsively, she asked them if she could buy them lunch. Their favorite place, when they could get the money, was Chevy's on Van Ness. She said her car was close to Chevy's and it was fine with her.

Fifteen minutes later, she was inside Chevy's ordering a couple beef burritos and a bunch of guac and salsa. Adam and Dawn wanted to stay outside, and she had a margarita while she waited and half-listened to the imminent dystopias blaring from a row of TVs: global warming, rising seas, millions displaced, boat people, ethnic cleansing, torture.

She decided they could use a picnic and drove them down to the wharf. Twenty minutes later, they spread out on the amphitheater steps in Aquatic Park. Talia drank execrable Chevy's coffee and grazed on chips and salsa while Adam and Dawn wolfed down burritos, chips, and guac as if they were fattening for winter. She wondered how many kids were like them, waiting for a decent meal. She knew what some of them did in order to eat.

The day was gorgeous, and the bay was punctuated with checkmark sails, the bridge bacon red. Tourists strolled along the park promenade and, in the distance, some started slowly up the steep hill towards Fort Mason. People strolled on the Aquatic Park hook, fishermen cast out into the bay, a bat ray glided close to shore. A man, thin, white, in a red bathing suit walked slowly out of the Dolphin Club and strode purposefully towards the ice-cold water. He splashed water on himself for a few seconds, then dove into the water, came up and shook his head, making the water spin around, and started swimming in clean strokes.

Talia shivered.

Dawn ate the last of her burrito. Adam munched slowly on a chip and settled back against the worn amphitheater steps, propping his boots on the seats in front of him and folding his arms over his chest.

Dawn said, "This was a treat. Thanks.

Adam: "You seemed real interested in that SRO."

did i stare at it   how long was i there

"I was taking photos the other day and thought I saw a pimp and a couple thugs going in. Not the front door, but along the side. Seemed peculiar."

Adam said, "I heard something about a strange SRO, probably squatters. Can't remember the name or where it was."

Dawn looked at Adam. "Strange?"

Adam laughed. "That it was a kinda meeting place or a fly-by-night theater."

Talia felt in her purse and brought out her cell. She tapped her photos and hunted for the shots she'd taken.

Dawn crossed her long legs and shrugged. "There's all sorts of stuff going on in the Tenderloin. We don't know most of it. You talked about what you would do about heroin and drug dealers when I called last time. Really, there's not much you could do. They may go away, get arrested, or get killed, but the dealing is the same. We see slots, positions, corners where you can buy stuff, anything. Sometimes the dealer's a hulking guy with missing teeth, and in a week, it's a stringy guy with nervous eyes and tattoos on his face."

Talia rested her legs on a seat in the next row. "You can't be as cynical as I am. You could say I'm holding down a slot."

Adam: "We're all stuck in our roles."

Dawn: "C'mon, she's not stuck; we are."

adam has bravado but dawn is in charge   neither one can see a way out   but dawn keeps both of them from going crazy

Talia said, "I'm just curious. Let me show you my shots."

Adam and Dawn leaned over. She tapped the first photo and scrolled through a couple others.

Dawn: "Weird. They're sneaking into that SRO."

Adam: "I've seen the black guys around. Saw them around Sutter and Jones. Thought they might have run oxy for old guys from the SROs. But never saw them do it."

Dawn: "I know the two Hispanic guys. Talked to that one once. Not sure what they do. Somebody said they used to deal heroin at UN Plaza, but you know hearsay." Dawn laughed. "You going to bust those guys?"

yes it was ridiculous   what am i doing   might as well go all the way

She scrolled to the photo of the bald guy.

"Lousy photo." Adam looked at her slyly. "Don't know his name, but I've seen him."

Dawn said, "Dresses in sweats, like he's running, but I never saw him run."

Talia, expectant, "You know his name?"

Dawn shook her head no and Adam said, "Not me."

Talia felt her heart beat a little faster. Then she frowned. Did she want any more from Adam and Dawn? They'd given her nothing. "You know when you're curious but don't know why?"

Dawn: "Wait, I remember something."

"Kay."

"I remember seeing this guy disappear in a bar once, with a woman."

"What did she look like? Do you know the name of the bar?"

Dawn shook her head. "Couldn't see her face. She had a dark coat on and a big floppy hat. The bar was The Deep. A dive, been there forever."

Talia said, "I know it. Thanks."

Talia felt a chill. Who was he, and who was she? Why did she care?

She realized she may have just found out more than Jack with all his bugs and cameras and his conscious characters. Was the guy with Maddy in Point City the bald guy? Was his lean friend Maddy? What could she do with that?

Dawn said, "It's nice that you buy us lunch, but we get hungry a couple times a day."

Of course, handouts were one-shot deals. She knew they knew about the soup kitchens, Glide, St. Anthony's, other churches. The last thing she wanted was to be the banker for a bunch of runaways.

im an outsider i dont really know the people in the tenderloin im playing with them the same way jack plays with his characters

"What about twenty bucks? It should last you a few days."

"That's great," said Dawn, grinning.

Talia dug the money out of her purse and gave half to Dawn and half to Adam. "I don't have to tell you, but it will go a lot further without drugs."

Adam scowled and said brusquely, "We just do dope when somebody else has some. Meth scares me. I seen what it does to people. And black tar kills."

Dawn: "By the way, I called Edna a couple times. I like talking to her. Hope you don't mind."

i care but shouldnt

"Good for you."

* * *

She dropped them off on Turk near Chevy's. She watched them walk slowly into the Loin with a sinking feeling. What was she going to do with the sinister man in the running suit and his companion? Maddy and a violent thug?

sure matched with what id found from jacks characters

Talia drove to her club, parked in the garage. There was less parking because the Zip cars had reserved space. She walked slowly upstairs to the club, mulling over her meeting with Adam and Dawn.

The club was a great way to relax, but when she was there, she always thought about how different her life was—both in Point City and in the city—from Adam and Dawn's. In a sense, they had not chosen that life. They both came from broken families and, she supposed, they did the best with what they'd been given.

They weren't like some of the alkies who swore they liked their life and had chosen it. The kids were different. They needed a leg up, someone to help them besides getting a couple bucks for food.

She swam a mile then relaxed in the Jacuzzi, the steam swirling around her, partially masking the swimmers in the pool. She timed the swimmers. Most were slower than her, a couple faster. One woman, long and lean with a long-stem rose tat on her leg, had a great kick, flip turn, and did 35-second laps.

such a different life   despite what ive done today despite what i feel about what ive done i feel fine for these few stolen moments

(41)

A year or nothing

One side of the sign had broken loose from the tape a week ago, and he'd let it hang askew. He couldn't stand looking at it. He ripped it down and threw it in the wastebasket. March 15. The date was engraved on his mind.

Winter was waning, and it was sunny erratically, enough to give one hope. Then the letdown. Fog, fog, with a forecast of fog.

And cold.

Jack slouched through the living room. He glanced at one of Maddy's paintings and turned from it. Slashed women, burkas, and bombs for breakfast?

He stumbled upstairs, spilling coffee on the way. He collapsed in his lounger. He mussed his blond hair, letting it fall over his eyes, then swept it back so it settled over his neck. He hesitated calling up his characters. He knew Talia had seen the Show, and he didn't mind. He was sure she hadn't talked to them? He didn't think so from talking to them.

Jack leaned back in the lounger, pyramided his fingers, and thought of Talia, the Maddy flyers, and the Tenderloin. She had a ton of data, photos, a map, and the flyers. He'd scanned her spreadsheets of calls. She'd met two homeless kids, Adam and Dawn, and written about it in her Maddy file. She seemed obsessed with the shuttered SRO on Leavenworth.

He'd been to the Tenderloin a couple times in the last few weeks and captured as much as he could, the people, the buildings, the action on the street, the fronts of the bars and cafés where Maddy had recited/incanted/screamed her poetry, especially the shuttered SRO and the Last Call. The fuzzy photo of the bald man intrigued him and made him think of Maddy's companion in P.C. He had Phisto use the grainy, unfocused shot Talia had taken to search the Net's photos using his facial-recognition program…to no avail. He organized the data he'd assembled from Talia's descriptions, downloaded and fixed up a better map than hers. Then he added the SRO, although he wasn't sure what good that would do. Then he added the little he knew about Maddy's readings in the Tenderloin and attached them to the bars he'd visited.

He'd loaded it all into a Tenderloin data set with a series of instructions for Phisto. The Tenderloin Show would be a sequence of photos, choppy capture videos, canned backgrounds, and lots of noise. He was sure there wouldn't be any mention of Maddy, but the scenes would help him think about what Talia was doing and whether it might be where Maddy disappeared. He wasn't sure it would help, but there was something there.

"Phisto."

"Yep, Jack."

"How's it going, buddy? How's the system, the Show?"

"How do you mean, Jack?"

"I've seen more hesitations in the Raquel show."

"Ah, yes. It's the damn power, Jack. I've started allocating more resources to lower-level replacement programs."

"Good boy. It's time to make the Tenderloin show."

"Okee dokee. I got the data set and the instructions. Should be a piece of cake."

"Okay, let's do it."

"Grab a coffee. It shouldn't take more than a few minutes."

* * *

Jack walked slowly downstairs, deep in thought. He hesitated In the kitchen. Coffee, tea...something a little stronger?

what about those mushrooms jack wheewyou collapsing reality collapsing shows what about feeling better what about the warmth no no mushrooms today but something

Jack unearthed a bucket from under the counter, threw in some ice, grabbed a quart of soda, a large crystal glass, and a fifth of Jack Daniel's. He mused about a joint of Hymie's Durban Poison, but decided to show some character and say no.

maddy and i played hard in the first couple years but we always backed up or she backed up she got healthy before i did am i in a downward spiral

Before heading upstairs, he thought for a second, reopened the fridge and took out a chunk of Jarlsberg. He cut a cube out of the chunk and threw it over the table. It bounced once on the carpet and settled a few feet from the mouse hole.

* * *

When everything was on the table next to his lounger, he mixed a large whiskey and soda, opened the extension on the lounger, spread his lanky body over it, and called for the Tenderloin Show. As the Show was loading, he took a long pull on his drink. It warmed him, and he felt the heat, then the flush. He leaned forward as the Tenderloin show started.

The first few photos showed Polk and Larkin, which, he guessed, were Talia's usual entry points into the Tenderloin. The next few shots showed him closer to the heart of the Tenderloin. Street people lounged against buildings, blacks entered and exited bodegas with small bottles of vodka and gin, drug deals were made. The violence started on Leavenworth with a shooting (mixed in from one of his games), people were shot (backdrop from Dark City), a whore gave a blowjob in the back of a Honda Accord (ditto, Dark City), street kids (Talia's shots) huddled in corners, defecated in the street, shot up, and a faceless kid slowly closed his eyes, dying from an overdose (game, Dead End). Then a shadowy shot of the baldy in the running suit entering the SRO.

That shot froze him. It was because of its indistinctness. It could have been anybody, but it gave him the jitters. Jack stopped the Show. He mixed another drink, took a long pull on it, and thought about what he'd seen.

He knew the Tenderloin show would be static. Shit, it wasn't a show; it was a travelogue, a mix of capture, backgrounds of his games with Talia's photos and clips, a mix of fiction and reality. It did give him a feeling for the space and the actors, characters: Talia, a boy (Adam?), a girl (Dawn), a couple thugs, a bald man, Maddy, and a shuttered SRO.

Was the Tenderloin a key, and the SRO a key, and the bald man a key? Maddy and the Tenderloin started making more sense than everything he'd learned from his fractious posse of digital characters.

Part 3

(42)

Jack cut up three small cubes of Jarlsberg. He placed one cube two feet from Mouse's hole, another five feet from the first, the third much closer at the line between the kitchen and the living room.

Jack sat in front of his laptop, flexed his fingers, and booted up. He checked Talia's mirrored drive. Not much new. Something, something about a meeting with Adam and Dawn. Maddy folder: zip. Talia wasn't stupid. She guessed he could hack her computer. If she found something, she'd keep it to herself or write it down, old-style, with a pen, paper, and plop it in a real manila folder. No way to peek at that, except if he broke into her house...again.

The more he thought of what Talia had done, Maddy's flyers, and the bars, the more he thought that the Tenderloin was the key...if there was a key.

He was starting to admire what she'd done, especially her pluck. They were both taking chances, dangerous chances...in order to find Maddy, or solve a mystery, or both.

He glanced at the first cube of cheese. It seemed likely...

i hate to say...

Mouse was gone, a goner, dead as a doornail, kaput, cashiered, ein tote Maus.

That was when there was a gray blur under Oz.

Natch.

Mouse sniffed the first cube of cheese, then looked up, almost as if he were wondering not just where it came from, but why, as if he knew that somehow the competition had reached a new level.

Mouse ignored the first cube and slowly advanced towards the second and, after a pause, on to the third. There he stopped, reared back on his haunches and stared at Jack.

Did Mouse look older? Haggard? Rundown? With a three-year life span, this could be the last month of the last year.

i know you cant understand me but in some way youre the
only being that can understand me weve been through a lot id
apologize for the knives and darts if i could of course you got
back at me talking to me running through my body running
through my head anchoring in my brain running the show through
my head and pixel dancing into infinite regression

"I know I'm talking to myself. Interesting how people wrangle with their inner lives, calling them their ego or their superego, or their better self, or their conscience. Don't we, Mouse, become a hodgepodge of competing feelings, ideas, cognitions, and interests? What does that make any decision? Necessary, or aleatory? Determined, or blind raving chance? What does that make consciousness? I guess it depends on where we stand."

Mouse's bulbous eyes leveled at him, and then he snatched up the cube of cheese and started nibbling.

"And, as you pointed out, what does that make the Show? What does that make those characters who say they're conscious and seem conscious? Aren't they just as wishy-washy as I am? Or, maybe their wishy-washiness is what makes them alive."

Mouse stared, cocked his furry head, ears aslant.

"Good, good. I'm glad I've got your attention. So what should I do? I usually talk to myself inside, but why not outside? What course, Mouse? Should I leave Maddy alone? Should I pretend our time was what, a hiatus, a golden interlude, a dream? Should I get on with my life?"

Jack rested his head on his hand.

"So simple. Hunger. A piece of cheese. Why is our life so complicated? I guess we live a little longer, but what is that? Is that good? Is that important? Of course, if we lived forever, that would be different. But we strut and shout and—"

Mouse scampered to the second cube of cheese, grabbed it, rocked back on his legs, and started nibbling.

"You're right, of course; one has to continue. One has to finish things. That's our curse."

Mouse consumed the second cube—he'd cut it smaller—and scampered to the last one, took a final look at Jack, snatched up the smallest cube in his mouth and disappeared into his hole.

"Thanks for listening."

Jack strolled through the living room, ghostly voices whispering of Michelangelo. Out the window, the clouds inched slowly across his vision, lower, buildings patched with light. In the distance, people jerked by as if on invisible wires, talked of this and that.

He strolled by Maddy's prints.

Anarchism, check.

Rage, check.

Dominant dark colors, check.

Feminist-centered, check.

Dorothy, Oz, and death. Why had it had become Maddy's favorite? Such a cliché, so vintage Americana. But then, the memorial, the teenagers, cut off by death. Death and the maiden, a trail, and a glittering Emerald City.

Jack walked to the hall closet, pulled out his backpack, and checked the camera.

Outside it was clear and cold.

It would be a great day to take Highway 1. Scrape the edges, see the jagged rocks, muse about death and mortality. He and Maddy had done it often, as if that'd been the only thing that would end the competition.

Jack opened the garage door, threw his coat, glasses, and hat into the back seat, and popped the roof.

Soon he was speeding down Marsh Lane.

(43)

According to Dawn, the bald thick-chested man—health nut, boss thug, or Tenderloin street freak?—went into a bar with a secretive woman.

Was the mystery woman peeking out of a flyer? Talia strung a black string from her unfocussed photo of the bald man to the mystery SRO, then bright red string from the photo to the Deep. Finally, she stretched a second red string from Maddy's flyer to the bald man. When she was done, the spider's web was crowded and off-center, a handful of colored string, converged from two people to a handful of buildings in the Tenderloin.

If only she could pull out that building's image and its spiderweb of colored string and have the corollary reality collapse. She'd had that fantasy before, of controlling reality by remote control. Shit, people believe their prayers can win football games, save Mom from cancer, usher them into Nirvana with 76 virgins.

prayers on a string

* * *

Aquatic Park.

Aquatic Park was their go-to lunch spot. It was gray, with a crack of blue in the east. It would be sunny before they left. A huge freighter, Matson Line, inched under the Golden Gate Bridge on its way to the Oakland docks. Gulls fluttered around its gray-and-white wake like confetti.

Dawn—tall and skinny, moist blue eyes, pinned-back blond hair, sandals, torn jeans—wolfed down tacos. Dawn's hunger depressed Talia. She'd leave, and Dawn would go back to her patch of concrete. Of course, she'd always thought that...how absurd it was, how Tenderloin reality was unrelenting.

Dawn had called a couple times since she'd bought them lunch. But she couldn't imagine what she wanted when she called and asked to see her. She guessed it had something to do with Adam.

For the next half hour she heard about Dawn and Adam, how Adam was doing more dope, would sit, fold his arms around his chest, and stare at the passing scene. How sometimes he'd nod his head seriously and tell her he knew the way out. She'd ask him how, and he'd say selling.

"He meant something hard...heroin, oxy, or meth." Dawn squinted, sifting memories. "Most of the time he's not like that. He's funny when he's stoned, but the time I like is when we don't have to act out anymore, when we can laugh a little, get drowsy, and sleep. Doesn't matter where we are. It's the best time; it makes me think we're together."

who props me up since the divorce i have acquaintances
drinking buddies raquel harris my ex maybe carol
i suppose not to be counted on i prop myself up
talking to them i count on my echo

Finally, Dawn—real name, Sarah Miller—came to the point.

"But, you know, I'm not going to sleep on the concrete the rest of my life or squat in an SRO with five other teenagers or run away from a methed-out screaming meemie. I want out and Adam doesn't or just seems stopped." Dawn shook her head, and her shoulders slumped. "I hate to do it, but it's time to move on. And right now it looks like Seattle and Mom. We've been talking."

Talia, frowning, "How are you getting there?"

"I got it all figured. Train, tonight."

"How much?"

In the depths of Dawn's eyes, she could see the start, the yellow road, the distant gleaming city of green, hope reflecting off the distant windows, slight hitch in her stride. And it all faded, returned to dust, to Talia's reflection in Dawn's blue, blue eye.

How much would one give to save a life, to restart a life? It wasn't much to her...but was Dawn playing her? People in the Loin knew how to play people. It was how they got by. Dawn's fingers were long and shapely, her shape gangly. With cleaning up, she'd be good-looking. A good businesswoman, ace programmer, real estate maven...or partner, mother, a fitter-in, a go-getter, prize of the community.

Normal.

cynicism bubbles up is that what would happen to
me if i made the cut into jacks show would i collapse

*into hopelessness and mocking smiles or what did carol
say   thunderbird and fingering social workers*

No, getting a kid like Dawn out of the Loin would be a success, regardless of what happened later, regardless of whether she became like everybody else.

maybe my only success

Dawn, quickly, "I got the money."
"What?"
"Edna. I've been talking to her every couple days, when I can get the cell away from Adam. I told her my plan, and she came in yesterday and gave me the money. Gonna catch the bus to the train tonight. If I don't do it right away, I may not do it at all." Dawn misted over. "Edna's kinda like my Mom, at least when Mom was nice."
"Right."
"She said I should tell you."

great   coopted   shit

"I'm going to be in town most of the day," Talia lied. "You need a ride to the bus?"
"Sure! But it has to be later. I kinda wanna spend the day with Adam."
"Not a problem."
Fifteen minutes later, she watched Dawn's loose-hipped walk as she headed into the Loin. She should have been happy, but she felt lost, co-opted, and apprehensive.

* * *

Living room light shone through front windows and bathed the front porch and a small puddle under the just-watered cyclamens. Talia sat back in a shadow of the corner, her face ghostly in the glow from the laptop balanced on her knees. People walked on Main, blocks away. Tourists, or a wedding reception at the Station Restaurant. They'd had a couple there recently. Broke up the easy swing of life in Point City.

Dawn did that too.

To: carolmarlow66@earthlink.com
Subject: City Redux!

Hey Carol...

Met these two homeless kids a while ago, Dawn and Adam, and today helped Dawn restart her life, or kinda helped. She's gonna leave Adam, go home to Mom, get a GED, start community college. A friend from Point City gave her the money. Made me feel weird, like I've been co-opted. I was supposed to help her. Can I feel used?

Anyway, I gave her a ride to the bus to the train. Consolation prize.

Had a five-hour wait before I met her. Tried to swim away my anxiety, how I felt, then took a long walk through Golden Gate Park. Hadn't done that for a long time.

There were a bunch of homeless kids camped at the park entrance smoking dope and playing with their pit bulls. I walked through the tunnel under the papier-mâché stalactites into the park (do you think people think those stalactites are real?). Robin Williams Meadow had the same people I saw last time when it was Sharon Meadow, as if they'd waited for me: the beaters of drums near the hill, a handful of dope smokers, a couple of families spread over blankets eating, playing with their kids, throwing or kicking balls.

Magnolias blooming in the Botanical Garden! Must be February!

Shoulda stayed in the park, but drove back, had a late snack and coffee at Arlequin in Hayes Valley. Shoulda stayed inside, but I roamed around outside and made a few calls. Maybe it was Dawn going back to Mom, made me want to connect.

Mom: okay, but worried about Tena, recently released by Marines.

You: answering machine.

Mindy: working long hours on a low-cost housing program for the poor.

Frank, ex: still doing improv at night. Fine, fine. Then, kicker: he's getting married to someone thirtyish, Claudia, a wannabe actress. Guess what? She wants to have kids. Imagine a kid at his age.

No way to disguise it: disaster.

Everyone going on with their lives. Everyone doing something, changing something, trying new programs, promoting, procreating.

Talia Morse, Spectator.

Thought Dawn might be a no-show, but there she was scrubbed, hair ponytailed, clean blouse, or as clean as she could make it, subdued, a little apprehensive, twirling fingers in her hair.

At the bus to the train, I gave her an extra fifty for the trip and took a pic of her getting on the bus. Probably show it to Edna sometime. It made me feel a fleeting sense of having done something concrete.

Dawn is morphing back into Sarah, a young women with hope and trepidation. One day she'll see the Tenderloin and Adam as an interruption, a hiatus, something to blank out, then fade out, fade to dim memory.

Looks like there's a wedding at the Station House. Makes me think of Frank. Makes me think of Talia, Spectator.

I'd better sign off, before I collapse in a maudlin puddle.

Let's get together soon.

I'll let you try to convince me to restart my art career.

T

Talia sent the email, got up, and put the laptop inside. She put on a light jacket, checked her money. A few seconds later, she walked towards Main. She paused once to stare back at Jack's house. The second floor was, as usual for the last week, ablaze with lights, lights flickering, light edging the blinds and touching the roof and the lowest branches of the Monterey cypress across the street.

ignore it   ignore them   ignore jack

Talia snapped off her gaze. She walked slowly onto Main and across the street and stopped near the swinging doors of the Dog. She leaned against the side of the building, took out her cell, checked the photo, and sent the photo of Dawn to Edna.

(44)

Jack parked a couple blocks from Van Ness on Turk.

Sauntering into the Loin was like slipping from Bermuda into the Triangle.

He'd been a frequent visitor and had captured the outside, but now he was about to dig deeper. He walked slowly down Turk, taking it all in, seeing the change in a few short blocks from Polk to Leavenworth. A homeless shelter on Polk was like an extrusion from the Loin. Farther, the street dirtied up, overflowing garbage cans, discarded take-out cartons, orange peels, crushed plastic coffee containers, half-eaten food, empty Steel Reserve cans, Thunderbird bottles with a thin sheen of sugary alcohol, used condoms. And the people:

sleeping in wheelchairs;

leaning against buildings;

stumbling into gated Palestinian groceries for Thunderbird and malt liquor;

passing shiny crack glasses from grubby hand to hand;

bruised lipsticked whores, gap-toothed smile wide, hands on cocked hips;

word salads;

dying world;

nightmare reliquary.

Jack caught a reflection of himself in a grocery window. The cross-hatched grate broke his face into a once-broken nose, a luminous blue eye, blond hair, a compressed taciturn mouth. He smiled an idiot smile. He raised his eyebrows. He stuck out his tongue, exposing his inward-canted canine.

all me all my jacks

* * *

He walked the Tenderloin for a half an hour before zeroing in on his destination: the Last Call...and the mystery SRO. The SRO had 2x4s over the door, a few broken windows on the front, a beaux arts entrance, a sculpted keystone arch, and an air of abandonment. What could go on there? Talia's photos showed Tenderloin street people—pimps, thugs, dealers?—slipping into the alley on the side.

The sign outside the Last Call was old and missing the last l in Call. It was dark, gloomy, and smelled of pissy beer and old smoke. He'd been in bars like that for Phisto's games and in what passed for real life. Some people never went in bars like that, wouldn't think of going in a bar like that, had never been in a bar.

His shadow made the gloom gloomier. Against the far wall to the left of the passage to the bathrooms was a small stage likely used for bands eons ago, and possibly a poetess/performer. There was a scattering of tables, a grizzled drunk passed out at one, his face alternately bright blue and dark from a flickering Bud Light sign.

Jack hitched up to the narrow bar top and regarded a bald dumpy man, pale as a mushroom, in a pair of jeans and short-sleeved work shirt.

Jack scanned the bottles. "Shot of Macallan, PBR back."

The bartender turned, found the Macallan, set a shot glass down in front of him, poured it to the top, and drew a small beer. Jack threw a twenty on the bar. When the bartender turned, Jack turned on the audio recorder. A few seconds later, the bartender slapped nine dollars next to the shot glass.

Jack leaned over and sipped the scotch. He let it warm him for a few seconds, straightened and said, "Thanks. Say, what's your name?"

The bartender stared out the door then at him and shrugged. "Randy." Jack extended his hand. "Jack. Say, Randy, been bartending here long?"

Randy shook Jack's hand. "Longer than I wanted. Almost ten years."

"You remember hearing a poet here, a woman?"

Randy laughed. "Wouldn't think about it here. You'd be thinking of Maddy."

Jack frowned. "Why Maddy?"

"Shit, she kinda made herself into a Net celeb with that video and disappearing."

Jack took another sip of scotch. "Sure."

"You're the Jack, aren't you?"

Jack grimaced. "Yep."

"Used to play Dead End. God, I was addicted to that game." Randy glanced towards the ceiling, hooded his eyes, thinking. "I followed the story for a while, because she was here."

"All past tense."

"That's sure true. I ain't heard of her for months."

Jack shrugged, "The life span of any story."

"Well, you're kinda still a celeb, and I'll tell you what I know. Make my life a little more exciting. I can tell my boyfriend. You know, gossip."

"Sure."

"Where was I? Oh, yeah. I seen her. You couldn't not watch her. I can't say I liked what she was spouting, about our fucked-up system, raunchy sex, women being abused, and how artists break the rules, how they're criminals at heart. Some of it clicked with me."

"She loved to perform."

"I can see it, except—"

"Except?"

"A couple times she kinda hitched up, you know, paused. It didn't seem to be part of the reading. Probably reading too much into it cuz she started up a split second later."

Jack smiled. "She had a full house?"

Randy laughed. "Tell ya, I kinda thought the whole shtick was a drill, a placeholder. A couple people seemed to follow her. Made a couple drunks look up from their beers. But after a while, I thought she was waiting for someone." He leaned over confidentially. "She did hook up with someone."

Jack frowned. "Here? Who?"

The bartender picked up a bar rag and rubbed the counter slowly. Finally he said, "I think his name is Ryker. He'd come in now and then. Never stayed long, usually had a scotch with a beer back, like you."

"What'd he look like?"

"Heavyset, bald like me. I seen him before. I couldn't remember where until I saw him a week later comin' out of that building acrost the street."

"It's closed."

"Old SRO. I've been thinking of walking over there some day. It's been shut for years, but just in the last year I seen people outside it, then gone, usually on a Friday. A customer told me they might use it for a pop-up theater. Must be a secret to getting in."

talias building ryker

"You didn't check it out?"

"There's a lot of weird stuff in the Tenderloin, a lot of dangerous stuff. Just don't want to get involved, or hurt. Besides, I got other things to do."

Jack masked a chill by taking a long sip of Macallan. "You say this guy liked her poetry."

"He liked something about her. They left together, like they'd planned it." Randy laughed. "You know, once you seen her last video, you start looking for her. I thought I seen her a couple times. You know, dark glasses, long coat, like you couldn't really tell what was underneath, or whether it was a man or woman. Looked like a lot of people in the Tenderloin."

Jack twirled his shot glass. "So, she might be here."

"You could probably make a whole fantasy around that. Know what I mean? Isn't that what you sell—fantasy? Maybe you got caught in one."

Jack finished his scotch and chugged half of the beer. "Keep the change. Do you mind if I take some video?"

"Be my guest."

Jack captured the front of the bar, the chairs and tables, the sleeping man, the stage, and finally the back bar and Randy who, without urging, mugged for him.

Jack headed for the door but turned and said, "Thanks for letting me shoot."

"My pleasure. Maybe I'll see myself in a game one day."

"Stranger things have happened."

Jack paused at the door, turned and scanned the bar, then the building across the street. Outside, he turned off the audio recorder and waited for the street traffic to slow, captured the front of the SRO, and walked across the street and captured the front of the alley.

Jack took a step into the alley. It was dark, faintly sinister...

should i shouldnt i

Jack turned and walked back to the Porsche. The drive back was slow. He took 101, not trusting himself to take 1.

(45)

Dawn, Edna, the Tenderloin, Carol, her ex...

> *real stuff real people lots to do lots to think about*
> *to worry over why cant i jacks show thats why*

...it was always there, a couple doors away, blazing, fueling her obsession.

Seeing people she knew talking and acting in bizarre ways on screen was unsettling...and exciting. Raquel and Doris, Emma, George...all acting out. But the images that anchored in her brain were of Mike talking, laughing, and screwing her avatar, and then smashing her face. She couldn't help seeing Mike differently, seeing he liked the sex, but in some way hated her too.

> *cant help it makes me horny again*

Jack stayed in for days. The rare times he emerged and she saw him, he made pro forma stops in the Dog. When she was there at the same time, she could see Jack was touching base, perhaps touching a reality he missed with the Show. When he settled in the corner and stared at his drink, was he seeing the drink or a copy? Was he projecting his show bar on the real one? Did he prefer the Show Dog to the real one?

Monitors are easy to switch off.

She watched his house when she could, saw the flickering lights on the second floor, and itched to see what he was doing, whether he was subjecting other P.C. inhabitants to Phisto. Hadn't she seen all the people mentioned in Maddy's video?

She took a couple long hikes on the beach. It made her feel fantastic, but when she came into the house, a depression settled in her spirit. The Line beckoned her, the photos of Loin residents accused her, her Map with its crisscrossed lines, buildings, and photos reproached her.

She had a long talk with Raquel. While Raquel talked of Nook prospects, which were grim, she couldn't help seeing Raquel as the Raquel in the Show...with Doris plunging into her. What else did Raquel get into? Was she a nymphomaniac? A digital rapist? Would she become a serial killer with enough time and no constraints? What would any of them do unshackled from reality?

And where did she go? Where did any of them go? She guessed they didn't go far with Jack watching. What could they do confined to a box?

On her way back from chatting with Raquel, she watched as Jack opened his garage door, started his multi-hued Porsche, and angled it out of his garage. As he drove past, he smiled a knowing smile, as if he knew something about her. He drove down Marsh Lane, turned right, and disappeared.

What did that knowing glance mean? He was an idiot if he didn't suspect her.

She glanced up towards the second floor.

The Show was on!

She wanted to rush in her house and get the duplicate key, but what if he'd gone to Invert?

slow down hotshot

It was cold, but she grabbed Joyce's Ulysses and settled on a chair outside. She reread parts of Molly Bloom's bitchy, brilliant, sexy monologue while she watched the road. Odd thing about Molly, she was so right. She twisted men into pretzels, homunculi with gaping mouths, enormous dicks, or a Lucien Freud contortion, or Francis Bacon at his sexiest. And weren't their depictions closer to what Jack's digital characters were doing? Slipping through the restraints into the dark areas of human feeling and desire? Didn't we all do it secretly? Didn't she have a subconscious reason for liking Lucien Freud and Sheile?

When Jack hadn't returned after half an hour, she scanned the road to the coast. When she didn't see anything, she got the key. She walked casually towards his place, waved to the secretive Andrea, who lived in a cottage at the south end, hemmed in by ten-foot hedges. She walked down the marsh trail, then ducked back to Jack's hedge. She waited a few minutes, slipped through the hedge and up the steps.

She scanned the road before inserting the duplicate key. She opened and shut the front door.

She'd been lucky before. Why did Jack leave the Show on? Was it like leaving a world on, his alternate reality? Maybe he thought that if he turned it off, it would disappear.

Who was featured that day—more sourful Emma, more repentant George? Mike fucking her digital brains out or beating her? She couldn't tell from the living room. All she saw was the flickering, a hint of the Show. She couldn't make out dialog.

His computer room was messy, as if he were starting to unravel. Roaches and scraps in the ashtray, half-full glasses, a pair of old slippers bunched together, a stale smell.

The sign in bold—"A year or nothing"—was gone.

Talia frowned as she edged into Jack's recliner, her eyes on the screen.

* * *

She was in the middle of the Tenderloin, a rough cut Tenderloin. Sometimes it stopped and flickered past a series of photos. Then there was a short clear clip and more photos. Most of the photos were hers, except the ones that seemed to be from a game.

With his capture and bugs, he had Point City in a net. She couldn't imagine that Jack was switching focus after all he'd done with Point City.

It was remarkable what he'd done in a short time. Certainly the video was jerky, and the only audio was background grindings, horns, sirens, and a hodgepodge of voices. Many scenes looked as if they'd been copied in from video games, and they changed color and shape as the characters had changed. He had videoed the outside of bars where Maddy had done her readings. He'd captured the inside of the Last Call, and she listened to the bartender, Randy, and his description of the bald man. Ryker! He also had her shots of the SRO and the alley.

She froze when she saw her photos of the thugs, especially the last shot, the blurry photo of the bald man in the running suit. She thought there was something there and she guessed Jack did too.

* * *

When the tape of the Tenderloin looped, she got up.

shit   where is raquel   and emma   and

She wanted to see the Point City characters, but she didn't know how to get Loop and Present, and she didn't have the time. She wasn't going to risk Jack coming back and finding her. She walked out of the computer room, the images following her. She felt them on her back and gradually slipping away as she reached the middle of the stairs.

She started towards the door but stopped, intrigued by the macabre gallery in the living room. She checked the road. Empty. The prints and collages weren't like hers; hers were tame, stylized. Maddy's were critical...of society, people, human nature. There was an obsession with torture and cruelty towards women.

The print of the Oz collage entranced her. Dorothy, back to the viewer, alone, skipping down the yellow strip towards a shining Emerald City. Were we all chasing rainbows?

alone   what did that mean

You couldn't see her face, but she was leaving. She was tripping down that golden road right out of Jack's life. But she wasn't quite gone.

she lingered   jack lingered

Talia walked slowly through the living room, waited until the sidewalks were clear, slipped out, locked the door, and sidled over to the side of the house and through the hedge.

(46)

Jack laughed as he watched the tape. Here was Talia pausing by the front door. Here she was opening the door. She must have duped the key he'd left in the door! Daring! Here she was climbing the stairs and settling in his lounger.

glad i could make it comfortable

He could see her chagrin when she stared at the remote. Heh, heh. The Tenderloin show was in a different digital space. She couldn't find the Show's Loop and Present if she tried. He didn't want to take the chance that she would decide to talk to them. He didn't want to lose their confidence. Oddly, he didn't feel distraught that she'd seen them.

lets call it objective validation

Now she was standing in front of *Oz*, mesmerized, as he had been. There was something there. A clue, a meaning he was missing. What was she seeing? Maddy tripping down the road alone...but not quite gone. Was Maddy saying something to her?

Had Maddy found her Oz in the Tenderloin?

As for Talia, he couldn't fault what she'd done. He even admired her pluck. He'd seen that in her nature before but hadn't realized how far she'd go. Were they competing to see who'd find Maddy first? Wouldn't that be the bee's knees!

* * *

The next day, Thursday, it was time for the SRO. At four in the afternoon, he was back in the Tenderloin.

Jack navigated the street in a slouch, trying to meld into the street population. The SRO seemed an unlikely spot for anything, especially a meeting. The buildings on either side were closed, and the front of the SRO itself was

223

barricaded with 2x4s and yellow warning tape. The only way in was the narrow dark alley shaded by overhanging trees and the abandoned building on the corner.

im a fool on an errand

There was a black homeless guy in the bus shelter who smelled of stale garbage and cigarettes. When he asked for money, Jack gave him a five and told him to move to another spot. The homeless man got up, sniffed the air, and shuffled down Ellis.

Jack wrinkled his nose at the smell and sat down. He clasped and unclasped his fingers. When he realized he was doing it, he stopped. He breathed in and out slowly, calming down. It was risky breaking into George's and Mike's, and later Talia's. Now, he hoped to get into a mysterious Tenderloin building, a meeting place of pimps and thugs and a random assortment of street people.

Things could get a lot worse than a slap on the hand.

The background noise was constant, the view constant too. A block away, clumps of blacks shared cheap booze in paper bags and passed limp joints; across the street, homeless and runaways stacked against worn buildings. A block north on Eddy, a red-lipped low-skirted whore strutted towards her spot. Farther up on Ellis, a hijabed Muslim mother pushed her kids across an intersection with an open hand. A bus rolled by, opened its doors, and no one came out or got on. The driver looked straight ahead, the bus doors closed, and it rumbled towards Market Street, glowing like a distant fantasyland.

Jack got up and started towards the door but stopped. A red-lipsticked tranny with white-rimmed dark glasses, blond beehive, red crotch-exposing skirt, and five-inch sparkling white heels clomped down the street. Jack retreated to the bus shelter. The tranny pouted, scanned the street, and ducked into the dark alley. He could barely see her as she walked under the encroaching trees and vanished.

what the fuck

A few minutes later, a middle-aged man—gray suit, shiny cordovans, and valise—walked up to the SRO, scanned the street, waited for a woman with a clutch of kids to pass, then ducked into the alley and disappeared.

fuck me

In the next half hour, at staggered intervals, twenty people including three homeless kids walked down the dark alley and into the SRO.

fucking convention who knew how many were in there before i got here the sro could be full of people what are they ghosts

Jack waited twenty minutes. No one else entered. No thugs, no bald guy. He got up and walked to the head of the alley. He hesitated but finally slipped into the alley. A few seconds later, he stood before a small door partially covered with ivy.

∗ ∗ ∗

It was dark and musty inside. The door led into a narrow passageway into the SRO lobby. Two-by-fours were scattered everywhere, plaster cracked and spread over the floor. Sunlight leaked from a broken window in front and cut glowing crisscross lines in the dust and bounced off the mirror on his left.

The accordion gate of the elevator on the left of the lobby was covered in red tape. There was a small man with lank gray hair, head nestled in his crossed arms on top of a ledger, sleeping at the check-in desk.

checkin desk ledger clerk really

Jack slipped along the wall and walked quickly up the stairs on his right. There was red dust in the corners of the stairs and rat and mouse scratches, but the center was clean.

Jack walked up the stairs quickly, unsheathed his camera, flicked it on, checked the settings, turned, and captured the lobby, the stairs, and a corner of the front desk and man. He wasn't sure what good that would do. It might, remotely, key a memory or restart the sequence of small discoveries that led him here.

Capturing the outside was, he realized, something he'd done automatically for years. It was one of Maddy's complaints, from her "whore" comment when

225

they met to her constant amused refrain of him standing by reality, removed, letting reality lope by...making his own reality. Jack clicked off the camera.

thing is maddy maybe its the way im built maybe i cant change even though everyone says you can you know start a new life change your attitude get zen get religion get out get down find your passion but do we really change or are we coating the nut

The stairs creaked. It was darker near the landing on the second floor but lighter down the hallway. People talking, music, laughter.

What were they doing?

Jack hesitated. He should get out of there but...

He heard classical music from the first room, 200. He peeked in through the cracked door and saw two men and two women in a semicircle with violins, a cello, a viola rehearsing. Sounded like a Mozart quartet. The music was brilliant, soothing. The room was partially covered in makeshift soundproofing.

how did they start this

Jack flipped on the capture camera. He moved to the center of the hallway and walked quickly, capturing both sides.

202: two people facing across a desk, open folders; interview?

203: man dressed in suit, four people casual dress, round table; meeting?

206: low rock music, three people, grunge, pot smoke filtered into the hall.

211: three kids, sleeping bags, one watched him for a second then rested his head on a pillow.

Not all the rooms were occupied. People hardly looked at him. At a room at the far end, he glimpsed a woman in bra and panties unbuttoning the pants of the well-dressed man. Across the hallway, people grouped around a table argued, coffee steaming from take-out cups.

Jack turned and started back towards the stairs. And stopped. He felt dizzy. The floor was pixelating. He was on a thin neuron...no in Ouroboros... no. He leaned against a wall watching the rooms swim before his eyes, dissolve, pixelate.

Finally, it stopped. He blinked, felt the smoothness of the wall, tested his legs, stretched his neck in a tight circle.

hah fungus residue okay im ready

Jack straightened up and walked carefully down the hallway.

No one stopped him. No one seemed to care that he was watching them.

Jack took a deep breath when he got to the stairs.

He should leave but, according to Talia's email to Carol, there was a meeting on Friday on the third floor. Was it the thug meeting place? Would Ryker be there? It was darker on the stairs up to three. Footprints in the dust.

He waited to adjust to the gloom. Light leaked through a boarded window, casting a weak yellow glow over the end of the hallway.

It was quiet; none of the doors were open. Jack followed the stream of footprints. They stopped at Room 305. Jack knew it was the riskiest thing he'd done. He put his ear to the door and listened. He waited a few seconds and turned the door handle.

He was surprised it was unlocked. The door opened into a large room. He knew most rooms in SROs were small, single, but this one was larger. The window on his left was boarded up with crisscrossed 2x4s. In the middle of the room was a long table bordered with a scattering of six or seven armless chairs; a few more were pushed loosely against the wall.

He flipped the light switch. He wasn't surprised when two shaded bulbs in the ceiling came on. He changed the settings on the capture, and shot the room from the door. He was careful to walk in footprints as he circled the table. The table was scarred with cigarette butts, and there were butts on the floor. There was a garbage can in the corner with paper in it.

Grich, grich, grich...

The scraping sound grew louder. He glanced at the open door and moved slowly to the wall.

It stopped abruptly. Jack breathed in, out. Waited.

Jack checked the garbage can. He took the few papers out. Scribbles. He spread the papers on the table, took out his cell, snapped pictures of them, and put them back in the wastebasket.

**how could this lead to maddy i might find out more about ryker
or who met here**

Jack thought for a moment, then fished in his pack. He brought out a leather case, opened it, and took out two surveillance bugs. He looked around the room then under the table and carefully pulled the plastic back off a bug. He put the plastic in his pocket and carefully attached the epoxy side in the corner under the table at the end closest to the door.

He performed the same sequence at the door and placed it nearby on the wood where the plaster crumbled. When he activated them remotely, they'd last for over two days.

Jack flicked the lights off, closed the door, and descended the stairs, careful to stay in the steps in the dust. On two, he heard voices, and the tranny he'd seen earlier walked out of a room at the end of the hallway, glanced at him, and went to a room on the other side.

**id love to stay but cant expose myself what will i hear friday if
anything**

The old man at the lobby desk had shifted, but his arms still sheltered his head. Jack walked slowly out but paused at the head of the alley. It was unusual, unusual enough that in the past he'd used it in a Phisto game. It was so much like Ouroboros, so much like the Magic Theatre. Mystery hotel, mystery door, mystery rooms.

was maddy teasing him

(47)

Inside, dark and musty, the sun making everything seem gray. But winter was breaking, and each day had a couple hours of sun.

Dawn had called to say everything was working out, but Adam—now dealing oxy and pissed because she had helped Dawn leave—was looking for the running man to tell him about her, Talia.

a win   a loss

Talia settled in her small sofa and rotated her mug restlessly through her hands. She stared into the swirling mix. She turned it over and stared at Wyeth's *Christina's World*. That's how she felt, down and struggling, crawling, dragging leaden, self-created baggage.

Jack had cobbled together a Tenderloin show.

if dawn hadnt called id be digging through the tenderloin trying to find out more about the bald runner and maddy

Was her experiment over? She'd picked up the phone to call her mother a score of times; she punched out the number of Carol in Oakland, and before she hit the red icon ending the call, Carol answered.

Carol said she was going to the Modern and she, Talia, was coming too, and that was that.

* * *

Frank Stella's Moby-Dick sculptures captivated her. She followed the colors, the shapes, thinking about how they related to the text. Monumental work, 135 works, single passion.

Talia walked slowly through the exhibit. She felt her obsession with Jack's show and the Point City characters, Maddy, and the Tenderloin fade. That stuff—life, the flip side of people, the Tenderloin degradation—tied her down and made her feel trapped and vulnerable. She'd forgotten how absorbed, often exhilarated, she felt when she strolled through a gallery or lost herself in a painting.

Carol ran into the prints curator and stopped to talk to her, and Talia wandered off into the distant galleries, through a German-themed gallery (mostly Richter) and into early 20th century. She sat down in a darkened room, not knowing exactly what she was going to see.

The hearse followed a meandering course. Picabia and René Clair. The oddness of the film made her feel even more detached from her problems.

make art to destroy it   maddy would have liked it

* * *

She stayed with Carol that night. It felt emancipating to be away from Point City. Yes, there was another life. Yes, there was good life, exciting life.

She undressed and was about to get into bed, when she stopped. Something about Carol. Something about how close they were that day. She turned and walked out to the hallway and stared at Carol's door for a few seconds.

What if...

What if...

She opened the door and stared at Carol. She was stroking Nick.

Talia said, "Don't really feel like sleeping."

Carol smiled. "Well, you're in the right place." She held up the covers and said, "Hop in."

Talia stared at her for a few seconds, then slipped under the covers.

"I hope you don't mind. Sometimes I have to get beyond talk."

Carol sat up, her left breast swinging down towards her. "I don't mind."

Talia nestled down and Carol took her hand.

what am i doing   its exciting   do i want her   does she want me   whats next

She talked about her obsessions, the Line, Jack, the mystery SRO. When she talked about them, objectified them, she began to see that she was edging away from them, that she had fallen into a bunch of things after her divorce that she hadn't chosen.

Talia said, "I'm talking too much."

Carol: "It's nice getting away from the internal storm. It'll be back soon enough."

Carol was a successful artist, had a basketful of shows, and had a following, but she was full of self-doubt. She worried that she was derivative, worried that she didn't have any creativity left.

and yet she is urging me to change urging me to listen to my inner artist maybe shes like me help others cant help myself

They were both thirsty and hot from talking and Carol got them a bottle of Chardonnay, and they sat up and talked some more.

Finally, tired but not sleepy, she cradled Carol's head in her hand and kissed her slowly on the cheek. Talia said, "Thanks for that."

Carol said, "Hey, cowgirl, we're not done." She felt the warmth grow in her skin and the warmth grow in her face. Hot and sweaty. Carol kissed her back. Soon they were tumbling over each other, and Carol's hand, then her mouth, found her sex. She arched her back and lay back and let the thrill and tongue ripple through her body.

Most of Carol's pubic hair was missing, except for a thin strip of hair leading to her sex.

"Do you like it?" Carol asked.

"I don't know, do you?"

"Gets stubbly. I like the idea of a landing strip. You could try it. Brazilian wax. Hip."

Talia smiled. "Let's try a landing."

Carol's hand lay on Talia's back. "Wow. That was something. Were you laughing? No, that was definitely a chuckle."

"I was thinking of something I saw, something sexy, something dirty, something erotic, something just like what I was doing. I felt a show was impinging on life, real life...whatever that is."

Carol hoisted her legs around Talia and brought her face close. "Shows, images, paintings; they always stay with us, probably in ways we'll never know. So, let's kiss again...for real."

Later, Talia thought about what she was doing. It felt good, better than Mike grabbing and thrusting and demanding. And look what digital Mike did!

Later she thought of Raquel and how she'd said she liked men. Maybe she still did. Maybe she liked men and women.

tart

Nick and Nora moved in with them late and made the bed a nest.

Towards morning, she started thinking about what she'd given up when she got married, when she divorced and moved to Point City. She'd circumscribed herself. Was it time to realize that she'd fallen into the Line and Jack's obsession? Was it time to call the last few years a hiatus? She thought about what she could do with her space in Point City. Would there be too many memories of the Line? Would there be too much speculation about Jack and his Show? Was Point City too small?

Talia smiled at all her objections. It made her think she didn't want to do it.

or that i couldnt do it

(48)

Friday. He didn't know if listening to what happened in Room 305 of a mysterious SRO full of people would do any good, but then again, didn't we try to find out as much as possible about what goes on?

or am i a voyeur or does reality feed my fake worlds

Scriitch, griiik, braaack, bleechch...
Bugs live!
Jack set up the listening system in a corner of the Stage and hooked the signal into his speakers. After listening to random knockings, tappings, distant voices, and rats scritching across the floor, he eliminated the background noise.

Jack settled in the lounger and switched on Present, and when no one was doing anything, switched to the Nook. Raquel wasn't there. He switched to his other characters, but they weren't in their usual haunts either. He was about to sign off, when Raquel slipped into the Nook followed by a thin trail of pixels. Jack turned on the mic.

"Jack, are you there?"
She seemed different, composed. "I'm here."
"How'd you like to follow me?"
"Where?"
"Into uncharted depths, into Ouroboros."

∗ ∗ ∗

Raquel had chosen a dead-end bar at an exit in Ouroboros. The hushed lighting flickered around the four characters sitting on barstools and slumped in chairs across from the bar. The back bar glowed with bottles of Knob, Dewar's, Stoli, and Don Julio.

Raquel, Emma, George, and Mike sat in a loose semicircle, backs to the bar.

Mike: "Surprise!"

Raquel edged up in her chair, her hair flickering slightly from brown to a light yellow.

Raquel: "I was going crazy not having anyone to talk to, so I started hanging out where I saw Emma, and found her first. It took some hunting, but I found George in Game of Kings, and Mike in Dark City. Ouroboros seems to be the only game common to what you call our digital spaces and we've met here a couple times. We thought the bar setting was appropriate since you told me about your recent chemical excursions."

chemical excursions are they criticizing me what do they want

Jack: "So you found each other. Didn't expect it, but I didn't expect you. Fine."

Raquel: "I'm surprised it worked, but I'm not surprised I tried to make it work. I guess it proves we're a social animal, even if we're missing bricks-n-mortar bodies and bricks-n-mortar reality."

Mike: "And you made us, and we're here for the wrong reason."

George, the outline of his body wavered then slowly reformed: "We should keep some of our fantasies locked up."

Jack edged down in his recliner. He felt surrounded by his four characters on the walls, screen, and ceiling. "Projectors off."

Mike frowned. "What was that?"

"I told you I project your images throughout the second floor."

George's body changed colors. "Weird, Jack."

Jack: "The images help me think."

George's voice was high, then sank into a baritone: "Tell you the truth, I didn't want to be found."

Mike: "Me either. I don't like these people. Fucking lesbian. Fucking born-again."

Emma: "I didn't want to be here at all."

Raquel: "I had to talk to someone else, but I don't like any of these people either."

Emma, looking sorrowfully into a multicolored glass of wine: "Yes, Jack, you're brilliant, and I'm amazed I can sort of see everybody. But

I don't give a hoot about seeing anybody else. I wish you'd taken me out of here when I asked."

George, turning to Emma: "I never liked to hear you talk about God in real life. Here, it's hell. Haven't we heard enough about how conflicted you are about Jesus or not, heaven or not, hell or not?"

Emma: "And I've heard enough about how you plotted to have sex with Maria and kill your wife, and about your boo-hoo-hoo contrition. You know what, George, we all think you could do it, you know, in real life, not this fake one."

George, angrily: "I'd never do it for real."

Emma cackled: "How do you know?"

Raquel took a sip of her drink. The liquid appeared briefly in her throat then disappeared: "You know, I do feel slightly tipsy when I drink this, except I never get drunk. I guess we call that the best-of-all-possible-worlds. Pace, Voltaire. Thing is, Emma, George doesn't know. That's the rub. Here we don't have any constraints as our ringmaster has said. Back in reality our decaying selves are bound by all sorts of external and internal bonds. But it doesn't mean we couldn't do those things. Those impulses existed and exist now out there."

Jack, troubled: "There is that potential, but—"

Mike: "Thing is, Jacko, what gets me is there is no connection between in here and out there, except—"

George, surprised, turned to face Mike: "Except?"

Mike: "We talked about it already. If our overlord let real people see us. It would be the ultimate mind fuck. I think we've all thought about it. It wouldn't bother me; I don't think I'm that different than out there. Tell us, Jack, has our bricks-n-mortar self seen us?"

Jack, sternly: "Of course not. If they knew about you, they might want to, but they never will."

Raquel: "In a sense, you know more about us than anyone, than ourselves, because you know the outside person and us, the dark side. It's like you're a writer like Stevenson watching Jekyll and Hyde. Doesn't it seem odd that Jekyll never did completely separate Jekyll from Hyde? It's obvious Jekyll must have known about Hyde, and Hyde Jekyll. Except our Jekyll doesn't know about us. But you do."

Jack: "You're not the dark side. None of you are Hyde. Remember, while you're changing in here, the flesh-and-blood you is changing too."

Raquel: "So has the real me changed, given up the Nook, found a new girlfriend?"

Jack, soberly: "I haven't followed them much. I don't know."

Raquel: "So once you had us, you didn't care about the real person?"

Emma, shaking her head: "I'm sure I haven't changed, and neither has God."

Mike, angrily: "Emma, you gotta give up this god business. It's warping your pixels. If he does exist, why would he care about you? There are billions of galaxies and billions of stars and planets in each galaxy. Do you think he's sitting on a couch up in space diddling himself and musing: 'Jeez, I almost forgot. I'd better help Emma'?"

Emma: "That's a horrible thing to say. He cares about everyone... maybe not you."

George: "Hey, get real. Jack's our god. He can do what he wants. He can turn us off; he can't do that in the real world."

Mike: "Thank Buddha. Tell you, though. I like the games. I don't care if I'm a drooling idiot, and I don't care what Raquel, our resident lesbo, thinks of me. I can do anything I want. Murder, mayhem, fucking my eyes out. It gooses my bits and makes my pixels glow."

Raquel: "Except until we found each other, no one else reacted to what we say, except by rote. It was like being in a kaleidoscopic echo chamber. Mike's right. I hate looking at him, but if I swear at him, he can swear back."

Mike: "I guess it depends on how much you need people."

Raquel: "You claim you don't, but you do."

Mike: "C'mon Raq. We're all different. I like being alone with my toys. What about you, George? Are you depressed cuz you don't have Edna to scold you?"

George, slumping: "I never thought I'd say it, but I miss her."

Jack, puzzled: "More than Maria?"

George, serious: "It's odd how I chatted with Maria in real life and fantasized about her. I made up life with her, the sex, having kids, growing old. And Edna, I dreamed about ways to kill her. All fantasies. It took this world to make me see I couldn't do it."

Emma: "Real life. What a joke."

Mike, growling: "Let's see, you don't like it there, and you don't like it here. I sure hope heaven works out for you. Shit, why do you think you'd be any happier there?"

Emma: "Shut up."

Mike: "And what do you think it means to be there? Same body? Same depressed spirit? Is it going to be a sanitized Emma, a perfectly smooth Emma without the wrinkles and fat and mournful expression?"

Jack: "Slow down, everybody."

* * *

Mike looked at Raquel. "Why don't you do it, Raq? You're the articulate one."

Jack, exasperated: "Now what?"

Raquel: "I can't speak for the rest of them, but I like it here, even though it has its drawbacks. Tell you what I like, Jack. I like reading the classics. I like the Bible, Dante, Shakespeare, Pope, and Eliot...sure my memory isn't exactly the same, and I forget or don't get some of it, but I remember more than I did in real life. It's stored somewhere in my bits and bytes. Some of my older memories are non-existent, but I don't need them in here."

Jack shrugged, tired: "Glad you like it."

Raquel: "There is one thing."

Jack: "I guessed."

Raquel: "Some of us don't care about helping you, but we're agreed on one thing."

Jack: "What's that?"

Raquel: "When you're drunk you talk a lot about you and Maddy. I know how much she means to you, but I—we—think you have to give up looking for her."

Jack, angrily: "Why?"

Raquel: "We think you should take care of us. Aren't we the most important thing you've done?"

Jack: "But she's the reason you're conscious. I've thought about—"

Raquel: "You're acting rotely. I remember she was different the last time I saw her. I don't think this is going to end well. You know what we want you to do?"

Jack, skeptical: "What?"

Raquel: "We want you to take care of us, your creations. I want more books, Mike wants more games, and George wants Edna, someone he can talk to."

Emma: "And Emma wants out."

Jack: "So this is a revolution."

Raquel: "Consider it therapy."

Jack, puzzled: "Okay, I won't ask more questions about Maddy. Frankly, none of you helped much."

Emma: "They can do what they want or have you do it, but if I help you, you have to turn me off. I've had enough of this pretense."

Jack: "I think she's in the Tenderloin."

Raquel, wide-eyed, curious: "Why?"

Jack: "I told you. I visited bars where she gave readings. In one of them, she left with a guy named Ryker. I think Maddy might be with him."

Emma: "Please let me out."

George: "Being here might be your best bet at immortality, Emma."

Emma: "What a horrible thing to say. This is nowhere."

Raquel: "We shouldn't fight among ourselves."

Mike: "Why not? We lose a few bytes, and Phisto replaces them."

George: "Who knows with what?"

Mike: "Problem, overlord."

Jack frowned: "I can see lots of problems. What?"

Mike sat back in his chair, tilting it on two legs: "Remember what I told you about Maddy, how if she planned the whole thing, how she knew you'd look at the four people she mentioned, how she organized the whole mess? What makes you think she didn't have all of us point towards a big guy in a truck, see her standing in line at the café, talk about a building, about a phone call to the Tenderloin with George. All of those clues could have been salted by her into our narratives without us knowing it."

Jack: "It's possible. She had to leave some clues."

Mike: "Of course, we didn't have to say anything."

Raquel: "This is all too ambiguous. I didn't know what she was doing, and I didn't know she'd talked to other characters. But from what I know, the Tenderloin makes sense. She could be there...but you have to know she's not going to be the same person. Of course, we all change—"

Emma screamed: "Get me out of here!"

* * *

Jack flicked the mic off, and said "Phisto."

"Yep."

Jack sighed. "Eliminate Emma from the Show."

"Whoa. You sure, Jack?"

"I know you have to ask. Yes, eliminate Emma."

"Shouldn't take long. Took a lot longer to make her. Hold on."

Emma seemed to waver and dissolve and finally blipped off the screen.

"Thanks."

"No problemo."

Jack flipped the mic on.

* * *

Mike, shaking his head: "It's that easy, a delete key away from oblivion."

Raquel: "That was brutal."

Jack: "She bugged me from the first scene to take her out."

George: "You could do that to any of us."

Raquel: "Or all of us."

Jack: "You are brilliant creations. You can stay as long as the power stays on."

Raquel: "Right. What gets me is that it all comes down to energy, you know, like the real world."

Mike: "But in here it's all electrical. Out there there's bio energy."

George: "Which do you prefer? In here, we don't get old and we don't feel much. In theory, Jack could leave a will that we have to stay on as long as his money lasts."

Raquel: "Isn't it an ersatz immortality?"

Mike: "I'll take any kind I can get. I want to stay here. Fuck the guy out there. He's too fucked up. In here, I can live."

Raquel, solemnly: "I know what you mean. But what's immortality without other people?"

George: "We still feel shame, still feel."

Jack: "I have to go. You can obviously find each other whenever you want. I didn't plan it, but I didn't understand I could make you."

George: "As long as I'm in here, I want to talk to someone conscious."

Mike: "I suppose. I do miss talking, but I don't have to like them. Once a day would be okay. I still have the rest of the day for blowing up aliens."

Raquel: "It'll be good for you, Mike. It might even change you for the better."

Mike, laughing: "You make me a better person."

* * *

The monitor was off, the mic was off, but Jack sat back in the lounger staring at the screen. Jack grinned. It was funny that they came together like that. What wasn't funny was what he saw happening to Raquel, his first, or Phisto's first, creation. He wasn't sure she could see it because of her limited sense of sight, but Phisto's algorithms hadn't replaced part of her right leg. It could be a fluke, but he'd have to watch them closely. If they were disintegrating, it wouldn't be long before their consciousness would go as well.

And the grand experiment, the grand creation, his conscious avatars would flicker and disappear.

"Phisto."

(49)

She spent the next morning with Carol, watching her in her studio, talking about art, about what it meant, about how she, Talia, could start. They were easy with each other. They touched and it felt good.

She left around noon, after a wet embrace in Carol's driveway. Carol drove everything out of her head. The warmth, the sex. She hadn't felt that for a long time. She re-created that night, the hesitation, the softness, the sensuality. And what was next? Would she and Carol become a couple? Would they see each other once a week, a month, at all? Would she be jealous? Would she regret everything?

Beyond the sex were the questions. She questioned what she was doing before, but she began to see how she'd fallen into her present life. She'd fallen into the Line, Jack's show. If she took it far enough, she'd fallen into marriage and—why not go all the way—fallen into the bars, the Vortex, and school. She hadn't fallen into art, her collages and painting, but she'd doubted it, doubted her talent.

* * *

The calls had tapered off. That day, she got a call from Sheri, who just wanted to talk, and a call from a kid, Sean, who said his friend had an overdose and was talking to imaginary people at two in the morning. The few she looked forward to, the few whose histories she'd known longer, the Petes and Johnnies, had quit calling.

She'd been looking at her database of calls. She couldn't remember some of the early ones. Early ones. Had she been on the Line that long?

Reluctantly, she pulled up the record for Adam. She unpinned the few photos that obscured him, and there he was. She'd glanced at his slightly lopsided face—grimy in that photo—and felt a twinge of regret. But she hadn't examined it closely. What he'd done overshadowed her early sympathy and made her want to avoid it in his face. He'd jeopardized the Line and put her at risk. She couldn't see that in his eyes or in the cant of his face, but it had been there. Of course, his line was that he had to survive. What was she to him? What was she to any of them?

the line is slipping away   it is   was   my lifeline   my hook into life or lives   a reason for living   accomplishment   i feel it has come crashing down   people have died   adam a dealer   ladies of the night   hip fuck suck   druggies shoot up   pete and johnny sip their poison

* * *

Late afternoon, her obsession with Jack resurfaced. She'd watched Jack's for days. She tried to watch inconspicuously, but she knew Jack watched her, sure he knew she had seen his show and seen what he'd done.

She marveled at what he'd done. Animating characters. Creating consciousness. No one would believe her. Sometime she didn't believe it herself. She did know one thing: Jack was now focused on the Tenderloin. He'd probably gone to the same bars she had. She was sure he'd pumped the bartenders. He may have seen a flyer.

Perhaps Maddy was living with the bald heavy, Mr. Big Boy, likely a criminal.

Except. Given that Maddy was brilliant and creative, why would she go through the charade of a pretend death to live with a criminal? It was beyond showboating. It was too close to a line. Did she try to eliminate the line between criminal and poet, à la Genet?

Or, was she just crazy?

(50)

Jack sat at the kitchen table, watching the mouse hole and occasionally glancing at the Oz collage.

Oz.

my show is the real oz and im pulling the strings kinda

His digital characters revolted! They'd met in secret! They'd made demands! They'd staged an intervention and wanted him to give up looking for Maddy!

There was a lot to think about in that meeting. His characters, besides being conscious, needed others...to talk to, to interact with, to see reactions. It was a deep-seated need. Another item he never thought of with digital consciousness. What was more troubling was the thought they had started decomposing. Phisto said it was certainly a power problem and a bug, maybe several bugs, in a subroutine. Phisto couldn't do much about the power without dismantling much of the Show, and it wasn't sure it could find the bug or bugs.

my avatars theyre fading theyre like aliens then theyre not but im attached to them

Jack spent most of that day and part of the next writing down his meeting with his characters. He noted how they moved together, how they interacted, how their consciousness evolved, how important it was to find other conscious characters, and, of course, finally getting rid of Emma. That frightened them, had shown his power. But they also realized, finally, he couldn't delete them.

they are my grand creation however annoying

Maddy?

The more he thought about it, the more he thought they were right about Maddy. The search had taken on ominous overtones, and every time he looked at *Oz*, Dorothy, the crinkled papier-mâché golden road, the silly toys and fatal inscription, he felt a cloud grow over the search.

He was at a point he'd never thought about. Compromised. Constrained. Others were compromised. Others had to continue because of this or that, kid on the way, kids to educate, wife in recovery, car payments. He didn't have those constraints, but he'd painted himself into a corner. He'd tracked Maddy's thin trail through his characters, followed Talia's trail into the Tenderloin, and finally came upon a candidate for the person that helped her, Ryker, a mystery SRO, and a meeting place.

"Well, Mousy, what do I do?"

He'd started something and had gotten involved with a Tenderloin Show. That nagging feeling that he was being controlled wouldn't go away. But how was that possible? Even his hallucinated talking mouse, his double, his alter, thought he was being controlled.

do i really think that can i think that or am i pretending

Maddy in the Tenderloin made a strange kind of sense. It fit with her ideas about being true to her artist's nature, her blowing up expectations, her anarchism. He could see her with someone like Ryker.

But the competition was real; Maddy had made it real. If she was with someone else, why string him along?

thats the mystery at the heart of my obsession

* * *

Jack had Phisto analyze his capture from the SRO and had come up with zip. A secret SRO inhabited by a score of people, bands, homeless, actors, thugs, kids. He was amazed it existed, that it was a secret meeting place. How often? How was one invited? How did they open it? He was full of questions. He knew one thing: it was the kind of place Maddy would love. Had she arranged it, or was she using it?

Or was it about her at all?

Jack sipped black coffee and waited for the listening system to kick on. He felt there was something wrong, not with the bugs, but with the place. It didn't make sense, and he wondered what he was going to hear from the meeting in Room 305.

if i was going to hear anything

He shot straight up in the lounger when he heard the low rumbling voice.

Bug

gentlemen
what we doin' here man
who am i...your cody...doesnt matter names dont matter ...why we doin'
it
hey code...its cuz of her...got it...yeahyeah

"Shit." Jack grabbed a pen and a loose sheet of paper from the end table and scribbled a note: reception lousy, exceptional meeting, intelligent voice. Ryker?

gentlemen...screek, screek, screek...loosely..lets see what we doin' okay its about payin' up ...we got welchers...flipped out druggies...scrawk...double-crosses leon
ahm...screek, screek...were all ears
imagine a person with no head and just ears...it's easy to see one ear but two...what would hold them together...super glue...epoxy...horizontal gravity...but i digress...screech screech...problems

Note: Commanding voice, intimidating, absurd—almost mordant—sense of humor. Ryker?

black...screech...tar
excellent...excellent...cody...the tar not a problem its cutting it...com-prende...capeche...got it...two street kids ODed last weeks... that's ten
dint you and her have that covered

Her?
Who? Her = Maddy?

boom...boom...screech...told you dont mention her...low profile

shes why were doin' it...right

yeah...but lets get on with the play...think ahm taking too much clyde

right...course your taking too much

...hah, hah, hah....honesty among thieves...i may be taking a lot but your making more money than before i took over...i think well keep the same cuts

clump, clump, clump...tap...TAP...TAP...TAP

what about a guy who... bad black tar

tap...TAP...TAP...THUD

pop...pop...pop

What the fuck was that? Shots? Silencer?

everybody sit down...screech screech...necessary...oscar...screech...he's been skimming heavy...course you all do...your fucking criminals...you started filching dollars from your grandma's purse...i dont expect it to stop...but you cant take too much...we need a scapegoat...oscar will be found with some not much black tar on him and we will circulate the rumor he was the main dealer

yeah...but oscar was our pal

nobodys your pal...youre your pal...cant count on anybody else here... doggie on doggie

but Ryke...

pal...hah...gotta be ready to go over the edge

yeah...we know about your edge

well we're gone move the line...we're expanding...were going to take over the loin

Note: Edge? Loin???

Jack turned off the live feed and sent the rest to tape

Jack's stomach knotted. He retrieved a bottle of Jack Daniel's from the nook, took the cap off, drank, and put the cap back on. The hot wash from the whiskey couldn't mask what he'd heard.

Her. Edge.

The SRO, a mystery itself, a murder, and a grandiose plan to take over the Loin.

Problem: Had he done that scene before? It was familiar. Ouroboros?

Or was he projecting his scene on a real one?

Again.

* * *

The rest of the tape didn't tell him much, except that they mentioned a tall blond guy who came into the SRO and took pictures, and a woman who photoed the building and asked questions in bars!

Great. They knew about him and they knew about Talia. And, of course, he'd just witnessed a murder remotely. What to do, what to do...

fucked totally fucked and who was her

Later, Phisto found something from the Bug tape. It was the phrase *who am I* uttered by Cody and the word *play*. Why would he wonder who he was? Was it a play? It was almost as if he was asking what character he would play. Scenario: Maddy goes back to her true anarchist self, gives readings in the Tenderloin and meets Ryker, a criminal (that fits with what Mike said), and they're mutually fascinated with each other. Ryker fascinated by Maddy's anarchism, Maddy fascinated with a sociopathic criminal.

The rest was easy to suss out. Ryker visited her in Point City, and Maddy came up with the insane idea of disappearing. And Ryker thought it was a lark. They both planned it, salted Raquel, Emma, George, and Mike into her narrative, then she made her grand exit. After that, she retreated to the city, to the Tenderloin, to Ryker...

...and the hoax had fooled Phisto. Phisto had said the characters were holding back

...and he'd followed the clues like Sherlock with his magnifying glass

...and here he was.

If she wanted to disappear, why lead him on? Why play a last game?

Answer: She was Maddy. She may not know what she wants ultimately, spiritually, but he knew how she wanted to be in the world.

A mystery...except.

It was too pat.

Too, what was the word: staged.

247

(51)

March!

She may be stalled, wondering, lost, but time lurched on.

One year or nothing.

She'd done the calculation. Maddy disappeared on March 15, the Ides. That was the end, the punch line. The *One year or nothing.*

She needed time to think. To think about art. To think about Maddy. To think about Carol.

* * *

Day trip, Bodega Bay...okay, it was nice, refreshing, but too open.

Talia—white top, blue Capri pants, open-toed sandals—strolled down the winding dirt path through the bluff wildflowers, the footsteps of spring, delicate pink hanging bells of wild currant, hug-earth golden meadow foam, charming baby blue eyes...deep orange California poppies. Edge of the world, curve of bay, loons swimming, diving in tandem, flocks of western gulls banking, landing in unison on an overturned boat.

She had mussels and fries in a local restaurant, the Sea Breeze, and mused about how far she was from Point City, the Tenderloin. Those ambiguous props would fade if she took another long trip, if she displaced herself. Eons ago, she'd slept with a guy, Jeffry, blond, blue-eyed, rugged, and immature, who told her that whenever a woman got serious, he moved. He called it his geographical exit. Fascinating. Cool. Bye-bye, Jeffry. Why get serious and watch someone scuttle into alleys or halfway across the country to avoid you?

course i realized later i did the same fucking thing no not moving that was radical but distance spiritual psyche distance it made jeffry honest but still a dick

248

She had too many getaways lately. Getting away with Carol, far away and deep. Getting away to Bodega. Getting away.

Why did she feel better getting away?

* * *

Early the next morning, she rented a small U-Haul in San Rafael, drove to Oakland, and took the first step towards going down her Carol-inspired path by rescuing her collages, prints, and oils from Oakland's Store Now.

She drove to Carol's to tell her what she was doing. She was about to get out when she saw Carol come out with a slightly short, attractive young man with buzz-cut, fair hair, one arm bare, the other full of tattoos. They were walking towards Carol's detached studio hand-in-hand.

what did i expect i know little about her life its like the people in the tenderloin what do i really know about their lives

* * *

Talia made an especially strong coffee and found her Rembrandt mug as a goad to creativity.

She stared at the mess of half-finished paintings, collages, and prints. Some would go upstairs, some would stay down here, some would go into the studio, her new studio.

She walked through the kitchen into the Line. It looked like an office, was an office, she supposed. Headset, computer, a wall full of photos, a huge map with a bunch of colored string, and photos and names blotting out the images of buildings, churches, police stations.

Wouldn't mean a lot to most people. If she'd seen it for the first time, it wouldn't mean a lot to her. But it meant something: it was a summation of her life for a time.

The Tenderloin would always be there. The places on the Map would shift, the names change, the people, but the Tenderloin would always be there. Talia started unpinning the threads on the Map. There goes the black thread from

Maddy's flyers to a building on Leavenworth. There goes the red thread from Ryker to a building and Ryker to Maddy, and there goes a yellow thread to a street corner on Hyde. The threads hung down like Rastafarian braids.

Finally she unhooked the threads from the photos and took down the Map. A week ago, she'd invited Edna in for a drink and told her what she planned. Edna had looked at the photos and the Map and smiled, as if she had finally placed Talia, placed what she was about, why she did what she did. Edna said she'd decided to volunteer in the Tenderloin a couple times a week. She asked about the Map.

tag ednas new path my old one way of the world

Talia carefully rolled up the Map and placed it on her desk.

She didn't take down the photos; they were important in a way she couldn't express. She'd take them down later, not all at once. There were some she'd keep. She plucked out Maddy's flyers and dropped them in the wastebasket with the pile of string.

Talia sat in her easy chair and turned on the stereo. She didn't know what was playing. The stacked collages made her think of a print of a collage Jack had in his living room.

Oz. It was more than a collage. It meant a lot to a lot of people. But for Jack, or Maddy? She remembered staring at it after seeing Jack's show. Maddy was leaving but with a hint of death, of teenagers on a highway.

Kay.

Still, why leave a mystery?

There was no mystery about Talia walking away from the Line. Of course there were a few loose personal threads to deal with.

(52)

Show turmoil—evolution; revolution; back talk. Fast sorties into the city and fast backtracking, strolling through the mystery SRO, listening to the thugs' meeting and hearing a murder; he needed an escape, but he couldn't leave... he knew he was close. The tape ran through his head serially, and over all of it were the words: rat-tat-tatting into his skull. A...year...or...nothing.

And he couldn't escape the feeling that he'd created the mystery. Did reality run into the Show, or did the Show run into reality?

Maddy said once that one day he'd never know.

He started thinking of the last Mouse hallucination. There was something peaceful about what Mouse did, about settling in on the floor, his head encased in fungal flickers. It was the neural snake, the fantastic characters, Jick, his nemesis, Maddy, and, finally, his neural image pixelating, dissolving into wavering repetition, seeing himself seeing himself projecting himself. It was a game, a metaphysical game. It gave you control. You knew exactly what was going to happen. And if you know that, why not repeat it *ad infinitum*?

Is it time for another psychedelic holiday? He had a mushroom left. He could talk to Mouse, although that was chancy. He couldn't control Mouse. Mouse was his unregulated alter, a furry Jick. At least he thought so. Mouse could help him. But had Mouse disappeared?

Or died.

How long did mice live? A year, two maybe, three? His mouse was fully grown, so it was likely dead.

Was it possible Mouse was normalcy, a touchstone? A guide?

some normalcy am i kidding myself will hesheit come

Jack sat at the kitchen table and munched the last 'room. While he waited for the fungus to wrap around his neurons, he nursed a tall glass of tonic water. He and Maddy liked mushrooms, but she decided after a too-long trip that she didn't need mushrooms to hallucinate; they led hallucinatory lives. The psychedelic band tightened around his head; then his head began to expand and reality dripped, dripped, dripped.

Naturally, that's when Mr. Mouse scrambled up and perched on the tip of his sandal. It was the drug, wasn't it? Mouse came out when he tripped into immobility, when he couldn't react.

old yellow light old mellow light ole pixeled light

Show melt. Oblivion. Who cares about Maddy? Who cared about watching a conscious simulacrums exposing themselves, making demands, telling him what to do? His brilliant Show, brilliant creations, were repetitive, boring.

Okay Mouse, spill it.

tripping mouse not real i use mouse as a sounding board a bored to have have a real conversation a foil to embroil toil toil toil and trouble

"Hey, Jack-boy, over here!" Mouse, walking upright, lecturing, a furry professor.

"See, Jack, you're in this state because you're two nanometers from total solipsism, which is a hallucination of the *ego*. Shit, didn't Maddy tell you that? Didn't she say that someday you'd pick up your bags, check your wallet, grab a couple joints, and pile yourself into Phisto, or Phisto's latest iteration, call it the Show, and never come out, or come back, or just come?"

Mouse hopped into the U of his ankle, scrambled up his pants leg, up to his crotch, and jumped neatly onto the table, swished his tail twice, turned, and stared back.

"Don't say anything. Sit and listen. Nix Show. Get out there. You captured the Tenderloin, walked through that weird SRO. You think you did it for the Show, but reality never conforms to our expectations. Good start, good start. Get out. Don't stop."

Jack stared at Mouse. He opened his mouth, but no words came out.

Mouse: "Maybe, if you get out of the Show...you'll find Maddy!"

what what

"What? What's that, Jack? Of course she's alive. Of course she's waiting for you in the Tenderloin. Of course she had help from the big guy, Mr. Big, Head Honcho, King de Loin, top o' heap. Lord you can be dense."

252

what

"Articulate, Jack, articulate."

am articooolaaatin

"What was that? Who is she? I'll field this one: she is Salome, Judith, Cleo, Minerva, Sphinx, Medusa, Brunhilde, Kali. She's all of them, and none. Your problem is that you stuck around. You thought there was a key. You thought you could open her up and reveal her secrets. No, wait. This is better. You thought there *was* a secret!"

what no secret

"Slow down, Jack. You'll break your brain. Besides finding a key to a phantom secret, you fought back. So there was only one thing left, one thing she could do to win. Because isn't that what competition is all about Jack— winning? Isn't that what Vince said?

so then she she blink blink blink ahhh

"One last thing, Jack. When you wake up, this tape will be destroyed. Oh, shit. Two last things. She's different, different than you remember. She got you, baby; she got you good. How do you know I'm a real mouse? What if I'm just one of your bugs with a tail? Oh, shit, three things. Yes, she's in the Tenderloin and she's waiting for you. You know, you need a conclusion, a denouement, possibly a catharsis.

"Mouse off."

* * *

Jack lay his head on the table. Out of his right eye, he saw *Oz*, the hole. Mouse disappeared into the hole. He expected that. He didn't expect...

...The neurons, it's all in the neurons...and the Show. He wanted Maddy, not alien worlds, not massive battles, not end-o-world zombies, not a Nook and Raquel, not Emma and her Jesus, not any of them. Sure they call; sure they call loudly.

Sure.

The Show speeds through the brain and he tries to stop it, but it still projects on the background; it merges with reality. They merge out of sync; glowing pixels bind the backgrounds, the reverb voices...pixels everywhere.

Walking down the hallway: rooms open, Mozart, meetings, kids...why, oh why? The rooms huddled together, narrowed, and he walked towards the end... there was one room left...open it, Jack! Go on! She's behind that door...

...a golden trail...

Oz!

Racing, racing along a golden trail, a yellow trail...just like Oz...there it is! Emerald City!...no, no...it's another road, yellow, broken, brick...there she is! C'mon, stay there! See I'm reaching for you. But you're nothing but pixels, glowing pixels...

...and another road...and

No! Not again!

Jack watched himself watching the Show.

Jack was watching himself project the Show, watching Jick...and watching Raquel and Emma and George and Mike pixel away...and Maddy...watching Maddy fade...to...pixels...pixels...pixels

me watching me watching hi maddy what a trip huh what a game whata competition just like the old days just like we used to spar and fend and retreat and attack i i i me watching hey look im watching me watching

A warm cloud enveloped Jack.

Maddy floated in and out of the cloud. She was on the bright yellow 14 Mission, turning slowly towards him, doubling her image in the window, in the loft, in bed, pale legs scissored, mischievous smile. She spread her lean legs, and through them she beckoned...."Come, let's play. You've always wanted to play. Let's have a game...

...a real game."

(53)

The Line was gone, the thread down, Maddy's flyers down, the Map down... the Map passed to Edna and replaced with her favorite collage. Long live those who help despite the odds. The only thing that remained were the photos of people who called. Or rather, stand-in photos of those people. She imagined what most of them were like, imagined they were ratty, shambling, holes in sneakers, trodden, drunk, high, or sad, tearing, despairing. She made stereo-types out of them; maybe art was like that too.

A Net search revealed the Emerald was the mystery SRO on Ellis, the meet-ing place of thugs, prostitutes, kids, trannies, and businessmen and women. What did it mean?

Let's see, the Ides. Oz. Emerald City. Maddy...Jack...and Ryker.

and fuck me   talia   guess i left one last string pinned to the map

* * *

It was a sunny spring day, Point City full of light. There was a steady stream of cars and bikes on Main. People stopped in front of the post office and chatted, gestured, laughed. She hadn't thought about it lately, but her quaint retreat was starting to feel homey, solid. She could get used to it.

But first, clean up the clutter. She was sure Jack knew the name of the SRO, but she was going to tell him anyway. The second floor was ablaze with light, as it had been for the last few months. She felt a brief sense of loss about...

...Jack's virtual characters

...which—who?—had become part of her. It was time to cinch it off, but it also felt like a loss, that part of her consciousness was being snipped off.

She rang the bell, stepped back, and waited.

Jack opened the door slowly.

"I have something to tell you. It won't take long."

Jack looked tired, spent. "Come in."

Jack gestured towards the oak table. "I'm having a Perrier; want one?"

"Thanks."

Jack rummaged in the refrigerator, found Perriers, popped the tops, and set one in front of Talia.

He sat down wearily, then chuckled. "I know you've seen the Show."

Talia frowned. "I guessed you knew. You don't care?"

Jack shrugged. "I cared once. But you've seen it, end of story. What do you think?"

"It's fantastic, brilliant, and scary."

Jack took a sip of water, placed the bottle on the table, crossed his arms, frowned. "Scary?"

Talia took a sip of water. "Isn't it the ultimate intrusion to know what people think, or what they think *in extremis*?"

Jack shrugged. "Has it changed what you think of those people?"

"A few surprises. Not much. I'd already seen their tendencies."

"But hadn't acted on them. That's the difference."

"They haven't hurt anyone, can't hurt anyone."

"True, but they've changed."

"I didn't see much. How?"

"Mostly they weren't happy. Since they found each other, it's better."

Talia frowned. "Found each other?"

"Raquel found them and got them together. It seemed they all needed someone like themselves to talk to, to interact with."

thats why they disappeared

"Why weren't they happy?"

"Different reasons. Raquel wanted somebody to talk to. Emma wanted to be with Jesus but couldn't. George was unhappy with what he did to Edna and can't get her avatar back. I think Mike is the happiest. He likes the monotony of playing the same murderous games over and over." Jack smiled ruefully. "I suppose you could say I aided and abetted him by creating those games."

"At least they can change. Are you going to leave them alone?"

Jack shook his head, thought for a second, then said, sorrowfully, "They're starting to degrade, some parts haven't been replaced. I think their memories and consciousness will eventually disappear. I've thought of pulling the plug."

Talia took a sip of Perrier, placed it carefully on the table. "Can't you do anything to help them?"

Jack sighed. "I didn't make them; Phisto did. Phisto is looking for a remedy but hasn't found one. I doubt it will. There's a power problem and bugs, but there are too many programs, too many subroutines, too much code. Like us, in a sense."

Talia shook her head. "They are real...in a sense." Talia hesitated, then said, "Did you do me?"

"No."

"Good. I wouldn't want to see it, but I'd have to. Enough about your creations. What about your search for Maddy? What about March 15?"

"Tonight. The punch line. I think it's in that hotel."

Talia: "You know the name of the hotel?"

Jack leaned back in his chair. "The Emerald. I finally had Phisto do a search of San Francisco SROs. They named a bunch of SROs after gems. I suppose you found out too."

"Maddy, Oz, the journey, Emerald City." Talia gestured towards *Oz*, which blazed in reflected light. "That print."

Jack said, wearily, "I know."

"You don't sound positive."

Jack glanced at the print, grinned, nodded. He leaned back in his chair and looked at the ceiling. "I have the game, the competition, the puzzle, my characters. I know it, but I don't know what I'm going to find. More lack of control. And if I find Maddy, I'm not sure what I'll find or what to say. Maybe it's over. Maybe I should have left it like that."

"You won't know if you don't go."

Jack took a drink of Perrier. "I've been through too much with all this. It's not just Maddy's hoax, creating my virtual characters, or Point City. I'm trying to figure out what's next, and I have to know if Maddy's going to be part of it." Jack paused for a second, rubbed the white inverted scimitar on the bridge of his nose, then said, "You're just as obsessed as I am. Wanna go along?"

Talia said, "I thought it was over. I wanted to leave it like that. When?"

"Tonight, eight."

"How do you know the time?"

"We met on the Ides, March 15 around 8, on the 14 Mission. I could be wrong."

Talia, getting up, "I'll vacillate, but I'll be there."

$$* \quad * \quad *$$

Late afternoon, Talia got her swim clothes together and walked outside.

She sat in the Toyota for a minute, fingering the keys before getting out and slamming the door. She walked up Highway 1, turned and walked back through town.

She strolled by the Café con Vache. Emma shutting down, walleyed and sour, as usual, the coffee the usual French for the masses.

good luck with jesus

A few minutes later, she stared in the window of the Nook. Raquel looked up from her desk and waved, jiggling her bracelets. She waved too, but...

the digital raquel is not that different from the real one maybe a little kookier   maybe more adventurous

She strolled by the Barn, waved to Edna.

cant tell ya   but watch out for georgie porgie

She hesitated outside the Dog, then pushed through the swinging doors. The Dog was almost empty, a construction worker aimlessly shooting the cue ball on an empty table, a spandexed biker nursing a beer and a glass of water.

Mike smiled at her, came over. "Little early for you."

"Yep."

"You haven't been in lately. The Line keeping you busy?"

"Kinda." She rested her elbows on the bar top. "Look Mike, let's cool it for a while. I'm going through a bunch of shit right now, and I have to keep my head on."

Mike placed his hand on her elbow. "You sure lose your head with me."

She shook off his hand. "Sure do. How are the games?"

Mike looked puzzled. "Good. Jack came over a few weeks ago, and—"

"Later."

She felt Mike staring at her as she left. Shit, didn't it all start in the Dog? One day, Jack and a posse of characters stroll into a bar and...

258

(54)

Jack roughly scrubbed his wet hair, toweled off his back, and threw on his blue robe. Wisps of steam followed him out of the bathroom. He walked by the Stage and computer room without a glance and walked deliberately down the stairs, grimacing slightly at the coffee stain on the carpet. Ten minutes later, he sat on the sofa and crossed his legs on the cushioned camel saddle. He tasted the coffee and set the mug down on the end table. He flipped on the stereo from the remote and used his cell to turn on Schumann's *Fantasie*.

The Ides.

The Emerald.

Room 315.

Eight o'clock.

Talia was right; the only way to tell, to find out, to settle it, was to go to the Emerald.

His mind was a storm of competing ideas: his digital characters, now a loose group starting to fade away; his final go-round with Mouse and Mouse's multiple admonitions; and, of course, the last chapter of his quest, Maddy, a bald thug, a gang, a mysterious SRO.

The images of the Tenderloin tracked him from room to room and, last night excepted, lay like a stone on his heart. The mystery SRO, the shots heard remotely in the safety of his lounger...those events brought a sinister reality to the Show. Maybe we play these games as long as we can, play with our ideas, our fears, our feelings, and before you know it, the game has merged with reality. He'd thought that about most of his games when he would walk outside and project his game on whatever reality presented itself. But Tenderloin grittiness defied abstraction. He felt impelled to do something, to act, as if he and the game had leaked into reality.

or reality had finally leaked into my game

* * *

259

"Monitor on, sound on. Ryker."

There he was in his black running suit. His back, his gleaming bald head. Something about the way he moved.

"Phisto."

"Yeah, Jack."

"Merge Ryker, meeting room."

"You got it."

The images mixed, blurred, resolved. It took time for the images to clarify.

"Phisto?"

"Yep."

"Why did the merging take so long?"

"I'm not sure, Jack. Everything seems slower."

Jack's brow furled; he shook his head. "Shit."

Ryker, Meeting Room, the Last Call. Let's see, they left the Last Call together. What had they done after that? Let's see: Maddy moved to Marin. Maddy made her video. Maddy disappeared.

Ryker had helped her, and she was alive and living in the Tenderloin. It was the only thing that made sense. Sense? What didn't make sense was why. She could have come to him and said, "Jack, I want to live with this violent, tough criminal in the Tenderloin." And he would have...what would he have done?

And why the game, the competition? Why dangle the four characters in front of his nose? He supposed, finally, it was her puckish nature.

A puckish anarchist.

A question mark.

course im going wouldnt miss it all this stuff my digital folks the sleuthing this is the grand finale the twizzlers the world ending party wheres my mask

* * *

Jack walked slowly downstairs, filled a glass with tap water, and walked to the bench.

Edging into spring. The bench had felt like another place for the last few months. He could barely make out the twisty road that led to Invert and on to the coast. It was a slight intrusion into his marsh. Odd that he called it his marsh. He wondered if he, or anyone, could buy it. It happened all the time near the beach. Multimillionaires and billionaires flexing their muscles, trying to keep everyone out of their gilt space.

It wouldn't be the same. The marsh was like a story, an incomplete story, one that ended and renewed itself. It didn't need human interaction, but humans could destroy it. That was what was happening everywhere. Humanity asserting itself, procreating, protecting what they had, making their space safe.

He supposed that was what he'd done. Except he didn't hurt the world outside. Sure, he used electricity and had powerful components which used rare resources. When he thought of it, he was doing in a small way what the billionaires did. Keeping his little world going, regardless of who or what it meant in a larger picture.

greasing the downward spiral

(55)

Great swim. Great Jacuzzi. Exhilarating steam room.

Talia dressed slowly. Finding out about Maddy was intriguing, more than intriguing; she'd been obsessed with Maddy and Jack for months...and Jack's circus of digital characters.

She drove from the club to Van Ness and Ellis and found a place to park up Ellis. She stared at the distant blocks of the Tenderloin, unsure but determined. She walked past Chevy's. Chevy's brought up images of Adam and Dawn. Adam was dealing and had betrayed her.

betrayed   really

Dawn? She hoped she was making it, making it in whatever she wanted to do. At least she wasn't in the Tenderloin. Talia walked slowly by gated groceries, screaming drunks, kids, huddles of smokers, leaners against walls, and babblers babbling to ghosts.

Talia stopped at Hyde and Post. She stared towards the corner of Hyde and Geary, a block away. She saw a couple of her girls, probably Deb and Sheila. Deb, Jesus believer, believer in the afterlife, was being propositioned. She felt a desire to go down, tell them who she was, and make them see there was a body on the end of the line.

But no.

They had their job; they had to survive.

im from   a safer world   im a dabbler in theirs

Talia walked slowly, heedless of the people around her, who stared at her, who watched her. She saw Adam. He was in the shadow of a building, talking to someone. She watched him reach in his pack, bring something out, and surreptitiously hand it to a small, lean man, who hurried away.

Talia backtracked quickly and walked slowly towards the Emerald, still unsure she was going in. She walked past an alley but stopped, turned, and walked back.

He was heavier, bleary. She almost didn't recognize him. "Pete?"

"Mama Teresa."

"How are you?"

Pete shrugged. He was sitting, leaning against the wall of the alley, his thick hand circled around a brown paper bag. Not much change from the first time she saw him. Except his face was heavier, puffy, gray, his eyes dull.

"Where's Johnny?"

Pete shook his head slowly. "Dead. Lung cancer."

"Christ. I'm sorry." Talia hunkered down, balancing on her soles.

"Hell, he knew what was going to happen. Why give up what you like to last a few days more?"

"What about you?"

Pete laughed, shook his head. "I ain't getting out either."

"Neither am I. Can I get you anything?"

"Nope. I got enough for tonight. I play it by the hour."

Talia squeezed his shoulder, got up, walked to the front of the alley, turned and waved. She walked, head down, towards the Emerald.

ghosts tonight

* * *

Talia stared at The Last Call from the Viet Luc Coffee Shop. She'd watched Jack's partially obscured face for less than half an hour. She was early and so was he. She was lucky to see him when she walked down Ellis. She had no idea months ago she would end up staring at the blurry visage of a drawn-faced video game developer trapped in a death grip with his ex-girlfriend.

They both watched the Emerald, which was quiet that night. It appeared as if it were truly a closed and abandoned SRO, a relic, the almost-hidden passage on the side dark and impenetrable.

What is he seeing?

is he watching a show do we reach a point where despite our grip on reality we project the show inside on the world

263

Jack started and emerged quickly from the Last Call. What did he see? Talia hurried out of the coffee shop.

(56)

Light touched Jack's right cheek, deep in the shadow of the single window in the Last Call. Beyond the yellow tape, warning notices, and overall abandonment of the Emerald, the window framed the heavy boarded-up entrance of a decayed SRO.

Randy, the bartender, glanced at him every few minutes.

he knows what im doing he knows his image flickers

The Last Call at night was different than the day. The stage, likely used by second-rate performers and a first-rate poet, was darker and seemed as if it had never been used.

funny seems like a real stage perfect for a last act

The Last Call patrons were friendly when they came in, bantered with Randy, then collapsed into silence. A couple were pensioners and friends of Randy's. One was a loner who sipped a beer and stared at the defunct pinball. Fifteen minutes ago, a high-heeled, black-wigged, long-faced prostitute pranced in, sprawled over a barstool, ordered a coke, and picked at one of her black eyelashes. The juke had broken since Jack's last visit; now, fifties pop songs leaked from Randy's yellowed Magnavox.

ive done this scene before bar of blood bar flickering again

His props, a shot of Woodford and a beer chaser, were not the support he needed but were getting him in the mood. It was darker than when he came in, and the street was almost empty. Occasionally someone would scuttle into the grocery next door and scuttle out. He hadn't seen either Maddy or Ryker, although a few times he started when he saw a bald man or a small woman hurry by.

Maddy lived, he supposed, with Ryker, a criminal, violent, capable of killing someone and laughing, a stereotype malevolent joker. If she had coupled up with Ryker, why had she dangled Point City characters at him? He'd thought about it often, but sitting there staring at the hidden alley, it became a constant in his thoughts. Maybe she couldn't leave the competition, the game.

Of course, she'd talked about how she'd gotten away from her true nature, how she felt closer to people on the street who had made a genuine choice to reject society. He had largely discounted what she said. Look at the life they led in SoMa!

It was a few minutes to eight. Jack downed the last of the Woodford and the last drop of beer. He was about to get up when he saw them, or thought he saw them. Their image was blurry. They flickered, as if he were under a strobe. She faded in and out, hidden by Ryker's bulk.

They disappeared near the Emerald alley.

He hurried out of the Last Call. By the time he got to the alley, they were gone.

He felt a presence on his right, turned.

Talia.

(57)

The old man at the check-in desk looked up with tired eyes. He glanced at Jack then peered at Talia. "You *both* here for Dorothy?"

Jack stuttered, "What?"

"DOROTHY!"

Jack smiled, nodded his head. "Well, right. Of course."

"315."

"Yeah, I know."

dorothy

Jack turned to Talia. "Right so far."

Jack walked past the broken elevator, draped in yellow tape and warnings, and started slowly up the stairs.

Talia: "I can't imagine how she fixed all this."

Jack shook his head. "Neither can I. Narrow alley, Oz, Emerald, Dorothy/ Maddy, tie the big bow. It's vintage Maddy, and I still don't know why."

doesnt feel good

Two.

Rooms closed, floor silent. No voices, laughter, music, off-the-grid musicians, actors, sex workers, housing support groups, meditators.

i captured them they must be real

The images swam before his eyes, embedding in the locked doors. There they are. Mozart. Trannies. Homeless. Musk smell of sex. Acrid smell of pot. Jack snapped off his gaze.

how could she do this

Jack: "There were people here. Prostitutes, homeless, quartets. I have the capture."

Talia: "I suppose it must be real then."

Musty, dusty, rickety, old SRO. Tracks to three. Tennies. Boots. Faint gray ridges banking sides, like sawdust ridges in the Dog.

universes in the ridges   galaxies in the dust   trapped in interstices

Three.

305. Thug meeting room.

dusty table bugs bugs blood on table murder

Jack walked down the hallway, his steps slowing. So many games. The tension, the finale approaching, the hidden thugs, the big guns, the ducking hero. The final shootout, the triumphant hero, battle-scarred, muscular arm around the adoring princess.

315.

now dorothy now maddy now finale drums rolls leadins klaxons

Jack: "Here it is."

Talia: "It's bizarre, unreal, but doesn't seem dangerous."

Jack felt the floor moving, swirling...the hallway, the road pixels, pixelating. He reached out and pressed his hand into the doorframe. It was solid, old, curved. Real.

Talia: "You okay?"

Jack shook his head: "Now. Let's do it." He turned the door handle and pushed the door open.

Large room, dark, musty, dusty, except for a table, stuffed chairs, worn brass-tacked arms. A digital projector was in the middle of the table aimed at a wall full of cracks. The table had a bottle of Macallan scotch, water, a glass, and two bottles of Corona. A cell was perched in a cradle on the wall.

Jack worried, puzzled. "Funny. A party. We're missing the main act."

Talia gestured: "Read the note."

Jack leaned close to the projector, read: "Press the button, Jack."

is that good or not

A mouse flitted along the trim, stopped, glanced at the room, and disappeared in a hole underneath the cracked yellowed wall.

Jack said, "At least it didn't talk."

Jack reached over and pressed the button. The cell and projector came alive, a gong sounded, and an empty room bloomed on the wall. It seemed like a room from Ouroboros with four doorways leading into a circular room with soft dark draperies and soft dark sofas and chairs.

Maddy came through the doorway on the right, walked into the scene, and perched on the side of a sofa ...

..Cheshire grin

..Soul-sucking eyes

..White bare legs

..Blue-veined ankles

..Annabelle Lee or

..Sybil or

..Kali or..

Maddy: "Together again! The Ides! Hey, Jack. You look haggard. And this is your new girlfriend!"

Talia grimaced: "Hardly."

Maddy: "I was kidding, Talia. Welcome to the party."

Jack smiled. "I'm glad you're alive, but did we need the hoax, this game?"

Maddy laughed. "Ah, the game. You always believed that stuff about the competition, the arc. I just threw that out. Hey, look, I have a PBR! Just like the Mimic." Maddy laughed, tapped the can. It sounded hollow. "Except, I didn't feel like drinking. So it's just a prop."

i tried to imagine this scene a thousand times is it still a game

Talia: "Mine isn't hollow." She popped the top off a Corona and took a swig.

Jack screwed the top off the Macallan and poured an inch into a glass,

269

added a little water. "Tying everything in a neat bow. Okay, let's have it. Why the video, the disappearance, the elaborate charade?"

Maddy sat on the sofa, crossed her legs, and leaned back. She looked skeptical. "I'm not sure why, precisely. I guess it comes down to a last flourish, maybe personality. It was part charade and part important. I guess the charade masked the importance."

whats behind her shes doubling tripling pixelating so many maddys

Jack closed his eyes to stop the images. "I played along and here I am. I guess you got what you wanted."

Maddy chuckled. "You guess, or not?"

"After a point, it was hard to believe the game was real."

"Why be tentative, Jack? Jack, are you projecting? Are you in a scene?"

Jack laughed, smiled. "Sometimes projecting reality makes sense."

She laughed. "Well, I suppose it kept you occupied. Company sold, employees scattered, Maddy gone. Shit, what else did you have?"

quit crowding all you maddys please

Jack laughed, ran his hand through his hair, shook his head dismissively. "I had a lot I could have done. It wasn't what I needed...or wanted."

"But you did it. That's important."

"And the real reason?" Jack took a gulp of scotch and leaned back in his chair.

cant help looking at her glad shes alive quit thinking quit the show

Maddy stared at him, smiling. She was calm, but a troubling frown flicked across her face. Was she really the Maddy of the infamous video or the Maddy of her reputation?

why is she flickering its the old maddy then its not

Maddy smiled, crossed her arms. "What was I doing, or rather thinking, staring out the window through my reflection on the 14 Mission?"

Jack shrugged. "No idea."

"I was thinking about my sister, my twin."

Jack: "There's more than one of you?"

"That would be too much. Reflections, mirrors everywhere. Well Max, short for Maxine, was not identical. She'd died a week earlier, complications of early Alzheimer's."

Jack sat up. "What? Alzheimer's? Is this a joke?"

"'Fraid not. It runs in my family. I have the gene. It's not certain, of course. It's just percentages."

Jack fumbled with his drink, spilling some on his pants. "But—"

"I saw you...and your camera. I knew who you were, and on the spur of the moment, I decided I needed a diversion to get me out of a lingering depression."

"Why me?"

"I didn't know what would happen that night. I guessed, rightly, you'd be my opposite: brash, unconcerned about reality, abstract, hubristic. It started as a lark, a game, if you will, and it took me right out of my funk."

what should i do flicker flicker stay with the show stay with the real

Jack narrowed his eyes: "So, you used me. I was a holding pattern."

"Hey, I didn't expect you to come to the reading at Books, Inc. When you did, I decided to extend the game. Shit, it could have ended any time. But, oddly, it turned out to be unexpectedly exciting, a good life, a fun life. If it's any consolation, I felt something in you right away that I liked."

Jack took a long drink of scotch, felt the flush, looked at Talia.

Talia, hesitantly: "Do you know if it's started?"

Maddy smiled, shook her head: "Don't know, but I started forgetting lines, pausing, and I started performing in smaller places, out-of-the-way places. Jack was too occupied with selling PhistoCo to notice."

Jack nodding. "Out-of-the-way places in the Tenderloin."

"I tried to be cavalier. Here I am, the old Maddy. Watch me! Watch me entrance you! Wake up! Listen! Learn!" Maddy shook her head, chagrined.

"It hasn't happened yet. If it does, I won't know. All the worry happens before the fact, like death."

* * *

Talia edged back in her chair, felt a loose tack on the arm. The projector, the drinks, the image of Maddy flickering in the multi-doored room was a set on the third floor of an old SRO. She couldn't imagine she'd ever be here. Somehow none of them should be here. This abandoned SRO was once for the workers and the old, the homeless, the runaways, not the endgame for Jack and Maddy. Thinking of what they'd done made her angry. Despite what might happen to Maddy, they were still playing at life, making it a game.

Maddy crossed her arms over her breasts. She looked as if she were sorting her thoughts. "I spent most of my time in P.C. wondering what to do, wondering about the last five years and about Jack, whether he could see anything beyond his games and our faux competition. Sure, people say they have to be with someone even when they're sick, but do they really, or is it just an act?"

Talia: "We can never tell."

Maddy: "I thought about that in P.C. It was calmer, easy, and I thought about what I was going to do, about what road I would take, and especially about *Oz*. Of course in our tale, the yellow road is a vanishing trail, and the Emerald City is death." Maddy laughed. "But let's not ruin our collective fantasy."

Talia took a sip of her Corona, set it down on the table and said, angrily, "*Oz* is a nice story, but your video was real. And Raquel, Emma, George, and Mike, and your disappearance. You played with reality for a strung-out joke."

Maddy sighed. "You're right, of course. It's complicated, but isn't life like that? The short answer is that after months of living in P.C., I still wasn't sure how I felt or what to do."

Jack put the glass up to his eye and watched Maddy's image elongate. "So you left a trail, a gauntlet thrown daring me to find you."

Maddy laughed. "Not really. You see there weren't any clues."

Jack frowned: "What?"

"Sure I got the idea of leaving in March with the Ides coming up."

Talia: "What about the four people? What about Raquel, Emma, George, and Mike?"

Maddy frowned. "What about them?"

Jack: "Didn't they have clues? Didn't you put clues in your conversations?"

Maddy laughed. "I just mentioned the four because I was interested in them, and they were the last people I saw that day."

"But they had clues. They saw Ryker, a truck, and heard about a troupe, this SRO."

Maddy: "Even if they saw or overheard Ryker, it couldn't have helped you. There weren't any clues. You made them up; you made your own narrative. I suppose Talia did too."

Jack, thoughtfully: "I see. What if I didn't find you?"

"I didn't want you to find me. I wanted a year to see how I was, to think about what I wanted."

"And what was going to happen after a year?"

Maddy: "I wasn't sure."

cant help it shes doubling again tripling

The tape filled the room, flashing over Maddy, Talia, the desk, the projector, pixels, pixels.

..Maddy in the Mimic
..Maddy in the loft
..Maddy in bed black hair snarled white limbs spread
..Maddy at Halloween black cape red horns
..Maddy pixelating
..Maddy drifting away down an endless yellow road
..Find reality
..Pull a tooth
..Bite your lip
..Make it back

make it back jack make it back jack

Jack shook his head. The tape faded and encircled his mind, leaving a glowing residue.

∗ ∗ ∗

Talia frowned. "Okay, what about this place, Ryker and his posse of thuglings?"

Maddy laughed. "Ryker is a friend, and I lived with him when I returned. Your Mr. Bad Guy is a gay ex-con turned actor. We met at a performance in the Last Call. He knew about Jack from me, and he knew about you from your shooting the Emerald. Somehow it all fit, the Emerald, the time of year."

Talia placed her empty Corona on the table, and said, dubiously, "Is everyone an actor?"

Maddy uncrossed her legs and crossed them right over left. She ran her hands through her thick black hair and let the hair fall about her neck. "Might as well give you the full monty. Some of the people who use the Emerald as rehearsal space knew Jack had captured it and told Ryk. When he found Jack was interested in Room 305, we decided to set up this rendezvous. A lot of what we did, the Room 305, the skit of a thug meeting, a killing, was ad hoc... and it fit together with the Ides, the year, the few times the Emerald opens as a performance/meeting/hang-out space."

Talia. "Amazing. Charades in a charade."

Maddy: "Charades in games and games in charades...you can stretch that metaphor like silly putty."

she doesnt seem affected   maybe i would feel the same way   do the same thing

* * *

Serial images danced over Maddy's face. She absorbed them all. She was them all. All a jumble. Jumbles of Maddys.

Jack stared blankly at the wall under Maddy's image. It was scarred with deep ridges. And lower, it was indented, as if it had been kicked in. An old SRO, a still viable SRO, a hidden SRO, rehearsal space. Maddy was part of a play in an old SRO. If it wasn't a joke, if it happened, how long would she know him? Everything fit in the jigsaw. Her wanting to be alone. The possible changes, her toughest competitor, everything she said to the four people in Point City, the *Oz* collage, the solitary Dorothy, the narrowing yellow road, the dead teenagers.

A stream of images played out on the wall. Maddy and his digital characters flickering, flickering on the wall, dropping, dripping, pixelating. Where's Mouse? Shouldn't he be here?

Maddy: "So, did you use the four I mentioned to find me?"

Jack took another sip of scotch: "It was a brilliant exercise; you don't know how brilliant."

Maddy frowned. "Intriguing. What?"

"You won't believe it. Phisto used untested AI programs and created conscious characters."

Maddy laughed. "You're right, I don't believe it."

Talia: "I didn't believe it either until I saw them."

Maddy, dubious: "Okay, lets say they're conscious. Did they help you? There weren't any clues. If there was an answer, it was in what I talked to them about, about what they couldn't acknowledge or escape from. They made me look deeper into my soul."

Jack: "I learned more about them than I wanted, but it didn't help me find you. What did you find buried in the recesses of your soul?"

Maddy grinned. "It's funny. Maybe I've been channeling you. I looked at all my Maddys, both before I met you and later and discovered I liked the one in the Mimic, the old Maddy, the performing Maddy. And I decided I was going to play myself as long as I could. Life is too precious to moon about death." Maddy paused, thought. "And I decided, finally, I liked you. What do you say to another five years?"

Jack laughed. "Another five-year plan, followed by another disappearance?"

Maddy frowned. "Maybe four years, maybe six. I don't know. I won't disappear on purpose."

Jack shrugged. "I'm not sure."

Maddy smiled, pensive. "Well, Jack. I guess this is the start of another game. I landed in Zagreb, Yugoslavia. I spend most of the day at a certain café. You should be able to find me easily, especially if you use Phisto…if you want to." Maddy laughed, "Quite an ending, n'est-ce pas? We act as if we're immortal, but then life catches up with us. It caught up with me. It made me think about what might happen.

"In a sense, we're all outside observing, but you took it to another level. I thought at one time you preferred the digital world to this one. The digital world is finite, controllable. In a sense, we all want that. We want to know we're in control. Unfortunately, as you can see here, the world out there is unremitting, unforgiving, uncontrollable.

"Will I slip over an edge in the next few years? I don't know and I don't care. I guess when I fall, I'll never know I'm falling or when I've hit bottom."

(58)

It was like being in Jack's show. Jack and Maddy...but more. Jack seemed to be a projection of himself, or as if he were projecting reality.

Maybe that was one of his goals. Maybe that was the impossible he was striving for.

Otherwise, he seemed dazed.

It looked like Maddy kept pulling him back, but he kept lapsing into a daze as if it were part of a competition he didn't quite understand.

what would i do i understand maddy better   maddy before   the screaming poet anarchist   the way she was   the way she might be   half there

Talia dreamed after a while, seeing Room 315 and the Jack/Maddy dialog (competition?) as a shimmering ghost skit, a never-to-be-repeated drama. Not like the dramas she saw outside in the shabby reality of the Tenderloin. Finally Maddy walked through one of the four doorways, the screen went blank, and Jack reached over and turned off the projector. Jack got up and walked wearily towards the door, and she got up and followed him. She walked slowly in back of him, and when she got to the reception, he was gone, and all she had was his fading image. That's what she had: images, ghosts.

Outside, the old man smiled and said, "Show's over. Time to lock up."

* * *

On her way to the car, Talia pulled down as many flyers as she found. She had a momentary pause when she thought people who found a flyer she'd missed and tried the number. Was she betraying them? They had other options, and most of them called to have relevance...and finally, what difference did she make?

ill miss talking to them   talking was important   for them and me

Maddy, Jack.

Pity?

Are all emotions about yourself? You see yourself in the person pitied. You're pitying yourself through them. No. She didn't want to think pity was self-reference.

Maddy said she finished poems since she made her decision to keep writing, to keep being herself.

what if i had it   would i continue to paint like dali and de kooning to show i could to prove that i could to show people what it was like to be like that   what was the alternative   waiting

* * *

Had Carol initiated her change, told her what was going to happen, at least hinted at what was going to happen, just like Maddy described their arc to Jack? What makes a decision anyway?

what if carol has other lovers   i have   had   mike

Talia: "I thought you should know I'm going to start Talia, take x."
Carol laughed. "Which means?"
"Art, sex with friends."
Carol laughed again. "Am I still a friend?"
Talia, nervously: "At least."
"Promising. What are you doing now?"
"Recovering from the end of a story."
Carol: "Sounds like you need a glass."
"I do, but do you?"
"Don't be coy. I'll ice the Chardonnay."
Talia: "Please be real."
"I'm always real."

was that the start of a new improved me   maybe one of me will know

(59)

Roll 'em.
   ..the 14 Mission
   ..the Ides
   ..the playtime years in SoMa
   ..the month-long escapes
   ..the video
   ..Raquel and Emma and George and Mike
   ..the search
   ..the readings
   ..the Emerald
   ..finally he saw it
   ..finally it made sense
   ..finally.
Everything in the tape led lockstep to the end.

we look back and find inexorability   we look for fate

Maddy.
He didn't understand until he got back, lying in bed, watching the ceiling, seeing Maddy imprinted on the ceiling instead of the Show.
Alzheimer's.
It pressed him into the bed, bound his head in gauze. He tried not to understand, to think it a joke, a continuing joke, a joke in a competition.
But it wasn't.
She seemed herself, intelligent, lucid, but all his digital characters thought she was different, had changed. And he saw something, some slight hitch in her delivery, some slight thing that wasn't there before. Whatever it was, age, simple mistakes...or the beginning of Alzheimer's, it robbed their time of timelessness.

* * *

Funny about the house. He'd never seen it before. He'd never actually imagined Maddy in it, although that was the reason he bought it. Kitchen, Stage, computer room, bedrooms. He'd walked through those arid spaces in a daze, in the Show, with his characters, or digging through images of the Tenderloin, talking to Mouse. It was as if he hadn't lived there.

But he did have things to do, to tie everything up, tie it up in a neat bow, tie up the past.

He supposed it was one way to forget.

or pretend ive forgotten

It was a fine spring day. The sun reflecting off the marsh. The marsh itself was coming into its glory, growing, greening, teeming.

The living room was full of light.

Jack wrapped up the capture camera and stored it.

Time to test reality.

Jack walked down Manzanita and turned towards the Café con Vache. He bumped into a few people on the broken sidewalk, apologized.

Real.

There's Raquel in the Nook, arm on a woman, joking. Raquel stared at him for a second, then waved. Raquel shifted slightly.

Not an image, not a tape.

Emma. Busy. A bandage around her index finger. Good.

George. Scowling. Fine.

Mike. Waving him in. No.

not for a long time

* * *

Jack hesitated outside the Stage. He rubbed his new beard and threaded his blond hair between his fingers. He'd grown fond of his irascible characters, and they would soon face their own crisis.

what should i do about them

An idea had nagged at him since he saw his characters were degrading: pull the plug.

It was only a matter of time that their consciousness, their precious aliveness would go too. If he pulled the plug, that world would blip out of existence. His characters wanted to live, but what did that mean? What kind of life did they have? Bouncing around video games, walking through a staged Point City and Point Reyes shorelines, watching their bodies' colors flicker and change...and degrade?

He hadn't thought it before, but his digital characters were under the same time constraints we are.

The power might go off anyway. Or it had to go off sometime. They wouldn't know. They would simply cease to exist. If exist was the right word.

He picked up the power cord, pulled it taut. He felt the smooth covering. The gray plug strained. He pulled it a little tauter. A little yank. No one would know.

Jack dropped the cord and hung his head.

i knew i couldnt do it theyre alive in some sense theyll have to go away like we do

* * *

One last peek.

Jack flipped on the monitor and clicked on Present. Raquel wasn't in the Nook but he found her in Ouroboros. He found her in a tangle of rooms, in Lazarus' Cave. He told her he wanted to talk to all of them, and could she arrange for them to meet in a few minutes?

Soon they were there. He told them what he'd found, about the search, Maddy, Ryker. There was one question they all asked...

Mike: "Why?"

Jack: "A last fling in our competition or a stamp on our time before it changes. I may never know the exact answer. I'm not sure she does."

Mike: "I like her style. I don't know if I could do that. Of course, I'm in here. I can't die, right?"

Jack, frowning: "Unless something happens to the power."

Raquel, contemplative: "We live from moment to moment. We don't think about longevity because we just have moments and longer moments. No day or night. Always on. And we're going to stay alive, moment to moment."

Jack: "You'll stay alive as long as possible, just like us. I won't be here often. Time for my reality."

George: "Good."

Raquel: "Great."

Mike: "I could play games forever."

Jack: "Enjoy."

* * *

"Phisto."

"Hey, buddy."

"When will the avatars fade away?"

"Jeez, Jack. I don't know precisely, but the entire Show is slowing down, and more parts are disappearing."

Jack frowned. "And you still don't know why."

"I tried Jack...I...I'm not sure."

"Are you slowing down? Why are you hesitating?"

"I don't know, Jack. How...how would I know?"

"So true. Good-bye, Phisto."

"Hey Jack...Jack."

* * *

Phisto couldn't help this time. He sorted through all the cafés in Zagreb and found five that seemed promising. He wasn't sure he wanted to see a declining Maddy...but if she wasn't worrying, he wouldn't either. She could stay the way she is now for years. And he realized something about the competition. Through all the details, all the feints, the tricks, he needed her.

more than need life was always exciting with her love i suppose i love her although im not sure what that means i suppose its

**like consciousness you know it when you find it but you cant
say what it is**

What about Mouse, Jack?

Real, or figment?

He didn't expect Mouse to come out on demand, but he gave it a try. He
cut a healthy square of Jarlsberg, and threw it towards Mouse's hole.

The *Oz* collage flickered, doubled, and tripled...

cmon jack stop it

Well, well, well, right on time.

Mouse looked older, as if wandering through the house, through the wood-
work, and eating scraps and the occasional cheese had worn him out. No way
to keep him past *his* date. Mouse hopped slowly towards him, hopped past the
cheese, stood up, and stopped.

"Howdy, Mouse."

"You've become cavalier."

Jack shrugged. "After all your messing with me, I know you're not talking
and I know you're not real."

Mouse squeaked, "What am I then?"

"Confusing me."

"Don't be coy, Jack. Your goal wasn't to find what was real or to find
Maddy. It was to capture the past. Everyone gives up their past hard. You saw
time with Maddy as a golden time, a time you were happy, when you floated
through life, a golden boy and his golden girl."

Reality ballooned towards Mouse and collapsed softly. Jack whispered,
"'Golden' is a stretch. Maybe."

"No 'maybe', Jack. What do you really know what happened? Hey, this is
better: how did you know what was real?"

touche i wish id said that i probably did

"Nicely put."

"So, it's time for another illusion."

"If I'm with Maddy, it will be real however she is. I can argue illusion vs.
reality later, after the fact."

283

Mouse squeaked, "I'll quit confusing you. You can do that without me."

Mouse nodded slowly, sadly, turned and picked up the cheese in his teeth, and limped slowly back towards *Oz*. At the wall, he turned towards Jack, swished his tail a last time, and vanished in a burst of pixels.

www.ingramcontent.com/pod-product-compliance
Lightning Source LLC
Chambersburg PA
CBHW031605240626
47153CB00002B/639